Dear Reader,

Welcome to the sixth title in the series of *Great Lakes Romances* ®, historical fiction full of love and adventure set in bygone days on North America's vast inland waters.

Like the other books in this series, *Bridget of Cat's Head Point* relays the excitement and thrills of a tale skillfully told, but contains no explicit sex, offensive language, or gratuitous violence.

We invite you to tell us what you would like most to read about in *Great Lakes Romances* ®. For your convenience, we have included a survey form at the back of the book. Please fill it out and send it to us.

At the back, you will also find descriptions of other romances in this series, stories that will sweep you away to an era of gentility and enchantment, and places of unparalleled beauty and wonder!

Thank you for being a part of *Great Lakes Romances* ®*!*

Sincerely,
The Publishers

P.S. Author Donna Winters loves to hear from her readers. You can write her at P.O. Box 177, Caledonia, MI 49316.

Bridget of Cat's Head Point

In memory of Hilda Stahl
whose spirit lives on in her characters, and mine

♥　　♥　　♥

Acknowledgments
I would like to thank the following people for volunteering their assistance in preparation of this work:

Doug McCormick, present "keeper" of the Grand Traverse Light, for a tour and consultation

Cyndi Gaudette of the Grand Traverse Lighthouse Foundation for research assistance

Reverend Bobby Dale Whitlock of the United Methodist Church, Caledonia, for information and advice regarding George Bennard

Cheryl McKenna, for research regarding Green Bay

Credits
I would like to credit Amy Lonier for the sketch of the Grand Traverse Light as it appeared before 1900, with thanks for graciously consenting to sign my heroine's name to the piece.

Notes
This novel is a work of fiction. Names, characters, places, and incidents are either the product of the author's imagination or, if real, are used fictitiously.

The term "monkey fist" as used in this work refers to a large nautical knot.

CHAPTER

1

South Manitou Island
June 30, 1899

The scent of citronella hung heavy in the air on the front porch of the Steffens cottage. While Bridget waited for someone to answer her knock at the screen door, she overheard the pleasant conversation and quiet laughter of the young people inside who had come to summer on South Manitou.

Within moments her new friend, Anna Steffens, opened the door. Her thick, dark hair was fastened in a French twist and her dusty rose dimity dress nipped in at a waist so tiny, Bridget might have been jealous. But she had long since abandoned the pursuit of the wasp waistline.

Anna's wide smile made Bridget feel welcome. Behind her stood an extraordinarily handsome strawberry blond fellow Bridget had never seen before. "Bridget, do come in. I'd like you to meet my cousin, Erik Olson. Erik, Miss Bridget Richards."

Bridget offered her hand. "Pleased to make your acquaintance, Mr. Olson."

He bowed and kissed her hand, holding it a moment longer than propriety allowed. The warmth of his touch penetrating her cotton mesh glove coupled with his attractive smile made her melt a little inside. She hadn't expected this much charm from the cousin Anna had described when insisting Bridget come to her party.

"The pleasure is mine, Miss Richards." The moment Erik saw Bridget, he knew Anna had not exaggerated. Bridget's pretty blond hair, escaping her Gibson Girl pouf in tiny curls that framed her face, the bright look of her blue eyes, and the blush on her round cheeks held immediate appeal. She was a good twelve inches shorter than his six-foot-one height, with a soft, round figure, so much more appealing to him than the skin-and-bones type that was in fashion. He was glad the evening was young so he could spend it getting to know her. "Would you care for some refreshment?"

Before Bridget could answer, he took a glass of lemonade from the maid's tray as she passed, and placed it in Bridget's hand. She was surprised and pleased that he already seemed to know she preferred it over the wine being offered.

"Shall we go to the back porch? There's a pleasant breeze there, and it's a little quieter for conversation."

"I'd like that," she said, allowing him to guide her through the front room where one of the fellows was cranking up the phonograph while couples paired off for the two-step. When they had settled on wicker chairs, he sipped from a lemonade glass that was waiting for him on the small table between them. There, also, were etched silver candy and nut dishes. Bold blue, green and yellow crepe paper swags stretched from each corner of the room to the lantern hanging from the center, lending the occasion a festive mood Bridget didn't yet feel. Her gaze returned to Erik, focusing on his entrancing blue-gray eyes.

He set aside his lemonade. "Anna says you live at the

light station year 'round. It must be quiet on an island like this, except for the summer people."

"It's different from the mainland, if that's what you mean," Bridget replied, thinking of the last time she had visited Glen Arbor. It was for her best friend's elopement three years ago. Meta was in the family way, and she and Nat had taken Bridget and Meta's brother, Fritz, ashore with them to be witnesses at their wedding. The mainland had churches and ministers and doctors, unlike both South and North Manitou Islands, which had none of those things. Sadness struck Bridget at the remembrance of her dearest friend's death last week from diabetes, an unhappiness she was desperately hoping to escape by coming to this party tonight, yet reminders seemed ever present. And despite her attempt to relax, motherless two-year-old Michael, whom she had cared for during Meta's long illness and was caring for still, was never far from her mind. She hoped the youngster would sleep soundly while she was away, and not tire his Grandma Ida by waking every hour and crying for attention.

"Have I said something wrong? You look as though you've just lost your best friend," Erik thoughtfully observed.

His words recaptured Bridget's attention, making her realize she wasn't upholding her end of the conversation. Too embarrassed by her lapse, and too discomforted by the accuracy of his assessment to reply with candor, she focused on his easy smile and offered one of her own. "Pardon my wandering mind, Mr. Olson. I was just thinking of the differences between the mainland and the islands." Quietly, she continued. "To tell you the truth, I think my time has come to leave this island. I'd like a

3

position as a nanny on the mainland. I've written a letter of application, but it's too soon to expect a reply." The moment she said it, she wondered what it was about Erik that had put her so at ease, she'd confided her most deeply-held secret in him. Until now, only God, to whom she'd prayed for guidance, and the Ferrises in Traverse City with whom she was seeking employment, knew of her plans to move.

Erik's brows raised. "You're looking for work on the mainland?"

Bridget nodded, a finger to her lips. "Please keep this between us. I haven't told another soul—not even my own mother."

"You can trust your secret to me," he said in a low tone, his wicker chair creaking as he leaned her way. "In fact, it's a remarkable coincidence that I just might be able to help you. My parents own a resort at Omena. They opened it last year, and it was so successful, they've expanded it for this season. They're still looking for nice young ladies like you for a few positions—a scullery maid, laundress, and a chamber maid who likes young children and can help with entertainment for them, if need be."

"Someone who likes children?" Bridget asked a little louder than she had intended, then clapped her hand over her mouth.

Erik grinned. "I'm going there tomorrow to help my folks for the season. You're welcome to come with me. The job is yours, if you want it."

Bridget's heart fluttered. Erik's offer was an answer to her prayer. "Oh, yes, Mr. Olson! I want the job!"

Erik smiled. He couldn't help thinking how much more pleasant his summer of toil would be, with Miss Richards working almost alongside him. He offered his hand. "Then it's a deal."

She shook his hand firmly. "A deal."

A harsh male voice intruded from the doorway. "Bridget!"

Nat Trevelyn's biting tone would have been enough to startle her, but his mere presence on the island when he had planned to be away the entire week hauling freight on his steamer completely flustered her. She almost spilled her lemonade before setting it on its coaster with a clank and jumping up. "Nat! I had no idea—"

He glowered first at Erik, then at her. "Bridget, come with me. I want to speak with you alone."

She stiffened, but managed an anxious smile. "Nat, I'd like to present Mr. Erik Olson. Mr. Olson, Nat Trevelyn, my longtime friend."

Erik stood, rising a couple of inches above Nat, and extended a hand. "Pleased to make your acquaintance, Mr. Trevelyn."

Nat ignored him, continuing to glare at Bridget. "Come along. It's time to go home."

Completely unaccustomed to such domineering, hostile behavior from him, she hesitated, casting a sidelong glance at Erik.

He eyed Nat warily, then calmly told her, "You needn't go now if you don't want to, Miss Richards. I'll see you home when you're ready."

"Thank you, Mr. Olson. I believe I'll stay awhile." She resumed her seat, fluffing the skirt of her dress. Folding her hands demurely in her lap, she hoped desperately Nat would disappear, but remained painfully aware of his continued presence.

Erik sat again, too.

"Now, where were we, Mr. Olson? Oh, yes, you were telling me about the resort." She spoke with studied nonchalance.

Wishing the obviously jealous friend would quietly disappear, Erik replied, "As I said, it was brand new last year, and has facilities for fishing, rowing, and sailing, and an excellent cook—Mrs. Little Bear, an Ottawa Indian."

Nat stepped forward, his face coloring as he bent over Bridget, giving away that he'd eavesdropped on their earlier conversation with his first words. "And you're not going there to take a position as a maid! You already have a job raising Michael. And as soon as I can arrange it, we'll be married." He took her by the elbow, his grip biting into her flesh. "Now come along."

With a quick, determined jerk, she twisted free. "Married? You've never even proposed!"

"You know you care for me. No sense wastin' time when Michael needs a mama and I need a wife."

Bridget's face grew hot. She loved Nat like a brother—maybe more. Her feelings had been in turmoil since Meta's passing. She needed time to sort them out. She couldn't consider marriage right now. "Meta's not been a week in her grave! My dearest friend! I could never dishonor your wife's memory the way you suggest, and I'm shocked to think you could, Nat Trevelyn. You should be ashamed of yourself!"

"And you should be ashamed of *your*self, making calf eyes at a man ya never met till tonight!" He eyed Erik with a look of sheer contempt.

"Nat, I think you ought to leave this minute," Bridget said icily.

When he made no move toward the door, Erik stood again, chest to chest with the intruder. "The young lady's right, Mr. Trevelyn. It's time for you to go."

Anna swept onto the porch, her sweet voice interrupting. "Mr. Trevelyn, there you are! I've been looking all over for you. I understand you're the master of the *Manitou Lady*. I wondered if I might have a word with you?"

Nat backed away, sending Bridget a furious look before turning his attention to Anna. "Yes'm. I own her. How can I be of service?" With obvious reluctance, he allowed her to usher him out of the room.

Still on edge from the tension, Bridget reached for the spoon in the candy dish, offering Erik a handful of the tiny mints, spilling some on the table when she helped herself. She quickly popped them into her mouth, chewing rapidly.

Sensing Bridget's discomfort, Erik swallowed the last of his candy and cast a backward glance, in search of Anna and Nat in the next room. Unable to spot them among the dancing couples, he turned to Bridget. "'Emperor Waltz' is playing. Would you care to dance?"

Bridget couldn't seem to take her mind off Nat, and concerns of Michael at home with Nat's mother crept into her mind as well. "Perhaps I'd better be going, Mr. Olson. I just don't feel in the mood for a party anymore."

"I'll walk you home," Erik said, offering a hand.

Rising, Bridget smoothed her skirt. "You needn't trouble yourself to walk me back to the light station, Mr. Olson. It's not even dark yet, and I'd hate for you to miss the fun here."

"I promised I'd see you home, Miss Richards, and I'm not about to let you leave alone. Besides, the walk will give us time to discuss your plans to work at Omena." He

7

offered his arm.

Pleased at his suggestion, she rested her hand lightly at his elbow and followed him through the parlor. She was relieved to find Nat nowhere in sight. Anna was absent, too, so Bridget paused to express her thanks and bid good bye to Anna's brother, Tom, before stepping into the balmy, dusky outdoors with Erik.

From above, came the cry of a whip-poor-will, melody to a chorus of crickets and the bass rhythm of a bullfrog from afar. The essence of citronella faded, overpowered by the moist earth smell as Bridget led Erik toward the wood-land path to the light station.

A mosquito buzzed about his head and he waved it away. "I'd forgotten about the pesky bugs up here in the north. I hope they won't be too awful at Omena this year."

Bridget kept one hand in motion, the other on Erik's arm, doing her best to keep from becoming a meal for one of the winged vipers. "I'm used to them. I don't think they could be any worse there than they are here."

Erik paused to slap his neck. "I believe you're right." Continuing on, he said, "Will you be ready to leave for Omena by noon tomorrow? Papa and Gramps are coming to fetch me on their steam launch, *Brede's Bargain*. They left Omena for Leland this morning and I expect them to be here by noon tomorrow. Otherwise, you can wait and come in a few days, when you're ready."

"I'll be ready by noon." She giggled softly, adding, "But do you think I can trust your papa's boat? *Brede's Bargain* doesn't exactly sound like the sturdiest launch on the lake." She laughed out loud, struck by a new thought. "Perhaps I should ask Nat to bring me on the *Manitou Lady!*"

Erik gave her a pointed look. "Don't be cruel, Miss Richards. I'm certain if you board Mr. Trevelyn's steamer, his destination will be anywhere but Omena. More likely, he'll be in search of the nearest preacher and carry out his plans to wed you, like it or not."

Bridget sighed thinking of the problem that awaited her on her next encounter with Nat. Sadness tugged at her heart remembering little Michael, knowing she would miss his laughter, his hugs, his jabber, the new words he would learn, and the growing up he would do while she was away. But maybe it was for the best, leaving him now. He'd become so accustomed to her, he now ran to her rather than his own father when they were both in the room. She didn't like knowing she'd come between them.

Erik laid his hand lightly atop hers, resting on his arm. "I believe your feelings for Mr. Trevelyn exceed the boundaries of friendship. Am I right?"

Their pace stalled while she looked up at him, his form silhouetted in the moonlight that was overtaking dusk, casting the handsome angles of his face in alluring shadows. "He's very special to me," she quietly admitted, "but I'm not about fall into his arms. He's hurting badly now from losing Meta. She was everything to him—she and Michael—and of course, the *Manitou Lady*."

The thought that had come to Bridget time and again since Meta's death resurfaced. It would be some time before Nat could honestly make room in his heart for another woman. He was desperate right now, grabbing at a convenient way out of the pain and the loneliness and the more practical problem of raising his son. She didn't want him to marry in haste when he might regret it for the rest of his life.

A bat's cry sounded overhead, and she caught sight of it through the branches of a nearby maple. She thought about that animal's blindness. Right now, Nat was suffering his own blindness of sorts, blindness to everything but his own urgent drive to put his life back in order again. Wife, son, steamer. Yes, she loved him, but she would not fall into a trap while the nature of her love was still in question. He needed time. So did she.

She focused on Erik again, and managed a smile. "It's kind of you to take me to Omena. I'll be ready by noon."

"Good. As soon as Papa and Gramps arrive, I'll come fetch you and your bags. We'll take rooms in Leland tomorrow night, so pack an overnight bag, too. Then we'll go on to Omena the next day. You won't regret it, I promise." Erik squeezed her hand, then continued on the path, making light conversation about his home back in Two Rivers, Wisconsin, his younger brother and sister in Omena, telling her of the fun they'd had last summer starting up the resort, despite the hard work.

By the time they reached the perimeter of the light station grounds, Bridget had all but forgotten her earlier problems with Nat, and the fact that she hadn't yet told her family of her abrupt plans to leave South Manitou. Now, these worries came flooding back full force.

But God quelled them quickly, for she had asked His guidance, and in her heart, she knew what was best for herself. She must go away for awhile and let time take its course.

And that course seemed to include a very attractive friend. She stopped a good distance from the keeper's quarters and turned to him. "I think it's best we say good night here, rather than at the door, if you don't mind. I'll introduce you to my mother tomorrow when you fetch me."

"Haven't you any brothers or sisters?"

"Oh, yes! Some are away, though. My younger sister, Charlotte, was married six days ago and is on her honeymoon. And my older sister, Aurora, is the wife of the assistant lightkeeper on North Manitou. I have a couple of younger brothers, Dorin and Eli, and they'll see me off tomorrow. You'll have to keep close watch on them or they'll be crawling all over *Brede's Bargain* the way curious boys do."

"And your father?"

Bridget shook her head. "Died several years ago in an ice storm in the Manitou Passage."

"I'm sorry."

Bridget shrugged. "My mother took his position as assistant lightkeeper, so we've managed to stay a family, thanks to Mr. Trevelyn, the head keep'."

"He would be Nat's father?"

She nodded. "The Trevelyns and Richards have been almost like one family, sharing the keeper's quarters for so many years."

Erik was beginning to understand the arrangements better, now that he knew Nat had been like a brother to Bridget, and more. That explained his jealousies, his assumption that she cared for him, and the quandary he could put her in. Erik wanted to take her away from the shelter of this island, show her another side to life. Perhaps she'd see there were more options for her future than she had ever dared to dream, and he could learn whether this attraction he felt for her would grow into something more.

He put on a bold smile. "You're going to have the summer of your life in Omena, Miss Richards. I guarantee it!"

Erik's promise set off a tingle of excitement deep inside that overrode her other worries for the moment. "I'll count on it, Mr. Olson."

"And I'll count on fetching you at noon sharp."

"I'll be ready." She took two steps toward the keeper's quarters, then looked back over her shoulder and waved. "Good night, Mr. Olson. And thanks."

Erik raised his hand in a parting gesture. "Until tomorrow, Miss Richards."

CHAPTER

2

Bridget took her time crossing the lawn of beach grass and sand to the two-story yellow brick keeper's quarters. The tower beyond was already sending forth its guiding light, warning vessels off its sandy island point while showing them the way through the Manitou passage. She wanted to remember the scene. Several weeks would pass before she would see it again, and in many ways, she was reluctant to leave this home of so many years.

The island was her sanctuary, closely circumscribing her life. Here, she knew what was expected of her. But God had put a new opportunity before her, and a still, small voice told her to take it.

She entered by the rear door that led down to the basement kitchen. It was empty as she'd expected, long since abandoned following supper dishes and evening snack time. But as she climbed the stairs leading to the first floor, she heard a voice she hadn't expected-- Michael's. He should have been in bed long ago. His childish words couldn't be misunderstood.

"Daddy! Up! Up!"

So Nat was there already. She should have guessed he'd be waiting for her. Reluctantly, she followed Michael's voice down the hallway to the front room.

But when she reached the doorway, her mouth fell open in surprise. In addition to Nat and Michael, who occupied the overstuffed chair to her right, a familiar guest from Glen Arbor was seated on the sofa between her mother and Ida Trevelyn.

"Preacher Mulder, hello. I didn't expect to see you here." Nat hadn't brought him back to the island for Meta's burial four days ago. Perhaps he'd had second thoughts and wanted the preacher to conduct a memorial service after all. The bag parked behind Nat's chair seemed to confirm that the minister would be staying the night at the keeper's quarters.

The room fell quiet and she could sense all eyes focusing on her in the uneasy silence that followed, finally broken by Preacher Mulder's well-modulated voice. "Hello, Miss Richards." He extracted his voluminous form from the soft sofa cushions with a quiet grunt of exertion, then offered a modest smile. "May I be the first to offer you best wishes. When I married Charlotte and Seth last week, I hardly expected to be back so soon to do the honors for you and Nat. Then, one can never quite predict what the Lord has in mind for His faithful."

The statements hit like a blow to her blind side. Before she could reply, her mother and Ida came to offer hugs.

"Best wishes, my daughter." Her mother wrapped her soft, plump arm about her. "This may not be the best of circumstances for a wedding, but happier times will come your way."

By contrast, Ida Trevelyn's embrace seemed all skin and bones, but the spare woman's words possessed warmth. "When I welcomed you to the family as Seth's sister-in-law last week, I hadn't figured I'd have the pleasure of welcomin' you as a daughter-in-law only a few days later."

Bridget extracted herself from the mothers, struggling to find the words to set things straight. Before she could find her voice, her mother spoke again. "Your bag is all packed so you can go with Nat on the *Manitou Lady* yet tonight." She indicated the one behind Nat's chair. "And by the time the two of you are back from your wedding trip, I'll have your trunk packed, too."

Bridget cast Nat a look of desperation, but he only offered a pleased, almost gloating smile as he came toward her carrying Michael.

She spoke directly. "Mother, Mrs. Trevelyn, Preacher Mulder, I'm afraid you're all mistaken. I'm not getting married."

"But Miss Richards . . . " Preacher Mulder's unfinished sentence hung in the air until her mother spoke.

"Nat said he'd proposed, and you'd accepted—"

"For the sake of my grandson," Ida finished for her.

"I can't believe you've changed your mind," Nat challenged.

Bridget bit her tongue, struggling to keep her anger in check. In the silent pause that followed, she glimpsed the vulnerable look in Michael's tired eyes and thought again about what he'd been through these last few months. Her ire lessened. She gazed at him a moment longer, then at his father, taking in the receding line of his dark hair, the endearing quality of his dimpled chin, the strength of his broad shoulders, and asked herself if she really should leave both father and son with whom she had shared so many joys and heartaches.

Michael broke her thoughts, reaching for her with his plump little hands outstretched. "Birdie? Mama?" he asked, his corrupted version of "Bridget" followed by the word his father had evidently been coaching him to substitute. "Birdie? Mama?" he repeated, waving his hands impatiently, his face starting to crumple, on the verge of tears.

She took him from Nat, and the child immediately wrapped his arms about her neck and rested his curly blond head on her shoulder. He felt so right in her arms, like he belonged to her. She wondered whether she could give him up for the whole summer.

Stroking his back, she spoke softly to him. "Bridget loves you, Michael, but I can't be your mama just yet. Your papa and I need time for the memories of your real mama to fade before you get a new one." As tears began to well in her eyes, she could feel him growing limp in her arms. Certain he was nearly asleep, she continued in a half-whisper, rocking him back and forth. "Bridget is going away tomorrow on a boat. I'll miss you very much, but your grandma will take good care of you while I'm gone. Maybe when I come back, I can be your mama." When she looked at Nat, his expression had turned unreadable. "I'll take Michael up to bed now," she said quietly.

Thankful for a few moments to collect her thoughts, she started up the stairs leading to the small room Nat and Seth had once shared that now held Michael's crib. She hadn't counted on Nat's footsteps dogging her. With him looking on, she gently laid Michael on his back and pulled the sheet over him, then turned to go.

Nat took her by the elbow the moment she stepped out into the hall. "Think what you're doing, Bridget. You can't just walk away from Michael and me."

When she gazed up into his troubled expression, the

careworn wrinkles about his eyes seemed deeper than before. Her heart ached for him.

And it ached for herself, knowing how very painful it would be to leave behind a man and a boy she loved dearly, but she had to go, had to get out from under the cloud of sorrow hanging over South Manitou. She must escape the emotional net that threatened to entrap her forever with a man she loved better than a brother, but not enough to marry. She needed the certainty that he wanted her for herself, rather than the substitute mother and wife he was so desperately seeking at this moment.

"I'm sorry, Nat. My mind is made up. I must go away. Nothing you can say will change my decision."

His head moved from side to side. "It'll be tough enough for Michael, with his papa out on the lakes for the next five months. I never woulda thought *you'd* abandon him. Not by choice. Not for the paltry excuse of a position at a resort. Why, come the end of the summer, they'll toss you aside just like old bath water."

Bridget took a deep breath, allowing her frustration to subside before making a reply. "Michael has two grand-mothers to care for him. His Uncle Fritz is fond of him, too," she reminded Nat, referring to Meta's brother who lived but a stone's throw from the little house Nat and Meta had called home.

"But Michael loves you best, 'n you know it," he reminded her.

Bridget simply turned and descended the stairs, Nat following close behind. In the front sitting room, Preacher Mulder and the two mothers stood in a circle, hands joined in a prayer that ended when she and Nat entered the room.

She focused on her mother. "Tomorrow, I'm going to a

resort in Omena to work for the summer. Anna's aunt and uncle, the Olsons, own the place. Her cousin, Erik, and his father and grandfather will take me over on their boat. I'll be leaving at noon on *Brede's Bargain.*"

Bridget's mother opened her mouth to speak, but Nat's quick reaction cut her off. *"Brede's Bargain?* I've seen that old fishing tub—last summer in Traverse Bay—the ugliest vessel on the water. Somebody painted her cabin with big red and white stripes." He gave a contemptuous laugh. "Shoulda saved themselves the trouble. Her boiler's in need of work, and so's her hull. If they haven't fixed her up, you'll be lucky to get from the dock into the passage, let alone all the way to Omena!"

Bridget stiffened, offering Nat a pointed look. "Be that as it may, my mind hasn't changed. I'm going to Omena tomorrow to work until summer's end."

Bridget walked the sandy beach, paused to look at the bay through the binoculars hanging about her neck, then turned and wandered back toward the tower. Erik should have come for her an hour ago, and *Brede's Bargain* should have long since arrived at the dock over town, but she'd just spent a quarter of an hour in the light tower with binoculars, and hadn't seen any evidence of a fishing boat with a red and white striped cabin.

A man called from the distance. "Miss Richards!"

She recognized Erik's voice before she turned to find him coming across the sandy lawn toward her. She hurried to meet him. Worry was evident on his furrowed blond brow.

"Miss Richards, I apologize for the delay. I can't imagine what's keeping Papa and Gramps, unless . . . " He

18

shook his head as if to rid himself of a troubling thought. "Like I said, I'm sorry. I really think they'll be coming into the dock any time now."

"Let's go up to the tower and watch for them. You'll love the view, and we'll be able to see them before they even enter the harbor." She started toward the tower door.

Erik hesitated, looking up at the parapet, then reluctantly followed. He couldn't help remembering his embarrassing experience on the Ferris Wheel at the World's Columbian Exposition six years back. He'd avoided heights ever since. "How tall is that tower, anyway?"

Bridget caught the doubtful look in his eye and laid a reassuring hand on his arm. "A hundred feet. It's perfectly safe, and the view is worth a million words— especially on a clear day like today." She offered a beguiling smile and his fear subsided.

The iron stair treads inside the tall white tower seemed never-ending. The spiral pattern almost made his head spin, but he kept his eyes on Bridget's bustle as he followed her up through the hatches to the balcony door. She pushed it open, stepped out, and held it for him. He swallowed, took a deep breath to calm his rushing pulse, and emerged into air several degrees cooler than on the ground.

Despite the lower temperature, a warmth rushed through him, setting up beads of perspiration on his forehead. His heart pounded. He leaned against the parapet wall and prayed his stomach wouldn't turn over.

At the balcony rail, Bridget checked again for any sign of a red and white striped boat, then turned to Erik. The sight of his pale face made her gasp. "You're whiter than an angel's robe! You really *are* troubled by heights, aren't you?"

Erik drew a deep breath and let it out slowly, but his heartbeat galloped on. "I think I should go back down," he said shakily.

Bridget offered him the binoculars. "Take one look, now that you're up here. The view is so pretty, maybe you'll forget your fears."

Despite his doubts, Erik took the binoculars, and couldn't help grasping Bridget's arm at the same time.

His steely grip caused her to revise her suggestion. "Maybe we *should* go back down now. Come on. I'll help you." Quickly, she put the binocular strap about her neck again. With a steadying arm at Erik's waist, she turned him stiffly toward the exit.

At that exact moment, Nat emerged on the balcony, closing the door behind him and leaning against it with the sole of one boot. The sight of Bridget's arm about Erik's waist raised the hair on the back of his neck. "I've been lookin' for you two," he said in his most accusing manner.

Beneath his condemning gaze, Bridget sensed her cheeks coloring, but made no move to separate herself from Erik.

Nat's unexpected appearance on the balcony, and his position blocking the escape made Erik's stomach capsize. "Please excuse me," he said, desperately gesturing toward the door.

Nat stood firm. "Not till I've had my say!"

Unable to wait a moment longer, Erik released himself from Bridget's embrace and dashed to the back side of the tower.

The sound of retching was unmistakable. Bridget focused sharply on Nat and stamped her foot. "How could you? If you'd only let him go down!"

"How'd I know he was about to—"

"Things aren't always what they seem," Bridget interrupted crossly.

"I discovered that last night at the Steffens's," he said with obvious disappointment.

On the back side of the balcony, Erik pulled out his handkerchief to wipe his mouth and mop his brow. Taking a deep breath, he returned to Bridget's side once again.

"Are you all right now?" she asked sympathetically.

"I'll . . . manage," he answered shakily.

Bridget turned to Nat. "I haven't changed my mind. I'm still going to Omena. You can't talk me out of it."

"I didn't come here to talk you out of it," Nat said defensively. "I know you're set on goin'." His gaze shifted to Erik. "I came here to offer you passage on the *Manitou Lady*."

Erik squared his shoulders. "We're going on my grandpa's boat, and that's final."

Nat sighed, pulling a card from his pocket and handing it to Erik. "You've got a mighty long wait, then."

Erik immediately recognized his father's calling card, and his handwritten message on the back side. He read aloud. "'Hull in repair, Leland. Come as soon as possible. Papa.' How did you get this?"

Nat leaned away from the door and adjusted his captain's cap. "Your pa sent it on the mail boat this mornin'. Evidently he and your grandpa developed a bad leak on their way from Omena around to Leland yesterday and their boat had to be put in dry dock. Like I said, I'll take you both to Leland."

Erik nodded. "Thanks for your offer, Mr. Trevelyn. I'd be most appreciative."

CHAPTER

3

Bridget set her overnight bag on the freshly varnished floor of the passenger cabin at the rear of the main deck and brushed her gloved hand across the smooth oak bench checking for cleanliness. She should have known Nat would keep the *Manitou Lady* spotless. As she sat on the edge of the seat, she was glad for the layers of petticoats and her own natural padding that helped cushion her, but the stays in her corset made it impossible to lean back in comfort.

The odor of coal smoke drifted in the open windows that lined the sunlit compartment, and she could hear Nat's and Erik's voices punctuated by the bell signals to Wilbur, the engineer temporarily replacing Nat's brother, Seth. Slowly, the *Manitou Lady* eased away from the dock.

In the distance, Bridget could see the shoreline curving toward the sandy lighthouse point. Gradually, the light tower and keeper's quarters came into full view. She stared a moment, storing the scene in her memory, fully aware that several weeks would pass before she would return to this pretty horseshoe-shaped harbor and the light station she had called home for so many years. An unexpected twinge of homesickness stirred inside.

Her gaze fell on the empty bench across from her and she imagined it as it had been a week ago, the day of Charlotte's wedding when Nat had crossed to North Manitou to ferry over some of the guests. Dorin and Eli had occupied it on the trip over, and on the way back to South Manitou, her older sister, Aurora, her husband, Harrison, and their friends, Cad Blackburn and Serilda Anders, had filled the cabin with happy chatter that had contrasted sharply with her own—and Nat's—grave concern about Meta. So much had changed in the few days since. Now, the only voice keeping her company was that of the throbbing engine vibrating through the wooden floor and seat, sending its pulse straight to her heart.

Unexpectedly, a shadow of a woman carrying a small bag appeared on the floor, drawing her focus to the doorway. There stood Anna Steffens in her sailor hat and dress. Her narrow skirt and boxy shirt collar enhanced her already attractive figure, and a knotted tie set off her long, elegant neck.

"Bridget, there you are!" She spoke all in a rush. "I've been up top, watching Mr. Trevelyn and Erik cast off. You'd never know they had cross words last night, the way they're behaving today." She dropped her valise on the floor beside Bridget's and flitted from one window to another, investigating the view from all directions.

"I didn't know you had plans to go to the mainland today," Bridget commented, thinking she shouldn't be surprised by her impetuous friend's sudden appearance. She'd known Anna just long enough to realize she acted on impulse.

"I didn't. But last night when your Mr. Trevelyn walked in—"

"*My* Mr. Trevelyn?" Bridget questioned sharply. "He's not *my* Mr. Trevelyn."

"He seemed to think so last night," Anna countered.

"Regardless, he's not *my* Mr. Trevelyn," Bridget insisted. "That was the point of your introducing me to your cousin, wasn't it?"

"I know we thought it was a good idea, but I had no inkling just how strongly Mr. Trevelyn felt about you. Anyhow, when he walked in and nearly started a scuffle with Erik, I knew I had to get them apart, so I drew Mr. Trevelyn aside on the pretense I needed to hire him to bring a cottage organ from Traverse City for Tom and me. Our parties would be so much merrier if we could all stand around the organ and sing, I told him." She perched on the bench beside Bridget. "The only problem was, I made it all up. I was planning to tell Mr. Trevelyn this morning that we'd changed our minds about the organ, but the more Tom and I got to thinking about it, the better the idea sounded. So I asked Erik if I could go with him on *Brede's Bargain* and stay with his folks in Omena while I made arrangements in Traverse City to purchase an organ from the Kimball Company. Of course, Erik said I was welcome. But as you know, things didn't quite work out with Gramps's boat." She grinned. "I'm glad. It's much more exciting this way!" She waltzed toward the door. "I'm going up top. Want to come?"

Bridget shook her head, thinking the less Nat saw of her in Erik's company, the better. "You go ahead," she said, reaching for the sketchbook and pencils she had tucked in the side pocket of her bag. Turning halfway through the book, she began to sketch Anna from memory on the blank page opposite her last drawing of Meta, Nat, and Michael.

Losing track of time, she concentrated on refining the minor details that lent a real personality to Anna's portrait—the sparkle of anticipation in her eyes, the exact curve of her heart-shaped lips when she was about to speak, the mole on the left side of her graceful neck.

A long time later, when discomfort from the hard seat made sitting intolerable, she closed her sketchbook and set it aside, ready for a few minutes on the upper deck. When she arrived there, she was unprepared for what she found. In the pilothouse, Erik was at the helm, while on the port deck, Nat and Anna leaned against the rail, standing so close their elbows were nearly touching. From the movement of their heads, she could tell they were carrying on an animated discussion, but their words were blown away before reaching Bridget. The sound she heard clearly however, was that of their laughter. It rang in her ears as she returned to the empty passenger cabin, dropped onto the hard bench, and again took up her sketching, eager to make revisions on her recently completed portrait. Her unexpected sense of jealousy confused her. Did she care for Nat more than she was willing to admit, or was she angry because Anna, who had already attracted the attention of every eligible young man on South Manitou, had now added Nat to her collection of admirers?

Bridget's feelings were yet in a tangle an hour later, when the *Manitou Lady* neared Leland. Still alone in the cabin, she slammed shut her sketchbook, tucked it away, and picked up her bag. Stooping to reach for Anna's, she paused, then jabbed it with the pointed toe of her shoe and marched out onto the lower deck.

In a boat cradle on shore, Bridget recognized the red and white striped cabin of which Nat had spoken. A man in a captain's cap and blazer, a tall older gentleman with splendid white hair, and a fellow clad in paint-stained work clothes were inspecting the hull—Erik's father, grandfather, and a ship's carpenter she assumed.

When the *Manitou Lady* was within a foot of the dock, Erik jumped off. Amidst the ringing of bells signaling the engineer, and the shouts from Nat in the pilothouse, Erik secured the vessel to the pier pilings.

While he was setting up the gangway from the boat to the dock, Anna came to stand beside Bridget. "Isn't the fishy smell here simply awful?" she asked, wrinkling her nose.

The odor reminds me of you, Bridget wanted to say, but instead, adapted a quote she had once read to fit the circumstances. "'She shines and stinks like rotten mackerel by moonlight.'"

"What's that supposed to mean?" Anna asked.

Bridget only smiled, then turned away and walked off the *Manitou Lady*. The notion that Anna had spent the entire crossing in close company with Nat, who from all appearances, had enjoyed it, dogged her every step. She took her time going ashore, hoping Erik would catch up with her. Instead, he and Nat flanked Anna as they ushered her ashore on their arms.

When they approached the cradled vessel, the elderly, white-haired man, slightly stooped at the shoulders, was the first to see them coming. "Anna!" He shuffled toward her, his arms opened wide.

She hurried to fill his embrace. *"Hvordan står det til?* How are you, Gramps?"

The old man's face glowed. "You remembered the Norwegian I taught you on my last day in Green Bay!" He loosed his embrace, his gaze falling on Bridget. He stared a moment, his blue eyes filling with tenderness that bordered on tears. "Freya?" The name was barely more than a whisper.

"Gramps, this is my friend from the island, Miss Bridget Richards. Bridget, my Gramps, Mr. Brede Olson."

She offered her hand. "Pleased to meet you, sir."

Gramps took her hand in both of his and kissed it. "Miss Richards, forgive me. You look like my beloved Freya did when we married. She's been gone for near thirty years now." Reluctantly, he let her go, then knuckled away the moisture in his eye.

Unsure how to respond, Bridget was thankful when Erik launched into an introduction of the blazer-clad man. "Miss Richards, my father, Kal Olson. Papa, Anna's friend, Miss Bridget Richards. She's agreed to take a position as a chamber maid and fill in as a nanny if needed."

Mr. Olson's thick strawberry blond hair was graying at the temples, but his strong jawline and easy smile bore remarkable similarity to Erik's good looks and obliging manner. He shook her hand heartily. "That's wonderful, Miss Richards. Mrs. Olson will be pleased! Now, if I can just solve the problem of this leaky hull."

"Mr. Trevelyn can advise us," Erik said. "He just replaced the bad wood on his own boat."

Nat, who had been inspecting the planks near the stern with the ship's carpenter, now joined the others, extending his hand to Mr. Olson. "Nat Trevelyn, sir. I can see you've got some serious wood rot."

"So I'm told. Do you think she's even worth saving?"

Nat pulled off his cap and raked his fingers through his hair. "I'll need more time to look her over." Changing his focus to Bridget and Anna, he said, "Ladies, you'd better take rooms at Mrs. Pickard's boardin' house for the night. Go up the hill to the main road. You'll see her sign. Tell her Nat Trevelyn and three other gentlemen will be joinin' her for dinner."

Though Bridget would have preferred staying to learn the fate of *Brede's Bargain*, she kept her silence and started up the hill at once. In her wake, she heard Anna arguing the same point with Nat and the Olsons. Soon, however, she was at Bridget's heels.

Mrs. Pickard's two-story gray home was clearly marked as Nat had said, her red "Bed and Board" sign hanging from a wrought iron frame in the front yard. Beneath it grew geraniums of blue, red, and pink. Bridget made a point to wait for Anna before opening the gate to the white picket fence and turning up the brick front walk.

Together, they climbed the steps to the broad front porch. While they waited for an to answer Bridget's knock, a delightful aroma of freshly baked bread wafted through the screen door. The delicious smell stirred Bridget's appetite, reminding her lunch had been long ago. She was about to check her timepiece when an auburn-haired woman appeared wearing a white ruffled apron over a black dress. She carried a small, sleepy child about Michael's age on her hip. Swinging open the door, she offered a generous smile.

"Welcome, ladies! I'm Mrs. Pickard," she said quietly, so as not to disturb the child.

To Bridget's surprise, the woman was only a few years older than she. Bridget stepped through the open door, with Anna. "I'm Miss Bridget Richards, and this is my friend, Miss Anna Steffens."

"Bridget Richards?" A hint of recognition sounded in Mrs. Pickard's voice. "You're from South Manitou—Nat Trevelyn's friend. I've heard him speak of you often. I feel as if I already know you!"

Surprised at the warm reception, Bridget explained, "Nat sent us to you. He'll join us later for dinner, along with three other gentlemen."

Mrs. Pickard's face lit with a smile. "So Mr. Trevelyn's in port! Meals are such a delight when he's at the table."

"Miss Richards and I also need a room for tonight," Anna said.

"If you'll excuse me, I'll put Timothy down, then show you a room," Mrs. Pickard said. A minute later, she led them up the stairs to a room on the front of the house.

Though sparsely furnished with a plain oak bed, two spindleback chairs, and a washstand, the room was immaculately kept, infused with the essence of orange pomander. In contrast to spotless white walls were the bright yellow curtains, a matching runner on the chest of drawers, and its green glass vase of brown-eyed susans. Somewhere down the hall, a clock chimed five.

"Dinner is in one hour," Mrs. Pickard explained. "I'm serving whitefish, chicken and gravy with biscuits, fresh vegetables, and strawberry shortcake with whipped cream." Taking the wash pitcher from the stand, she added, "My daughter, Carrie, will be right up with warm water."

When she had gone, Anna closed the door and turned to Bridget. "Did you see the look on her face when she heard Mr. Trevelyn was coming?"

Bridget nodded, reluctant to even think about it.

"She's a widow with her cap set for the master of the

Manitou Lady," Anna stated.

Eager to drop the touchy subject, Bridget sat down, pulled out her sketchbook and pencil, and began drawing the flowers and vase in an effort to take her mind off her jealousy.

A knock on the door signaled the arrival of warm water. Anna washed her hands and face, then flopped on the bed. "Too hard," she muttered.

"At least we won't be rolling into one another tonight," Bridget said, determined to look on the bright side.

Ignoring the comment, Anna got up to wander about the room. Moments later, she stood beside Bridget, watching her complete her drawing. "You're a good artist. May I look at your work?"

Bridget discreetly ripped out the sheet with her unflattering sketch of Anna and handed her the book. While Anna leafed through the pages, Bridget slipped the drawing into the pocket of her bag and washed her hands and face for dinner. As she wiped her face dry on the fluffy, fresh-air scented towel, she wondered again whether any truth existed in Anna's assessment of Mrs. Pickard.

At six o'clock, Bridget and Anna entered the dining room with several other guests. Mrs. Pickard seated Nat at the end of the table, opposite herself, putting Anna and Bridget on either side of him, and the Olsons beside them. Four gentlemen boarders filled the remaining seats, and Bridget couldn't help noticing their subtle glances at her and Anna.

At the Olsons' end of the table, conversation centered on Erik's father's decision to burn *Brede's Bargain* and purchase a sailing yacht in its stead. Though Gramps grumbled, and Nat suggested that a few new ribs and planks would make the old steamer seaworthy again, Erik's father held his ground.

Bridget's interest in Olson's boat and her pleasure in the excellent food on her plate were overridden by her disquietude over the occasional smiles being exchanged between Mrs. Pickard and Nat. No mention had been made of a Mr. Pickard. Perhaps Anna was right—Mrs. Pickard was a widow with her sights set on the widower at her table.

Nat finished the last of his strawberry shortcake and laid his napkin aside. "My compliments on a fine meal, Mrs. Pickard. Will you be servin' coffee later this evenin'?"

Her gaze took in all her guests. "Everyone is welcome to coffee later."

Nat stood and pushed in his chair. "I'll look forward to it. Now, if you'll excuse me, I need to tend chores on my boat."

Bridget left the table also, intending to go with Nat and ask about Mrs. Pickard, but Erik intercepted her halfway to the front door.

"It's a fine evening for a walk. Care to join me?" The curve of his upturned mouth and the charm of his splendid blue-gray eyes unexpectedly gave her pause, but the spell was broken by Anna, rushing past at a near run.

"Mr. Trevelyn! Wait!" The slamming of the screen door punctuated her words as she hustled off the porch and down the front walk, leaving four disappointed gentlemen boarders in her wake.

With a new purpose, Bridget focused on Erik once more. "It *is* a fine evening for a walk. If you'll wait a moment, I'll fetch my sketchbook. I'd like very much to have you pose for me."

When Bridget returned with her drawing pad and pencils, she found Erik sitting on the front porch swing with Gramps. The twinkle in the old man's eyes when he looked at her roused a sense of kinship within.

Erik rose, offering Bridget his arm. "Ready for our walk?"

Bridget placed her hand at his elbow. "Yes, but I'd like to make a suggestion, if you don't mind." Her gaze on the old man, she said, "Mr. Olson—"

"Call me Gramps," he said with a wink.

Bridget smiled. "Gramps, I'm going to make a sketch of your grandson, but I think the composition will be much more charming with you in the picture, too. Will you come and sit with him while I draw?"

Gramps knew he should let the young people go off on their own. They were far past the age of needing a chaperone. Besides, since the first moment he'd seen Bridget, he'd thought her the perfect match for his Erik. If he let them alone, maybe something would develop between them.

But her looks and her nature, so like Freya's, drew him like a magnet. In her company, he felt young again, and more lighthearted than he had in months. Should he deny himself a few minutes' pleasure, when Erik and Bridget would have the entire summer together? "I know a place down by the water. A very pretty picture it will make. I'll show you."

With an Olson on either side, Bridget strolled down the hill toward the lake. She looked for some sign of Nat aboard the *Manitou Lady*. By the time they had arrived at the beach, Anna, Nat, and Erik's father had appeared on the lower deck, waved to them, then disappeared below. Anna's presence there irked Bridget, but she pushed the troublesome feeling aside, determined not to let it spoil her evening.

Several yards north of the dock, a willow tree offered a picturesque background for Erik and Gramps, who posed casually. She listened avidly to Gramps's tale of Askeladden, about a poor man and his three sons, Per, Pål and Espen. When his story ended, he joked about the seasons God had bestowed on his homeland, then spoke reverently about the importance of Jesus in his life, especially when his wife had died.

Now Bridget knew why she felt such a kinship with Gramps—they both belonged to Jesus. She worked as quickly as possible, capturing the gleam in Gramps's eyes and the respect in Erik's; showing the hollow that had come with age to the old man's cheek and the strength of Erik's jawline; mirroring the wisdom in Gramps's creased forehead and the confidence of Erik's youthful countenance.

When dusk settled in, she closed her sketchbook. "I'm ready for some of Mrs. Pickard's coffee. How about you gentlemen?"

Gramps slowly rose from his log seat, stretching his legs. "I'd better fetch our bags from *Brede's Bargain* and stow them on the *Manitou Lady* before darkness falls."

Erik sprang up. "I'll get them."

Gramps put up a staying hand. "I want to climb aboard her one more time before your papa condemns her to the wood pile."

At the cradle, Erik held the ladder steady while Gramps climbed up, then he turned to Bridget. The roses in her cheeks were fading with the dimming light, but her hair, the shade of cornsilk at sunset, framed her fair face with a luminescent halo. Her lips, curved in a gentle smile, made him want to kiss her, but their friendship was far too new and casual for such a bold show of affection.

Bridget saw the look of admiration in Erik's eyes and was thankful for their new companionship. His physique, akin to a Viking god, gave him outward appeal, just as his respectful, accommodating nature gave him an inner beauty. She wondered if the time would arrive, under a Leelanau summer moon, when he would take her in his arms and bestow on her a gentle kiss. The desire surprised her, and quickly took flight at the appearance of shadowy figures in the distance—Anna, Mr. Olson, and Nat on their way to Mrs. Pickard's for coffee. She stepped back from Erik. Gazing up at *Brede's Bargain*, she looked for some sign of Gramps.

Erik, too, squinted into the darkness. "Gramps, did you find the bags?" he hollered.

A shuffling noise sounded overhead, then he appeared at the gunwale. "Erik, catch!" He tossed down his bag, then Erik's father's, then descended the ladder, seemingly more winded than the effort warranted.

"Gramps, are you all right?" Bridget asked.

He bent forward, clutching the left side of his chest.

CHAPTER

4

"Just . . . a little spell," Gramps said, forcing out the words.

"Sit down," Erik said. Bridget helped him lower the old man to the beach. "Where's your medicine—the Revivo?"

Gramps groaned, fumbling in his shirt pocket. Erik reached in and quickly extracted a small envelope, took out a tiny tablet and put it in the old man's mouth.

Bridget laid her sketchbook beneath the boat cradle and kneeled beside Gramps. "You'd better lean back against the brace of the cradle," she said, helping to reposition him.

The old man rested quietly, the only sounds his labored breathing and the *peent, peent, peent* of a nighthawk overhead.

For the first time since Bridget's arrival, the stench of fish nets on drying racks, enhanced by the damp night air, irritated her. She stroked Gramps's forehead and offered a silent prayer, asking God to give him strength. A few minutes later, he sat up.

"I'll go to Mr. Trevelyn's boat and turn in now," he said weakly.

Erik caught the questioning look in Bridget's eyes, but he knew better than to argue with a man who was too stubborn to even see a doctor. "We'll help you, Gramps."

With Bridget's aid, he escorted the old man down to the dock and onto the boat. A few minutes later, he had settled his grandfather in one of the four hammocks Nat had hung across the lower cabin. Bridget laid a light blanket over him.

"You young folks go have your coffee. I'll be fine," Gramps said, turning back the top of the blanket and lacing his fingers on his chest.

"We'll stay with you until Papa comes, no argument," Erik gently countered.

"Hmph," was the only reply.

Erik found space for Bridget at the end of one bench that wasn't overhung with hammocks, then he sat on the floor at her feet listening to his grandfather's irregular breathing. Gradually, it produced a steadier rhythm. When he was certain the old man was asleep, he motioned for Bridget to follow him. On the deck, he leaned against the stern rail, looking out onto the quiet lake. Bridget came beside him, and he turned to her, his brow furrowed. "I don't have any faith in that patent medicine."

Bridget shrugged. "But if *he* believes in it . . . "

"I suppose you're right." He lapsed into silence, his hands clasped, his head bowed in prayer.

Feeling the need for prayer, also, Bridget looked up at the brilliant array of stars, proof of God's power and presence, and spoke the words they inspired. "Father God, be with us this night. Grant us the grace, peace, and strength to face tomorrow. In Jesus' name, Amen."

"Amen," Erik added, reaching for her hand. The contact provided a comfort surpassing words, making conversation unnecessary for the next several minutes until his father and Nat approached on the dock.

"Bridget!" Nat called from several yards away.

"Hush!" she answered, anxiety rushing in to shred her peace and serenity. Erik released her hand, and the last fragment of inner solace vanished.

Nat clambered aboard, coming face to face with Erik. "What's goin' on here?" he loudly demanded.

"Hush!" Bridget said again. "Gramps is sick. He's trying to sleep."

"His heart?" Mr. Olson asked with alarm.

"Yes," Erik answered. "He seems all right now, though."

"I thought it was odd the three of you didn't come back to the house for coffee when darkness fell," Mr. Olson said.

"Bridget, I'll walk you back to Mrs. Pickard's now," Nat said in a tone that brooked no argument.

Ruefully, she glanced at Erik, then went with Nat, fetching her sketchbook from beneath the boat cradle on the way.

By the time they reached Mrs. Pickard's front porch, Bridget's stomach ached from the tension-filled silence. When Nat took her gently by the elbow, she wanted to pull away, but the hint of tenderness in his hazel eyes prevented her.

"I'm sorry 'bout the way I acted," he admitted. "It's just that . . . "

"You don't trust me," she said, unable to hide her irritation.

"I trust *you!*" he argued. "I don't trust *Erik*."

"You trusted him at the helm of the *Manitou Lady!*"

The corner of Nat's mouth curled upward. "I knew where his hands were, then."

Bridget pulled free, tempted to kick him in the shin, but she restrained herself. "He's been every inch a gentleman with me. Your jealousy is uncalled for."

Nat raked his fingers through his tousled brown hair. "I can't help it. In a couple months, you'll be my wife. Like it or not, I'm gonna look out for ya."

"You won't be able to look out for me in Omena, so you'd best start trusting my judgment now," Bridget stated, letting herself in the screen door without saying good-night.

Thoughts of Nat's jealousy were still rankling when the scene in the front parlor caught her by surprise. Anna was sitting on the sofa singing to Mrs. Pickard's two-year-old son.

"Little boy blue, come blow your horn, the sheep's in the meadow, the cow's in the corn. Is this the way you mind your sheep? Under the haycock fast asleep?"

Bridget was surprised at Anna's easy way with the small boy. She sat down beside them and smiled at Timothy. "I thought you'd both be in bed by now."

The child buried his head against Anna's shoulder, then peeked at Bridget and laughed.

"A few minutes ago, Timothy was crying too loud for anyone to sleep, so I asked Mrs. Pickard if she'd like me to try quieting him," Anna explained.

Seeing Timothy, Bridget couldn't help missing Michael. She held her hands out to the small fellow. "Can I hold you?"

He leaned toward her, then pulled back and giggled.

"He's such a tease," Anna said.

Mrs. Pickard entered the room. "Timothy, are you ready for bed now?"

When she reached for him, he shook his head and started to whimper.

"I'll try putting him down," Anna offered.

Bridget rose with her. "Good night, everyone. I'm heading up to bed."

"I'll be up soon," Anna promised.

In the bedroom, Bridget set her sketchbook and pencils on the floor beside her bag and changed into her nightgown, then searched in the pocket of her valise for her comb, finding instead the ugly sketch of Anna. She tossed it face down on the sketchbook and dug deeper in her bag, then discovered she had left her comb out on the chest before dinner. She had let down her hair and was sitting on the bed when Anna came in.

"Timothy's finally asleep. Now, maybe we can all get some rest." She stooped to open her bag, but instead, reached to pick up the piece of paper lying on the sketchbook nearby.

Bridget gasped, bolting off the bed to grab for it. "Give me that!"

Anna whirled away, unfolded the drawing and examined it. She focused sternly on Bridget, then her dark eyes lit with mischief. "You've almost got it right." Picking up a pencil, she hastily added a dunce cap and hairy chin wart to the mustached illustration of her, then propped it on the chest. "That's more like it," she said, standing back to examine the results.

Again, Bridget reached for the drawing, but Anna stepped in her way, blocking her. "Listen to me." Her brown eyes turned serious. "I was a fool, the way I behaved with Mr. Trevelyn earlier. I should have known you didn't mean it when you denied he was *your* Mr. Trevelyn. I didn't intend to hurt you. Please forgive me."

Bridget shook her head in disagreement. "*I* was a fool for making that silly drawing," she insisted. "Will *you* forgive *me?*"

Anna looked at the picture once more, then started to giggle. Her laughter was so infectious, Bridget soon joined in, dissolving in happy tears.

Moments later, she ripped the drawing in two, gave one half to Anna, and together, they tore the paper into confetti-sized pieces and deposited them in the wicker wastebasket.

Dusting her hands of the last particle of paper, Anna said, "Now that's over, I must tell you something. I've discovered why Mrs. Pickard is so pleased to have your Mr. Trevelyn in port . . . "

Anna talked long after she had exhausted the topic of Mrs. Pickard's recent loss of her handyman husband. Even after she had blown out the lamp, she continued to chat, telling of a suitor she had once planned to marry. Her parents had liked him so much, they hadn't even objected when they learned she would be converting from her own religion to his, but the change became unnecessary when disaster struck and the wedding plans were canceled.

When the opportunity arose, Bridget told Anna of the spell Gramps had suffered. Anna bolted up, paced the floor in alarm, and spoke as if her world would fall apart if anything happened to her dear grandfather. She explained how each year, he spent all winter and spring with her family in Green Bay, and summer and fall with Erik's family in Omena and Two Rivers, Wisconsin, thereby becoming a very cherished member of both households. Sometime after the hall clock had struck midnight, Bridget managed to allay Anna's concerns for her grandfather's welfare and convince her to come to bed and get some sleep.

Morning dawned cloudy, but Gramps's seeming recovery and Mrs. Pickard's pleasant breakfast supplanted thoughts of wet weather in the offing. Soon after the meal ended, Nat put the *Manitou Lady* underway while Bridget and Anna stowed box lunches from Mrs. Pickard's kitchen in the cabin.

Nat's course, rounding the tip of the Leelanau Peninsula, brought into view Cat's Head Light, its creamy white brick keeper's quarters topped by the white tower and its copper roof. Bridget quickly sketched the scene, including the flag flying on the pole in front of the house, the oil house, barn, shed, and privy, and the children and dog frolicking on the grassy lawn and stony beach of the barren point.

Discussion arose of the fog signal building being constructed, and mention was made of the additional labor needed to keep the steam whistle it would house operational. Word had already circulated among those in the light service about the search for a new assistant.

By late afternoon, beneath threatening clouds, the *Manitou Lady* had rounded Omena Point and entered the cove. Bridget realized that, unlike the crossing to Leland, Anna had spent little time with Nat this trip.

With the shoreline coming clearly into view, Erik joined Bridget at the starboard bow of the upper deck. "There's my parents' place, The Clovers Hotel," he said, pointing to a complex of grand white cottages overlooking the bay about a mile south of town.

"All of that is The Clovers?" Bridget asked in wonderment.

"The Main House, the Big Cottage, the Little Cottage,

and the Bay Cottage," Erik said, pointing to each in turn.

Opening to a new page in her sketchbook, Bridget began putting her impression of the resort on paper, the tower of the main house, its gables, and veranda; the lilac bushes past blooming, the apple orchard in the distance, the tennis courts and croquet lawns, the small barn and ice house, and the surrey that was coming to the dock to meet them.

Within minutes, the *Manitou Lady* had tied up, Bridget's trunk and bag had been offloaded, and she was on her way to the Main House along with Anna and the Olsons—and Nat, who had insisted on taking a closer look at her place of summer employment before casting off for Traverse City.

A tall, elegant blond woman with keys jangling from her trim waistline emerged from the Main House the moment David, the surrey driver, halted at the foot of the front steps. A boy and girl in their late teens, bearing remarkable resemblance to Erik, stood either side of her.

When everyone had alighted from the surrey, Erik made introductions. "Mother, Ingrid, Ole, this is Miss Bridget Richards and Mr. Nat Trevelyn of South Manitou Island. Mr. Trevelyn was good enough to offer us passage when *Brede's Bargain* sprang a leak, and Miss Richards has come to take a chamber maid position. She's willing to entertain the children when necessary."

"How do you do?" said Ole and Ingrid in turn.

Mrs. Olson focused on Nat. "How can I ever thank you for bringing my men home? You'll stay to dinner, of course."

"Thanks, ma'am, but I'd best be on my way to Traverse City. There's somethin' you can do for me, though." He

42

placed his arm around Bridget's shoulders. "Take mighty good care of Miss Richards. I aim to make her my wife, come summer's end."

Mrs. Olson renewed her smile. "My hired help receives the best of treatment, I can assure you, Mr. Trevelyn. Go see for yourself. David will wait here to drive you back to your boat." To her children, she said, "Erik, Ole, Ingrid, take Mr. Trevelyn to see the hired help's quarters." To Bridget, she said, "Come to my office."

"I'll be back to say my good-byes," Nat told Bridget.

When Anna and the Olsons had gone off with Nat, Mrs. Olson turned to Bridget, her smile replaced by a dour look. "This way, Miss Richards."

Thunder rumbled softly in the distance as Bridget followed Mrs. Olson inside to a small room. While the older woman paused to gaze out the large curtainless window overlooking the dock and the *Manitou Lady*, Bridget took in her surroundings. Mrs. Olson's modest desk was so tidy, it appeared unused. Even the blotter showed not a trace of ink, but the air was redolent with the odor of it. Then Bridget's gaze fell on the wastebasket. Larger than average, it was nevertheless full to overflowing with drawings of prehistoric beasts. Something about them, and the spartan quality of the place, was off-putting. And when Mrs. Olson turned to her to speak, so was her look of complete disdain.

"Miss Richards, have you ever worked as a chamber maid?" she asked curtly.

"No, ma'am, but—"

"Or a nanny?"

"No, but I've—"

"There's no work for you here." Mrs. Olson abruptly

turned away, gazing again out the window where dark clouds over the bay were beginning to spark with lightning.

The pounding of Bridget's heart seemed to match the increasing rumble of the thunder. "Mrs. Olson, I've made many a bed and can keep house tidy enough to please even the strictest light service inspector. For months, I took care of a two-year-old little boy. Those experiences ought to count for something."

Mrs. Olson turned to her again, her face set in hard lines. "I said there's no work for you here, and I meant it."

With one last idea, Bridget asked, "Do you know of any place in Omena that might hire me?"

"I do not. Get on the surrey and go with Mr. Trevelyn to Traverse City."

Mention of the town at the bottom of the bay stirred a new notion. Bridget had already sent a letter of application to the Ferrises, a family there on Washington Avenue. She would go in person to inquire. Genuinely grateful not to be working for such a disagreeable woman, she put on a smile. "Thank you for your suggestion. Good bye, Mrs. Olson."

The moment she stepped outdoors, lightning flashed overhead, thunder boomed, and the clouds opened up. Quickly, she climbed aboard the surrey to escape the fat raindrops. "David, I'll be returning to the *Manitou Lady* along with my trunks," she said, then settled on the back seat to wait. A few minutes later, Nat and the others came dashing toward the Main House, Anna taking cover beneath Nat's jacket. Anna's laughter at his teasing remarks rankled as they hurried for the protection of the veranda, unaware of her presence.

Erik was the first to spot her in the surrey. "Miss Richards, what are you doing in there?"

"I'm going on to Traverse City with Nat to look for work, if he'll take me. Your mother won't hire me."

"What?" Erik said in complete disbelief. He bounded off the porch and into the surrey, followed by Nat.

"Your mother won't hire me," Bridget repeated.

"Surely there's a mistake!" Erik countered. "Let me talk to her."

"Bridget said she's goin' with *me*, Olson," Nat cut in. "That's the last I wanna hear of it. David, take us to the dock!"

"Yes, sir." The driver slapped the reins and the rig lurched forward.

Erik climbed off without so much as a good bye, his long strides carrying him swiftly up the steps and into the Main House. Anna, Mr. Olson, and Gramps waved from the porch.

Mechanically, Bridget waved back and smiled, but inside, her thoughts spun in circles. What if the family in Traverse City didn't want her? She had but a few coins to her name, enough to tide her over for a day or two. Then she must find work. She must! She pulled a handkerchief out of her pocket and fidgeted, purposely avoiding looking at Nat, though she could feel his gaze on her.

Nat had only seen Bridget looking this forlorn once before—the day Meta had died. Secretly, he gloated over the fact Erik Olson would not spend time near Bridget this summer. The idea of proposing marriage again was so strong, he could barely keep the words from spilling out. He could easily find a preacher in Traverse City on a Sunday evening. They could be married tonight! Only with great self-control did he refrained from voicing the suggestion.

As much as he had disagreed at first with Bridget's plan to spend the summer on the mainland, he'd tempered his opinion about it since talking briefly with Anna on the trip from Leland today. Regardless, he didn't like seeing Bridget so hurt over broken promises. He'd like to pop Erik Olson for building up her hopes, only to let her come crashing down!

Gently, he reached out, lifting her chin until her gaze met his, then he pulled the goofiest face he could, the kind he used on Michael whenever he hurt himself. A smile teased at the corners of her mouth. "That's better. Now forget about the Olsons. It was just a temporary job. You'll find a better one in Traverse City tomorrow. It'll all work out for the best."

Bridget could hardly believe the change in Nat's attitude. It made her want to reach out and hug him, but she kept her tight grip on her handkerchief. "Thanks for reminding me God has a reason for everything."

Though Nat still hadn't figured out God's reason for taking Meta home to heaven, he pushed aside the question to focus on Bridget's problem. "God had a reason for bringin' you to Omena, and a reason for not lettin' you stay. Time 'll reveal His purpose."

In her heart, Bridget knew Nat spoke the truth, but she couldn't help feeling impatient for the Lord to unfold his true plan for her.

CHAPTER

5

With Nat's help, Bridget put her trunk in temporary storage at the Germaine Brothers Hack, Bus, and Baggage Transfer Line and found comfortable lodgings for the night on Washington Street at the home of the Doyles, two elderly sisters endowed with a most congenial nature.

The following morning, dressed in the navy blue serge skirt Aurora had given her for Christmas, and a new narrow-sleeved white waist, she set out for the Ferrises, who had advertised for a nanny.

The attractive rambling home a block away, at number six twenty-two, couldn't be more than a year old, she thought, approaching it on the walk. Its newly seeded yard boasted a pretty children's playhouse. If the family inside were half as appealing as their home and yard, Bridget knew she would be very happy here.

With high hopes, she proceeded up the front walk and cranked the doorbell. Moments later, a maid answered, the ruffles of her stiffly starched apron standing in stark relief to her pencil-thin figure, long nose, and even longer face.

"Yes?" The maid's arrogance was effectively conveyed in a single word.

"I've come to inquire about my application for employment as nanny. I sent a letter—"

"There's no work here," she said curtly, closing the door before Bridget could inquire further.

The turn-down haunted her all the way to Front Street. Once there, she canvassed the entire business area. Neither the baker, nor mercantile proprietor, nor milliner, nor seamstress, nor a dozen other shopkeepers needed assistance. She was thinking of quitting her search for the day when the enticing aroma of chocolate emanating from an open doorway drew her to a small establishment.

"Newtons' Candy Shoppe" read the sign in reverse painting on the front window. Inside the busy store, she could see a corpulent, balding gentleman in white shirt, pants, and apron—Mr. Newton, most likely. His tiny rimless spectacles seemed lost on his wide, sweaty face as he worked a batch of fudge on a marble slab, turning it over and over again with a spatula, explaining the cooling process to a cluster of patrons. Behind the glass case, a wide-set woman waited on other customers. Strands of gray hair had escaped her chignon, dangling against her cheeks. She shoved them back and continued filling the scoop of the candy scale with the choices of her finicky shoppers while several more people stood three deep in front of the counter, impatiently waiting their turn.

With a confidence born of desperation, Bridget marched in the door and threaded her way through the throng of candy-seekers, stepping behind the counter. "Who's next? Can I take your order, please?"

Barely sparing her a side glance, the woman said quietly, "There's a fresh apron hanging on the wall, and an extra scoop on the corner table."

For the remainder of the morning, Bridget worked

alongside the lady, their conversation consisting only of essential information regarding location of the numerous varieties of candy: hand-dipped chocolate-covered cherries, creams, and mints; nut delicacies including peanut brittle, pecan pralines, cashew clusters, and chocolate-covered Brazil nuts; and fudge slabs flavored in vanilla, chocolate, and maple, with or without walnuts.

During a lull after the noon hour rush, Mr. Newton turned to Bridget. "Where did you come from?"

The woman answered for her. "Ben, I told you a hundred times if you didn't hire an assistant, I'd find one myself. Folks from all over Michigan are coming up north on holiday this time of year, and I'll go downright crazy if I don't have help." She put her arm gently about Bridget's shoulder. "This woman here is an angel, come to preserve my sanity, Miss . . . "

"Richards," Bridget quickly supplied. "Bridget Richards. Pleased to make your acquaintance, Mr. Newton."

"Newton?" he said with a chuckle. "He was the last owner. Success drove him out of business—too much hard work. He sold to me and Lottie last winter. Our name is Marshall. I'm Ben. Some day, my sister will change the name on the window. Thought it best to just leave the old name for now. Newton had a real fine reputation. We need to trade on it for awhile."

Lottie untied her apron and hung it on a wall peg. "I'd best go upstairs and see to lunch. I hope you'll join me, Miss Richards. When we're done, Ben 'll take his lunch break."

"I'd love to take lunch with you," Bridget replied.

"You can wash the stickiness off your hands upstairs in

our apartment. I'd appreciate your help setting the table." To Ben, she said, "By the time you have that new batch of fudge all sliced and set in the display case, we'll be back to take over."

Bridget followed Lottie up a set of steep, narrow stairs to a small sitting room. Against one wall stood a table with an open Bible. A crucifix hung on the wall above. Two overstuffed chairs, a velvet pillow pinned with the beginnings of bobbin lace, and a bookcase filled with the works of Joseph Conrad and others furnished the candy-scented space.

No sooner had the door closed behind Bridget, than Lottie turned to her and heaved a tremendous sigh. "Thank the good Lord for sending a bold one like you through the door. All week, I've been after Ben to get me help, and he's been putting me off. I thought I'd go plum out of my mind in another day or so, up at five cooking the candy and dipping the chocolates, open at nine, waiting on customers till six. I've had no time to even place an ad in the paper."

"Working for you is answered prayer, Miss Marshall. I was desperate for a position," Bridget said.

"Not near as desperate as I am to have your help. My feet hardly fit into my shoes, they're swelled up so. And the summer season hasn't officially started yet—not till tomorrow, Independence Day! Come with me to the kitchen. We'll talk more while we get lunch on the table."

Bridget thought she knew now why God had brought her to Traverse City. Lottie Marshall needed her as much as she needed the Marshalls.

While Bridget set out napkins and poured milk, she began explaining how she had come from South Manitou expecting to be employed at Omena. Her story was inter-

50

rupted by the ringing of the telephone that hung beside the back door—two short rings. Bridget looked at Lottie expectantly.

Lottie shook her head. "Just ignore it unless you hear four short rings. That's our line. Now what were you saying about Omena?"

"I'd been promised work there at The Clovers Hotel, but when I arrived, the job was filled, so I came to Traverse City in hopes of finding something else."

Lottie nodded in understanding. "Seeing as how you don't live in Traverse City, you'll have to accept room and board here with us as your starting salary. I've got a little chamber downstairs that will be just right for you." She sliced the sandwiches and put them on the plates. "In a couple more weeks, providing business stays brisk, I can add a small wage."

"Those arrangements sound fine," Bridget said, thankful for the rapport she had struck up with Miss Marshall in such a short time. With the aroma of the candy shop surrounding her all day, and the pleasant fellowship of the Marshalls in the evening, she was certain she'd be content.

Later that afternoon, a gentleman of about thirty with a perfectly trimmed mustache and goatee entered the store during one of the rare lulls in traffic. Ben was the first to greet him. "Mr. McCune, you've come to replenish your supply of caramels."

"Good afternoon, Mr. Marshall. Actually, I haven't need of more caramels just yet." He removed his top hat, nodded to Lottie, then settled his gaze on Bridget. Something in his penetrating focus discomforted her, and his smile, though pleasing, seemed forced. "Miss Marshall, you have a new assistant."

"That I do. Miss Richards, this is Mr. Kenton McCune, Attorney at Law. Mr. McCune, Miss Bridget Richards of South Manitou Island. She'll be staying with us and helping out for the summer."

"Pleased to make your acquaintance, Miss Richards."

"Likewise, Mr. McCune," said Bridget, taking notice of his precisely tailored blue pinstripe suit, the tiny red feather tucked into the band of his silk-lined hat, and the perfectly manicured fingernails on the hands that held it. "I'd shake your hand, but mine are all sticky right now."

"Then we'll close on the handshake another time. Perhaps this evening." To Ben, he said, "If you'll be at home, I'd like to return *Almayer's Folly* and borrow *An Outcast of the Islands*."

"I'm pleased you found Joseph Conrad to your liking. Come about eight," Ben said.

"I'll do that," said Kenton, his focus returning to Bridget as she replenished the plate of caramels in the candy case. "On second thought, maybe I *do* need more vanilla caramels. Miss Richards, would you weigh up half a pound for me?"

"With pleasure, sir." When she handed him the box, he pressed a coin into her palm. "Keep the change, Miss Richards. Good day." Briskly, he strode off.

Bridget stared at the silver coin. "But this is more than twice what he owed," she told Lottie.

The woman dismissed her concern with a flick of the wrist. "He can well afford it. Do as he said, mind you, and keep the change for yourself."

After dinner had been served and the kitchen put in

order, Lottie said, "Miss Richards, I'll show you the room I had in mind for you." Bridget followed her downstairs where she opened a door off the back hall.

The space was just big enough for the cot already in place and the trunk she would bring out of storage at the Germaine Brothers Hack, Bus, and Baggage Transfer Line. Compared to the bedroom she had shared with her sisters at the keeper's quarters on South Manitou, it seemed tiny, but its sparkling white walls, varnished oak floor, and pressed tin ceiling made for pleasant surroundings. "I'll go now to the Doyles's and fetch my overnight bag. After the holiday, I'll have my trunk delivered."

She had just finished her sentence when someone knocked on the apartment door. Lottie opened it to Mr. McCune. He appeared as fresh as the fragrance of sandalwood soap that entered with him. His casual clothes—tan wool pants, white shirt, and bow tie seemed less daunting and more attractive on his well-proportioned form than the morning suit had. Even his smile was warmer and more natural.

"I've come to return this book to Mr. Marshall," he told Lottie. His gaze shifted to Bridget and his smile widened. Offering his hand, he said, "And I see my timing is perfect to collect on the handshake you owe me."

Bridget placed her hand in his, finding his grip comfortably firm. "You have a quick memory, Mr. McCune."

"And an eye for a pretty lass," Lottie teased. "Your timing is good for more than just a handshake, Mr. McCune. Miss Richards is on her way over to the Doyles's on Washington Street to fetch some of her belongings. I'd be mighty grateful if you'd walk her there and home safely. I'll take the book up to Ben and tell him you'll be along in awhile to borrow the other one."

He handed Lottie the novel, his attention still on Bridget. "It would be my pleasure to walk you to Washington Street. 'Pleasure is like the flow'r, Frail and fleeting ever; Now decks the bow'r, Now 'tis gone for ever.'"

Lottie chuckled. "I hope you like poetry, Miss Richards, because Mr. McCune is mighty eloquent that way."

He began again in lofty strains. "'Eloquence flows like droppings of sweet poppy syrup.'"

Lottie gestured toward the door. "Off with you, now. I'll go up and put on fresh coffee so it'll be ready by the time you're back."

Kenton McCune opened the door for Bridget, and as they stepped out together, it was as if the portal to his mind had opened as well, allowing every reasonable thought to take flight. He struggled to think of something significant to say, but everything that came to mind seemed mundane.

More than ever, he felt the intense awkwardness that beset him each time he was alone with a pretty young woman. His head was full of poetry, and in the courtroom, he had no trouble pleading and winning cases for his clients, but he didn't want to spout poetry now. He wanted to carry on a normal conversation, yet his dreadful lack of social skills kept his tongue clamped against the roof of his mouth.

In desperation, he loosened it to open with the only question in mind—concerning his newly discovered interest. "Have you read any of the works of Joseph Conrad?" The words came out in such a rush, Kenton wanted to dissolve into a puddle and evaporate.

Bridget sensed the anxiety that had overcome Mr.

McCune in the last few minutes. The tension was thicker than molasses on a January night. And Mr. McCune *would* raise the subject of Joseph Conrad. Bridget knew only that he was a British writer, nothing more. Begrudgingly, she admitted her ignorance.

"I . . . haven't had the pleasure." To avoid further awkward silence, she proposed a familiar topic. "Have you ever been to South Manitou Island, Mr. McCune?"

"No. Sorry." Kenton's clipped reply led to more silence. When they had walked another block, they came upon a baseball game on a city lot, the happy voices of young boys at play. A new thought erupted in Kenton's mind. He made a conscious effort not to talk too fast. "I haven't been to your island, but I understand your baseball team is hard to beat."

"How did you know?" Bridget asked in amazement.

"It just so happens I play baseball myself, right here in Traverse City. You're coming to the Independence Day game at the park tomorrow afternoon, aren't you?"

"I don't know. I haven't made plans for tomorrow."

"The Marshalls will be coming. They'll bring you. I'll discuss it with them when we get back. There's a parade in the morning and picnics and games all afternoon, and fireworks over the bay after dark . . . " Relief apparent, he chatted on.

When Bridget retired to her small chamber later that evening, she couldn't help thinking how pleasantly the hours with Mr. Kenton McCune had passed. Conversation had flowed all evening once they had conquered their initial awkwardness, and when they had returned to the Marshalls' apartment, she had listened with interest to his discussion with Ben about Joseph Conrad's tales of sailing on the south seas.

Following a pleasant night's sleep, she arose looking forward to Mr. McCune's return. Together with the Marshalls, they watched the Independence Day Parade. Afterward, he accompanied them on an outing to the park down by the bay where they enjoyed a picnic lunch of chicken salad sandwiches, lemonade, and Lottie's chocolate fudge cookies. Bridget managed to make a quick sketch of him before he joined his baseball team.

She watched every play with interest. Kenton McCune proved himself to be a surprisingly good batter, hitting in two runs for his team before they went down to defeat to their opponents from Greilickville. She roughed in a sketch of Kenton at bat, showing a homerun hit high in the air instead of the grounders.

Later, he watched the evening fireworks with her and the Marshalls. Reflections off the bay made the spectacle even more sensational.

As the grand finale boomed forth, lighting the sky with sparks of red, white, blue, pink, and green, Bridget thought of similar celebrations on South Manitou, and realized that for the first time, she was wondering how Nat had passed the day. She wondered, also, how Erik and his family were celebrating at The Clovers.

Those thoughts took flight as she and Mr. McCune helped Lottie and Ben fold the blankets and carry them back to the apartment. Ben and Lottie immediately took the picnic basket and blankets upstairs while Mr. McCune lingered at the door to bid Bridget good night.

Kenton couldn't remember a more enjoyable Independence Day than this one, despite the fact that he had been born and raised in the cradle of American independence at Concord, Massachusetts. He gazed into Bridget's eyes, blue-gray in the frail light of the street lamp, and a most wonderful feeling came over him. "'O deep eyes, darker and softer than the bluest dusk of August violets, darker and deeper like crystal fathomless lakes in summer moons,'--Augusta Webster. Forgive me for spouting poetry, Miss Richards, but this has been an extraordinarily pleasant day!"

He was gone so quickly, she couldn't even bid him good night!

Preparing for bed, she paused to look at the sketches she had drawn of him and couldn't help smiling. This *had* been a pleasant day.

She turned to the previous pages. The drawings of The Clovers Hotel, and of Erik and his grandfather in Leland reminded her of how unexpected changes had come to rule her life. In the past two days, she had been too busy to even think of the Olsons and Omena.

When she had changed to her nightgown she kneeled beside her bed. "Dear Lord, hold Gramps in your safekeeping and grant him strength," she prayed, hoping the old man had regained full health. "Bestow your blessings on Erik and his family at The Clovers Hotel, and on Nat and the *Manitou Lady*, too."

As she lay in bed, the image of Erik's mother came to mind, and when she drifted off to sleep, she couldn't help wondering about the uneasy atmosphere, and strange drawings in the woman's office.

The following morning Bridget rose early to help Lottie and Ben with the candy-making. Ben taught her how to melt the chocolate and paraffin in a big copper vat, stirring with a paddle to maintain a creamy texture. Lottie showed her the art of dipping the cream centers using a toothpick, and how to put a swirl on top to indicate vanilla, chocolate, or strawberry.

When the store opened at nine, eager customers crowded up to the counter, keeping her too busy to notice time passing. At ten o'clock, a wagon with the words, "Germaine Brothers" emblazoned on the side, stopped in front of the store and the burly, leather-capped driver strode in, elbowing his way to the counter. "Trunk for Miss Bridget Richards. Where do ya want it?" he asked, pulling a red print handkerchief from his torn shirt pocket to mop beads of sweat from his dirt-streaked forehead.

Bridget's mouth fell open. She had planned to telephone Germaine Brothers during her lunch hour to make arrangements for delivery of her trunk.

"I say, where do you want it?" the man asked irritably, stuffing the soaked handkerchief back into his tattered pocket, ripping it some more.

"I'll show you," Bridget said. Within two minutes, he had deposited the trunk at the foot of her bed. "What do I owe you, sir?" She searched for the change Mr. McCune had left when he overpaid for his caramels.

The driver lifted his cap to push his unruly brown hair beneath. "All paid for," he said with a gap-toothed grin. Indicating the flap of his shirt pocket, he added, "Bums and beggars know this ain't much of a shirt, but I'd lose even this old thing in court if I charged twice fer bringin' it here. Now come with me. I got somethin' else that b'longs to you. If I don't deliver it, I'll lose more'n my shirt. I'll lose my hide!"

Bridget followed him to his wagon. He climbed aboard and handed down a long green box tied with a huge red ribbon.

"Good day, miss!" With a shout to his team, he pulled away.

Quickly, Bridget carried the box to her room and opened it. Inside lay a card atop a dozen long-stemmed red roses. "Welcome to Traverse City. K. McC.," had been penned in florid strokes. Hastily, she tucked the card in her pocket and took the roses up to Lottie's kitchen to put them in water, wondering how Mr. McCune could have known the Germaine Brothers had held her trunk.

By the time Ben locked the door at six, Bridget's back, legs, and feet ached so much, she had no will to spend another half hour cleaning up the store, but she managed to do her part. Then she dragged herself up to the kitchen and somehow stayed on her feet long enough to help Lottie put the fried potatoes, biscuits, and creamed beef on the table. She couldn't help wondering, though, how she would hold up for three more long workdays. Sunday, her day of rest, couldn't come soon enough.

She was helping with the dishes, drying one of Lottie's rose-bordered china plates when a knocking commenced on the back door.

Bridget set the plate carefully in the cupboard and hurried to the back kitchen window, immediately recognizing the caller in the alley. "I'll be right down!" she shouted. To Ben and Lottie, she said, "It's Nat Trevelyn, a dear family friend from South Manitou."

"Invite him up for coffee," Lottie quickly replied.

On the way downstairs, Bridget fussed with her hair,

trying to force stray strands back in place before opening the door.

The moment Nat saw Bridget, he knew she was exhausted. He had seen her this way before, when she'd stayed up all night to care for Meta. "You look as though you're being worked to death," he said testily. "Haven't you had any sleep since the last time I saw you?"

Too tired to defend herself against his criticism, she spoke pleasantly. "Hello, Nat. Won't you come in?"

He stepped into the back storage entry, glanced through the open storage room door at the shelves laden with sacks of sugar, blocks of chocolate, and bottles of flavoring, then settled his gaze on her once more. "The Doyles told me you'd moved here. Where do you sleep? On a cot in the cellar?"

"No. On the dirt floor in the corner with the rats, mice, roaches, spiders, and ants. I've made a lot of four-, six-, and eight-footed friends in the last two nights." When Nat's countenance darkened, she smiled. "Just teasing. I have a room of my own. I'll show you." She led him into the back hall and opened her door.

He rapidly assessed the lodging. "Aside from havin' to remember to enter sideways, it's not bad," he concluded. His gaze settled on the trunk. "I went to Germaine Brothers to fetch your trunk and bring it to ya tonight, but when I got there, it was gone. Have any trouble gettin' it delivered?"

"It was easier than I expected," Bridget said casually.

His hazel eyes met hers. "How much are they payin' ya to work yourself to exhaustion?"

Too weary to humor him further, she answered candidly. "Room and board . . . with the promise of a modest wage if business stays brisk."

He scowled.

She smiled. "I like my work. I like the Marshalls, too. Come upstairs for coffee. I want you to meet them."

"Good, 'cause I wouldn't leave till I had," Nat remarked.

In the kitchen, Lottie moved the vase of long-stemmed roses aside and served coffee and a plate of cookies and candy. Nat complimented his hostess on the fine confections, spent several minutes describing his business hauling freight on the *Manitou Lady*, then looked Ben square in the eye. "You're not payin' Bridget near enough for the amount of work she does."

Ben replied pleasantly. "I was thinking the same thing. Lottie, from now on, see Miss Richards gets fifty cents a week raise."

"A dollar 'd be more like it," Nat countered. Feeling the sting of Bridget's kick to his shin, he added, "But fifty cents will do for now." Shoving aside his empty coffee cup, he said, "It's time I got back to my boat."

Just then, the phone rang—four short rings. As Lottie rose to answer it, Ben said, "Bridget will fill a box with sweets for you before you go, Mr. Trevelyn. That's one of the benefits of working here."

Nat nodded, his attention distracted by Lottie's end of the phone conversation. "Marshall residence . . . oh, hello Mr. McCune . . . yes, her trunk came . . . her roses came, too . . . just a moment." She gestured to Bridget. "Mr. McCune would like to speak to you."

Nat was about to demand who Mr. McCune was when Ben spoke again.

"Kenton McCune is a friend of ours from church. He came from out East to practice law after he graduated from

Harvard."

Nat nodded, then listened intently to Bridget's end of the conversation.

" . . . a home run? . . . Seven to six? Good for you!"

Lottie told Nat, "He plays baseball for one of the Traverse City teams. He's quite a hitter. They must have won again tonight." She picked up the coffeepot. "Are you sure you won't have another cup?"

Nat shook his head, then rose impatiently, interrupting the phone conversation with a loud announcement. "Bridget, I'm going now."

She cast him an anxious look, then said into the mouthpiece, "I have to hang up. My company is leaving."

Over the phone, she heard her caller say, "I'll ring you again soon. Good bye."

She hung the phone on its bracket and faced Nat with a smile, her weariness now gone. "Come down to the shop. I'll get you some candy."

Despite Nat's brooding countenance, and his silent shrug when she asked what kinds of candy he would like, she filled a large box with samples of caramels, nuts, creams, and fudge, then saw him to the back door. "Don't eat this all at once," she cautioned lightheartedly, offering him the chipboard box.

He paused before taking it, his look still sullen. "Seems to me this McCune fella's way oversteppin' his bounds. He can't have known ya more than a day or two, and already he's delivered your trunk and a dozen roses. What's the meanin' of this?"

From her pocket, Bridget pulled the card that had come with the flowers and handed it to Nat. "Mr. McCune was simply being gracious to a newcomer. Don't worry, Nat.

You're the best friend I've ever had—next to Meta."

He handed back the card, his cross look softening. "I'm goin' home day after tomorrow. I'll share this candy with Michael and your mama and the others."

Mention of her mother and the little boy kindled a flicker of homesickness within. "Kiss your son for me, and tell Mama I'm fine, will you?"

Nat nodded, and somehow managed to keep from saying he'd prefer having her return to South Manitou and do those things herself. These last few days, she'd been a real source of worry, and now there was this McCune fellow to think about. But Nat had slowly come to accept that he couldn't keep constant watch over her. He brushed a silken tendril away from her eyes realizing he cherished her—his best friend—as much as ever. "I'll be back again in a week, maybe sooner," he promised. "Don't go spendin' all your evenings with McCune."

Bridget kissed her finger and touched it to his cheek. "Fair sailing, Nat."

CHAPTER

6

"I'll take five pounds of assorted creams, and all the chocolate fudge in your case!"

At the sound of Erik's voice, Bridget looked up from the box she was filling with nuts. His wide smile sent a thrill through her, and her trembling hands nearly dropped the order of chocolate-covered peanuts.

Anna stood beside Erik, grinning. "He's only joking, you understand. It's the *vanilla* fudge we want."

"I'll be with you as soon as I finish with this order," Bridget said, hurriedly tying string around the box and making change.

Again, she focused on Erik and somehow gained control of the flutters in her stomach. "How did you find me?"

His brow raised. "I have ways." He wanted to tell her how miserable he'd been over their abrupt parting, but he would wait until later.

"Your whereabouts was no secret after Mr. Trevelyn stopped by The Clovers this morning and told us he'd found you here last night," Anna said. "He's quite worried about you."

"He practically bribed us to pay you a visit," Erik said.

Anna's eyes rolled heavenward. "As if a team of oxen could keep *you* away. You had the rig out and turned south before Mr. Trevelyn had even cast off."

Bridget laughed.

Lottie, just finishing with a customer at the other end of the counter, chuckled also.

"Lottie, come and meet my friends from The Clovers Hotel," Bridget said. "Miss Anna Steffens and Mr. Erik Olson. Anna, Mr. Olson, this is Miss Marshall, my employer." At the marble cooling table, Ben cleared his throat loudly, so Bridget hastily added, "And over there is Mr. Ben Marshall, her brother."

"Pleased to meet you," Erik said, then settled his gaze on Bridget once more. "When do you get off work?"

Bridget checked the time on the wall clock behind her. "Not for another four hours, I'm afraid. Then there's the cleaning up to do."

"I'll do the tidying up tonight," Lottie offered. "You're free to go at six."

"We'll come back and take you out to supper at the Columbian House," Erik promised.

At his cousin's insistence, their first objective, after finding Bridget, was to place an order at the W.W. Kimball Company for the organ Anna wanted. After poring over the catalogue descriptions and listening to the salesman's guarantee, she at last decided on the best model available:

the six-octave organ in black walnut with French bevel plate mirror, red silk plush center panel, lamp stands, and pedals covered with Brussels carpet and brass heel plates. Then she insisted on purchasing all new music, the most popular tunes of the day which she had played in Wisconsin on her piano.

Her choices were not so quickly made at the seamstress's shop where he waited two hours while she studied fabrics and patterns, and had her measurements taken for a new costume. At five minutes to six, he managed to get her aboard the rig and drove down the street to fetch Bridget from the candy shop, arriving at the front door precisely on the hour.

Bridget stepped out the moment he pulled up. As he handed her into the carriage, he couldn't help admiring her silken hair, light as the sun, poufed out and pinned in a golden knot atop her head, and the soft blush of roses on her round cheeks. He knew it was selfish, wishing he had the evening alone with her, but he couldn't help it.

Bridget settled beside Anna on the seat, noticing the gracefulness of Erik's lithe form as he climbed in beside her and set the carriage in motion. He looked far more handsome than when she had left Omena, her life suddenly thrown into turmoil. Now that he was beside her, she wasted no time raising the topic that had troubled her ever since.

"I've been worried about your mother. She was quite distressed the day we met. I hope things have improved for her."

His sober expression foreshadowed his reply. "She's still distraught. It concerns some illustrations she made for a Professor Evenson. He was a teacher of mine at the

University of Wisconsin until he moved out East."

"Pen and ink drawings of dinosaur skeletons?" Bridget asked.

"How did you know?" Anna wondered.

"I saw a wastebasket full of them the day I was in her office."

"They're stashed away under my bed in the hired help's quarters now," Anna informed her. "I moved there from the Main House just to put some distance between me and Aunt Katrina, she's been so difficult at times."

"We never know from one minute to the next what her mood will be," Erik told Bridget. "The moment you left, I went to find out why she hadn't hired you. To make a long story short, she was to have been paid for two years' worth of work on the dinosaur illustrations once they went into publication. On Saturday, she received a letter from Professor Evenson saying his book had been canceled because his publisher in Boston went bankrupt."

"That put her in a real snit," Anna said.

"She threw out all her drawings and decided never to have anything to do with them, or Professor Evenson again," Erik said.

While he brought the rig to a halt and set the brake, Anna took up the story. "Aunt Katrina was feeling so provoked, instead of conducting interviews to hire new help at The Clovers, she went and hired the first people she could find. Mrs. Zack, the woman who's supposed to help entertain the little children, is a grouchy old hag! On Independence Day, she frightened little Sarah Osbeck so badly, her folks couldn't bribe her to stay in the nursery—not for two candy canes and a lollipop! The poor little darling screamed at the top of her lungs until her folks let her come with them on their surrey ride. The Osbecks went home the very next day even though they were to have stayed the whole week. And they told Uncle Kal they'll never stay at The Clovers again. Aunt Katrina should have hired you instead, Bridget, and I even told her so!"

Bridget mulled over what Anna had said while Erik helped her and his cousin down from the rig. She could understand Mrs. Olson's keen disappointment over her artwork, being an amateur artist herself.

Erik escorted them to the door of the restaurant. The aroma of home cooking greeted them, and just inside, the pie safe filled with lemon meringue, strawberry rhubarb, and coconut cream pies piqued Bridget's appetite.

The atmosphere was inviting, with burgundy velvet drapes tied back at the windows, the electrified brass and crystal chandeliers glowing softly, and snow-white linens spread on the tables. Quiet conversation mingled with the soft tinkling of ice water as a waiter filled a glass for a man at a small table nearby. Bridget took a second look at the customer. With a start, she recognized Mr. McCune! After a moment's awkwardness, dreading the encounter in the company of Erik, a new thought came to her and she stepped up to the attorney.

"Hello, Mr. McCune!"

He glanced up from the menu he was studying. "Miss Richards, what a pleasant surprise! Meeting you so unexpectedly makes me happy as a beggar with a bag of gold!"

Something in his tone raised a flicker of doubt about the serendipity of the occasion, but she ignored her suspicion. "Would you join my friends and me for dinner? I'd really like for you to meet them." She beckoned to Erik and

Anna.

Erik reluctantly stepped forward. As much as he disliked the prospect of dinner with this slick-tongued, tailcoated fellow, an inner voice told him Bridget had a reason for including him in their party.

She made introductions. "Anna, Erik, this is Mr. Kenton McCune, Attorney at Law, a friend of the Marshalls. Mr. McCune, my friends from Omena, Miss Anna Steffens, and her cousin, Mr. Erik Olson."

Erik offered his hand eagerly. "Pleased to make your acquaintance, Mr. McCune. In fact, I could use the advice of a good lawyer right now. You *will* join us, won't you?"

"I would be ungracious doing otherwise."

Conversation flowed pleasantly over plates of scalloped parsnips and carrots, and baked chicken with the most delectable herb seasoning Bridget had ever tasted. She was careful to notice that while Anna gave her chapter and verse of the various fabrics and patterns she had considered at the seamstress's shop, Kenton carefully explained to Erik that he had only just met Bridget while shopping in the candy store. Then he launched into the topic of baseball and a lively but companionable discussion with Erik ensued.

By the time Anna began describing the parlor organ she was purchasing from the W.W. Kimball Company, Erik's and Kenton's topic had turned to the academic and cultural atmosphere of Boston. Over a piece of coconut cream pie Erik explained his mother's publishing problem.

"Is there any way you can help Mother get the payment she was promised?" Erik asked Kenton.

"Did she enter a written contract with this Professor Evenson?" Kenton wanted to know, his forehead creasing with concern.

"She signed some sort of agreement," Erik replied with certainty, "but I can't say whether it was with the professor, or the publisher."

Kenton opened a small gold case and laid an embossed card on the table. "Send it to me, along with the drawings, and I'll see what I can do."

"Thank you, Mr. McCune," Erik said, picking up both his card and his meal check. "You'll be receiving them soon."

Kenton slid a coin beneath the rim of his plate—a generous tip for all four of the twenty-five-cent dinners—and shoved back his chair. "I've enjoyed your company." His gaze lingered a second on Bridget, then he shoved back his chair. "Until we meet again."

Erik paid the tab and helped Anna and Bridget into the surrey. "Can I interest you ladies in a drive along the bay before we call it an evening?"

Wishing for a few minutes alone with Erik before he left the city, Bridget said, "Let's go to the park and watch the sun set."

"Good idea," Anna said. "I'm exhausted from shopping. I'd just as soon sit on a bench and feed popcorn to the gulls."

"The park, it is," said Erik, setting the surrey in motion.

While Anna settled herself on a bench with a bag of popcorn, Bridget strolled with Erik by the water, his quiet companionship and the beauty of the bay making conversation unnecessary.

Far offshore, two sailboats, their canvas reflecting the flamingo hue of the evening sky, seemed suspended on a silver sea that fused imperceptibly with the horizon. High above, a gull screamed and dove, creating a pool of ripples in the glassy water that spoke in whispers to the sandy shore.

Bridget moved closer to Erik, aware of his manly essence magnified by the moist evening air. Looking into his irresistible blue eyes, a fondness flickered within, and she fought the urge to reach up and caress the strong lines of his Norseman's cheek.

Erik gazed into the kindest eyes he had ever seen, and sensed a web of kinship surrounding him, subtly trapping him in a fondness that was threatening to become much more. He took her hand in his, and the pleasure he found in the innocent affection seemed to defy description.

Hand in hand, they followed the water's edge. By Erik's side, Bridget sensed a belonging within that she'd never known before, a warmth she wished would last beyond this meeting.

In Bridget's company, Erik found a peace in his soul that had been missing since their last parting. How he wanted to make it last, to take her with him to Omena, but knowing the absurdness of his desire made him all the more determined to treasure these rare moments.

The spell that had seemingly been cast over them was gently broken by the sound of a child's laughter as he darted toward the water, and the cautioning voice of an old man. The sight of him brought another gentleman to Bridget's mind.

"I've been praying for Gramps," she said.

"And the Lord has listened. Gramps hasn't had any chest pains since we were in Leland."

"Then I'll keep praying," she said, knowing in addition to Gramps's health, her prayers would include Erik and his mother.

Reluctantly, he turned away from the shore, taking Bridget in the direction of Anna. "I hate for the evening to end, but I'd better see you home now. I'll be late enough getting back to Omena as it is."

When Erik reached Front Street, he parked the surrey—and Anna—several feet beyond the candy store and walked Bridget to the front door of the Marshalls' apartment. Looking again into the fair, round face that seemed too pretty to leave behind, he summoned the words that had been ever on his mind these past few days.

"I've been suffering since you left Omena, knowing how I let you down."

"Tonight more than makes up for the past," Bridget quietly assured him.

Erik couldn't help wanting to go on making up, if every meeting could be like this one. Bridget didn't realize how effectively her forgiving spirit was feeding his fondness for her, and he wasn't about to tell her, not yet. Such admissions would seem too forward for two people whose friendship was so new. Yet in some ways, he felt as if he'd known her a very long time.

So much had happened in the last few days, Bridget had all but forgotten her anguishing departure from Omena. But she would not soon forget the geniality she was sharing with Erik right now.

"I wish I knew when I'd see you again," he lamented.

Bridget felt the same, but different words slid off her tongue. "God puts us where He wants us to be, if we let Him. When the time is right, our paths will meet again," she assured him, despite an overwhelming reluctance to say good night.

"Until then," Erik said, backing away slowly.

As he drove off, Bridget couldn't keep from whispering a selfish prayer. "Lord, *please* bring Erik this way again soon!"

CHAPTER

7

Anna's bag was packed and she was already waiting on The Clovers Hotel dock the following morning when Nat Trevelyn and the *Manitou Lady* steamed into the cove to pick her up and take her home to South Manitou Island. She was glad to be leaving the problem of her Aunt Katrina behind, yet at the same time she worried whether the woman would be able to withstand the demands of operating the resort for the entire season.

Those thoughts were pushed aside once she had boarded Nat's boat and fallen into a conversation with his sister-in-law, Charlotte Richards Trevelyn, just back from her honeymoon. The new bride was full of chatter about an idea of hers to sell excursion tickets on the *Manitou Lady* for Buffalo Bill's Wild West Show in Traverse City. They seemed to develop an immediate kinship that made their trip around the peninsula to Leland pass in no time at all.

After a lunchtime stopover at the fishtown, where Anna and Charlotte were treated to smoked salmon served in brown paper on the deck of the boat, Nat and Seth put the *Manitou Lady* underway once more on a course straight for South Manitou. The two hours in transit passed quickly, and soon Anna was at her cottage home.

On Saturday night, she and her brother, Tom, invited their summer friends over for another party, but it seemed dull compared to the one a week earlier when Anna had introduced Erik to Bridget and Nat had come storming in, fit to tear the place apart. She could hardly wait until her pump organ came to liven up the gatherings.

Sunday afternoon she went riding on Gala, her mare. The sun shone brightly, and the smell of juniper mixed with the essence of recently fertilized fields filled the balmy air. Her route took her west into the center of the island. There, she came upon the cemetery where she found Nat kneeling beside a fresh grave. Quietly, she dismounted and approached him, stopping a few feet away from the place where he had laid a bouquet of daisies and wild roses.

He was bent over, his chin resting on hands clasped in prayer. Tears moistened his cheeks, leaking past eyelids squeezed tightly shut. His receding hairline, the little wrinkles at the corners of his eyes, and the tiny ridge between his brows made him appear older than his twenty-five years.

She recalled her own loss several months ago, the pain she had suffered, and finally conquered. She could help Nat through this tough time. She had brought him relief from his sadness on the trip to Leland eight days earlier, and she would do it again, but not now.

From a fencepost, a red-winged blackbird sent out his *seee-yer* call of alarm. Even before Nat opened his eyes, he knew he was no longer alone and pulled his handkerchief from his pocket to dry the tears for which he felt no shame.

Then he saw her, the only person who had been able to lift the weight off his heart and make him forget Meta for awhile. Last Saturday on the trip to Leland, she had been pesty like a little fly, keeping after him to laugh a little until his world had turned briefly carefree.

But he didn't want that untroubled world right now—didn't want to smell Anna's sweet essence of violets, or admire her dark hair shimmering in the afternoon light, or gaze upon her cheeks so delicately sculpted no artist could create a look as beguiling. Nor did he want to gaze into her brown eyes. But he did, and found in them not the bright mischievousness of last Saturday, but a moist, melancholy, mournful look reflecting the pain he felt within.

Anna knelt beside Nat. Though her throat had choked with emotion, she managed somehow to speak. "You loved her very much, didn't you?"

Nat pressed his lips together and willed his tears to dry up, but they rolled down his cheeks in spite of his efforts. "Yes," he said in a ragged whisper, "more than life itself."

Anna brushed away her own tear with the back of her hand. "I'm . . . so . . . sorry."

Memories flooded back to her of a night when her own heart had broken so badly she'd thought it could never be whole again. Silently, she thanked God for repairing it and restoring happiness to her life. One day, Nat, too, would leave sadness behind, but he needed some time for deep sorrow.

She prayed silently for God's comforting hand in his time of sadness. When a few minutes had passed and she felt in control of her voice once again, she said, "Tell me about Meta, will you? I'd like to know her."

Nat remained silent, thinking back to his first memories of her, unsure he wanted to share them with a summer island visitor. But Anna waited patiently, her lips parted in an encouraging half smile, an expectant look in her eyes, and after several minutes he began putting his thoughts into words. "My first recollection of Meta is when she was a little girl with two long blond braids hangin' down her back. Nothin' special, really, just another farm kid. I was a lot older and really didn't pay her any mind until she was almost finished with the eighth grade. That's when I first noticed she was growin' up . . . "

Anna listened with interest as Nat told about the only girl he had ever loved, the only girl he had ever courted, the only girl he had ever kissed. She listened, too, to his description of their elopement, to how much he had missed Meta when he was away on the lakes, and how they had anticipated the birth of their son, Michael, who arrived seven months after their wedding.

Then he spoke of her bout with diabetes. "She was always fair, but she got even more pale then. It seemed like she never could get enough to drink. Always had a glass of water in her hand, and spent a lot of time in the outhouse.

"When I'd get close to her, I noticed a kind of sweet smell to her breath. And when she blushed, it went all the way to the roots of her hair.

"She was tired, too. After awhile, she couldn't keep up with Michael. Her mother came to help. My mother came, too, and Bridget. I don't know what we'd 've done without Bridget.

"Near the end, Meta had awful pains in her gut, then she went into a coma, and the next day . . . she was . . . gone." Nat couldn't keep his chin from trembling. He buried his face in his hands.

Anna dabbed fresh tears from her eyes. "Her suffering was over. You can be glad of that."

Yes, Nat thought, *but she shouldn't have gotten sick.* He wanted to shout at God for allowing such misery into his and Meta's lives, but that would do no good. He let the moment of anger pass, then continued on with his story. "We buried her the next day. It was a cloudy Monday mornin', kind of cool and wet."

Anna remembered the drizzly day three weeks after she had come to the island for the summer. Soon after arriving on South Manitou, she had befriended Bridget, and Bridget had mentioned the funeral. Anna listened now to Nat's telling of it.

"Meta's father, and her brother, Fritz, had worked late the night before, diggin' her grave and makin' a pine box. Her mama and Bridget washed her and dressed her and fixed her hair and laid her on a piece of blue velvet. I kissed her and went out of the house. I couldn't even watch them close the lid. When Pa Schroeder and Fritz put the nails in, it was just like they were pounding them into my heart.

"Pa Schroeder and Fritz and my father helped load the casket onto the wagon and we took her to the cemetery. Michael was with us, and I'll never forget what happened next.

"We were all standin' around the grave. The casket had already been lowered down, and there was a pile of dirt beside the hole. I was readin' scripture. All of a sudden, I heard Bridget gasp. I looked up, and there was little Michael, runnin' toward the hole!

"I tried to catch him, but he got clear to the edge of the pit, right by the pile of dirt. All of a sudden he plops down on his little fanny, lets out a squeal, digs both hands into the soil and tosses it into the grave."

Nat was smiling now and Anna smiled, too. She could see the little boy in her mind, feel her heart stop at the thought of losing him in the same grave that held his mother, imagine the relief and humor when he sat down to play in the dirt. "Here lies Meta Schroeder Trevelyn," she mused aloud, "wife of Nat, mother of Michael. Her life was short, but filled with love. May she rest in peace."

"May she rest in . . . peace," Nat repeated, choked with emotion. After a moment's meditation, he started to get up and realized his pants were damp from sitting on the ground and his legs and back were so stiff he couldn't straighten them.

Anna rose easily and let out a quiet laugh. "You look like a Viking sentenced to carry Norway on his shoulders for betraying his fellow warriors to the Icelanders."

He rubbed the muscles in the small of his back, finally managing to unbend. "Do you have a Norwegian myth for everything?" he wondered, remembering the tales she'd told on the crossing to Leland a week earlier.

"If I don't, I make them up," she said with a laugh.

He smiled briefly. "You'd better get on home now, or your folks'll be worried about you." He held the bridle of her horse while she climbed aboard, arranging the skirt of her riding habit over the side saddle.

"I'll see you in a couple of weeks, when my organ comes. I told the man at the Kimball Organ Company they were to ship it to South Manitou aboard your *Manitou Lady*. They're expecting you to come for it."

"I'll bring it. Off with you now." He slapped the mare's hind quarters and she eased into a gallop.

Nat watched Anna and her horse until they disappeared around the bend in the road. Slowly, his legs limbered up

79

and he struck a pace toward home, realizing the burden of grief he had carried in his heart was decidedly lighter now than when he had first arrived at the little plot where the oaken cross bore Meta's name.

Bridget dabbed perspiration from her upper lip, stuffed her handkerchief into her apron pocket, and continued to stick lollipops into the countertop display stand while Lottie waited on the first customer of the day. Even with the electric fan to cool the candy shop, the second week of July had turned too hot for dipped chocolates. In their stead, the Marshalls had taught her to make candy canes, taffy, and lollipops in a variety of flavors. She had even become somewhat of an artist, putting clown faces on the largest lollipops. Rain or shine, they were always sold out by the end of each day. Today being Friday, she had made a few extras.

The door squeaked open as she stuck the last lollipop in the stand. When she looked up to wait on the customer, Mrs. Olson was staring at her.

Bridget gulped air. From the dark shadows beneath the woman's eyes, she was obviously worn out. The look of disdain Bridget remembered so well from two weeks ago in Omena had become one of defeat.

Taking a deep breath, Bridget forced herself to employ a pleasant tone. "Good morning, Mrs. Olson. Can I help you?"

"No," came her curt reply. "I mean, I don't want candy. I came to ask if you'll work for me." When Bridget remained silent, she said, "The job you wanted at The Clovers is yours. You'll earn twice what you're making here."

Bridget thought of Erik. She hadn't seen him since his

visit over a week ago when he and Anna had taken her out to dinner. She missed him and wanted badly to spend the summer with him, but how happy would she be, working for his mother? Despite her low wages, the Marshalls had already made her feel completely at home. And she enjoyed her walks with Mr. McCune on evenings when baseball didn't interfere.

Bridget's gaze focused on Mrs. Olson's tired blue eyes. "I'm flattered by your proposal, but I can't work for you."

"Excuse me," Lottie interrupted. "Miss Richards, can I see you?" To Mrs. Olson, she said, "We won't be but a minute." Taking Bridget by the wrist, Lottie hustled her into the back room and closed the door, a look of urgency replacing her normally placid expression. "Don't be a fool, Miss Richards. You've *got* to go to Omena."

"But I don't want to," Bridget insisted.

"That woman needs you . . . badly. Can't you see it by the look of her?"

Bridget remembered the day she first started working for Lottie, how tired the older woman was then, and how rested she was now. "You need me, too."

Lottie waved off her argument. "I can get another girl to work here, but you won't get another chance to help Mrs. Olson. God told me to hire you, and he's telling me now to push you out the door."

Bridget wished she could be as sure as Lottie was about God's message, but she couldn't get Mrs. Olson's careworn look and edgy disposition out of her mind.

Lottie grinned and shook her finger at Bridget. "Don't make me fire you, Miss Richards, 'cause I'll do it if it's the only way to get you back to Omena."

Bridget chuckled. "All right, I'll go, but it will be on

my own terms." She marched back into the shop and leveled her gaze directly on Mrs. Olson. "Room and board, three times my current wage, Mondays and Tuesdays off."

Mrs. Olson's Adam's apple bobbed. "All right. How soon can you start?"

"She'll be on the six o'clock excursion tonight," Lottie said, referring to the last of the boats that ran three times a day to Omena.

"Thank you." Mrs. Olson started for the door, then came back to the counter. "I changed my mind about the candy. I'd like five pounds of your vanilla fudge, five pounds of the chocolate . . . and all the lollipops on that stand."

"I'll box it up," Lottie said to Bridget. "You'd best start packing."

Reluctantly, she hung up her apron and started putting away her belongings, retrieving several items from the apartment sitting room and kitchen which had become almost as much hers as they were Ben's and Lottie's. Her trunk was packed by mid-morning, and she rang up the Germaine Brothers to arrange transfer to the six o'clock boat to Omena. She also rang up Kenton McCune in his office to tell him of her abrupt change in employment.

"Let me take you out for luncheon," he suggested.

Bridget didn't want to turn him down, nor did she want to miss her last noon hour with Lottie. "Why don't you come here instead? Twelve o'clock."

"I'll see you then."

Bridget worked alongside Lottie until quarter to twelve when she went up to the kitchen to set the table, pour the milk, and make sandwiches. At twelve, Bridget heard the voices of Lottie and Mr. McCune as they came up the stairs. She hung up her apron and checked the table, quickly laying out the napkins she had forgotten.

When Kenton came through the door, she was reminded what a handsome figure he cut in a gray pinstripe morning suit, with his mustache and goatee trimmed to perfection and his caramel brown hair combed back from a center part that was straight as a lance.

He smiled when he saw her, and handed her a small book. "My going-away gift for you, Miss Richards—*Tales of Unrest* by Joseph Conrad. It's his most recent story."

Bridget opened the front cover and read his inscription. "'Unlike the title of this novel, may you find peace and tranquility in Omena.'" He had signed it the same as when he'd sent the roses—K.McC. "How thoughtful. I'm looking forward to reading it. I wish I had some small token to give you in return."

Kenton pulled a newspaper clipping from his coat pocket and handed it to her. "I know something you can give me. A promise to see Buffalo Bill's Wild West Show with me. According to that advertisement, it's coming to Traverse City on Tuesday, the twenty-fifth."

"How convenient," Lottie commented. "Miss Richards will have Mondays and Tuesdays off."

Kenton's brows raised hopefully. "Then you'll go?"

Bridget smiled. "I'd love to."

Lottie pulled out her chair and sat. "Now that that's settled, let's eat."

Bridget was lucky to find space on a bench aboard the six o'clock boat. The vessel was loaded with families and couples, young and old, just off the train in Traverse City and bound for Sutton's Bay, Omena, and Northport.

Their happy chatter filled the air, and though Bridget still felt pangs of regret leaving the Marshalls, she trusted Lottie's reasoning that God held something new in store for her.

A breeze off the bay cooled the passenger deck, offering relief from the stifling heat of the city. In the evening sky, wispy, fair weather clouds hung against a realm of aqua, promising an appearance of the moon and stars in full regalia once darkness set in. She thought of Erik and their last meeting, when he and Anna had visited eight days ago. He had been on her mind daily, and she had hoped to have seen him before now. Undoubtedly, work at The Clovers Hotel had kept him away, but now that she was joining him there, her Leelanau summer was about to begin.

CHAPTER

8

When the boat approached The Clovers Hotel dock, Bridget worked her way toward the bow to look for Erik. Passengers stood three deep at the rail, but she managed to catch a glimpse of him along with Gramps and David, the surrey driver.

She'd never seen Erik looking more handsome, his strawberry blond hair tousled by the breeze, shirt collar open, sleeves rolled up to reveal strong, tanned forearms. His face was ruddier, too, giving him the appearance of a real lakes man.

Her heart skipped a beat and the unexpected reaction sent a rush of warmth through her. She was glad he wasn't able to see the color invading her cheeks.

Reclaiming her small bag from beneath the bench where she had stowed it, she worked her way to the exit at the midsection of the ferry, finding herself in line to disembark behind a cigar-smoking man in a straw hat. The large paunch at his belt line got in the way when he transferred his leather briefcase from one hand to the other, pulled out his handkerchief, and mopped the sweat from a broad forehead deeply creased with lines.

His wife and three daughters were with him. The two

youngest girls were perhaps ten and thirteen. The white, square collars on their drop-waistline dresses—pink for the younger, blue for the older—flapped in the warm breeze.

Their older sister was all of eighteen with the perfect Gibson-girl look—a willowy figure, shiny auburn hair puffed out and smoothed up into a knot, and an oval face made attractive by dark, wide-set eyes, a perfectly straight nose, and a bone structure as beautiful as the models in the *Harper's Bazar* fashion plates.

The youngest girl, pink hair ribbon fluttering in the breeze, rose up on tiptoes again and again to peek through the crowd. "There he is, Clarissa! Erik's waiting for you!" she said to her oldest sister. "Are you going to kiss him hello on the cheek when you see him?"

"Of course she is, Polly," the middle daughter said, tossing back her dark ringlets and looking down her long bespectacled nose with disdain.

"Well, Clarissa? Are you gonna?" Polly wanted to know.

"Of course!" Clarissa answered with agitation. "I always kiss him hello in Wisconsin. This is no different."

"I wonder if he's kissed any girls since The Clovers opened this summer," the middle daughter mused.

"Rachel, that's enough talk about kissing," her plump mother warned, tugging at the waistline points of her gray linen jacket. Her traveling suit had obviously been custom-tailored to fit her pear shape at considerable expense, and the diamond pin on her lapel was no cheap paste imitation.

Despite the broad brim of the woman's straw hat, Bridget caught another glimpse of Erik through the crowd and couldn't help wondering how many young ladies had made friends with him on their visits to The Clovers Hotel.

The ramp banged down on the dock and the debarking passengers surged forward. Somehow, Bridget managed to move ahead of Clarissa and her family. Then Polly ran past.

"Erik!" she cried, arms outstretched to Erik.

He strode toward her, a wide smile on his face. "Hello, Miss Polly! I see you've made it safely from Manitowoc." He hugged her briefly, then his gaze and his smile settled on Bridget. He reached for her bag and put his arm about her waist, pulling her close to his side. "Miss Richards, I'd like you to meet a friend of mine, Miss Polly Hackbardt. Miss Hackbardt, Miss Richards." As Rachel and Clarissa joined their sister, Erik placed a kiss prominently on Bridget's cheek.

"I don't like you, Miss Richards!" Polly sulked.

"Polly!" Clarissa scolded. "Is that any way to behave toward Erik's friend?"

"He's not supposed to kiss *her*. He's supposed to kiss *you!*" Polly insisted.

"Hush, before I take you over my knee," Clarissa threatened. Turning to Bridget, she offered a hand expensively gloved in imported lace. "Please forgive my little sister. I'm Clarissa Hackbardt."

"Pleased to meet you," Bridget said, clasping a slender hand that went completely limp on contact.

Shifting her attention to Erik, Clarissa boldly planted a kiss on his cheek and said in a sultry voice, "I'll see you later."

"I'll be spending this evening with Miss Richards," Erik quickly informed her.

Clarissa offered a cunning smile. "We'll see about *that*." Taking Polly by the hand, she strolled off toward the

87

waiting surreys.

Erik shrugged off the remark, then focused on Bridget, giving her a little squeeze. "Come on. Gramps is waiting to see you, and David is here to take us up to dinner. By the time we're finished, your trunk will be in your dormitory room and you can unpack."

The Hackbardt sisters were claiming the back seat of David's surrey when Erik and Bridget walked up. Gramps handed the Manitowoc girls into the carriage, then turned to Bridget, his face splitting in a smile.

She smiled widely in return. "How are you feeling, Gramps? I've been worried about you."

"I feel wonderful! Seeing you again makes me light-hearted as a boy," he teased, his hand covering his left shirt pocket.

He helped her aboard the carriage and climbed in beside her. Erik took a place at her other side while Mr. and Mrs. Hackbardt climbed into the center seat. David set the carriage in motion toward the Main House.

"Miss Richards, you're looking pretty as a September peach, and just as sweet," Gramps said. "Must be the candy business agreed with you."

From the seats behind her, Bridget heard the distinctive sound of throats being cleared. She could almost feel the eyes of the Hackbardts boring into her back, but tried to ignore the discomfort. "Your compliments are most kind, Gramps. I did enjoy my time in Traverse City, but I expect I'll enjoy The Clovers even more."

"I was worried you might not be on the boat," Erik said. "Mother promised you'd be here, but the way she's been behaving lately, I never know whether to believe her. She's been acting so strangely, I asked Anna to come back and help out for a few days."

"Anna's here?" Bridget asked.

Erik nodded. "She'll help you get settled in and show you what to do. But dinner comes first."

Moments later, they arrived at the Main House. Erik took her inside, past the guest dining room where he paused while she admired its decor. A polished oak floor, large round tables covered in white linens, and a giant crystal chandelier furnished the long, narrow room that held the mild fragrance of lemon oil. Mrs. Olson had painted a striking border of rosemaling near the ceiling, and its wide front window, overlooking Omena's cove and Grand Traverse Bay, offered a view no visitor could fault.

A minute later, she stepped into the small, staff dining room, its only view that of the service drive. Through the screened back door floated cooking odors from the kitchen, a separate building set behind the Main House. While Erik went to get their meal, she took two glasses off the shelf and filled them with lemonade from the icy pitcher on the sideboard, then settled down at the plank table to wait. When he returned with their dinner plates and sat across from her, she needed no fancy linens, scenic vistas, or hint of lemon polish to make for dining pleasure. His smile brought a far greater joy.

Erik knew he was grinning like an idiot, but he couldn't seem to help himself, nor could he take his eyes off Bridget--the most welcome sight at The Clovers Hotel since she'd departed for Traverse City. "When I realized there was a chance you'd be arriving this evening, it spoiled me for work for the rest of the day!" he admitted unabashedly. "On Monday, I'll take you for a drive if you'd like." He chuckled. "You haven't been here thirty minutes, and already I've planned your first day off!"

"I'm glad," Bridget said. "My only plans for the day were to read and to take my sketchbook and walk around the grounds looking for interesting scenes." She sipped her drink, then asked, "Where is your mother? I thought she'd be looking for me as soon as I got off the boat. I should go and see her after dinner."

"Mother and Father are registering the guests. I told them Anna and I would show you around," he said, spearing a piece of fish with his fork.

When Bridget had eaten her fill of the batter-dipped perch, home-fried potatoes, fresh spinach salad, and cherry pie, Erik took her to the women's end of the servants' dormitory building.

Anna came out to greet her. "You're a welcome sight! I thought Aunt Katrina might be pulling my leg when she said you were coming."

Before Bridget could respond, Mrs. Olson came striding across the lawn, a scowl set on her face. "Here's a list of chores." She shoved a scrap of paper at Bridget with a jittery hand. "See that these guests get what they want. Then make sure all the beds are turned back by ten. Anna will show you where to find everything."

"Yes, ma'am," Bridget said, disappointed that Mrs. Olson hadn't extended even one word of welcome. Considering the shadows beneath her eyes—darker than when she'd been in Traverse City earlier that day, Bridget could tell Erik's mother was under tremendous strain.

The woman focused on her son. "I have a chore for you, too. Miss Clarissa Hackbardt would like to go for a rowboat ride. She's waiting for you in the parlor at the Main House."

Erik sighed. "Can't her father—"

His mother cut in. "Her father got as far as the front porch, fell into the first chair he came to, lit his Havana cigar, demanded an ale from the keg he brought up from his brewery in Manitowoc, and buried himself in the evening newspaper. He's half owner of this place, and has a right to expect you to keep his daughter happy. Now go do your job."

"Yes, Mother." To Bridget, he said, "I'll talk to you later."

"And I'll see you in my office at six sharp tomorrow morning," Mrs. Olson told Bridget.

"Yes, ma'am."

As mother and son walked off, Bridget read Mrs. Olson's list aloud while Anna peered over her shoulder. "'Make up cot, Room 10. Four pillows, Room 23. Two towels, Room 15. Sweep parlor, halls, Main House—'"

"I just swept the Main House!" Anna cut in. She tapped her finger to her temple. "Aunt Katrina isn't right. Yesterday, she told me three times to polish the silver—*after* I had polished it." She shook her head in frustration. "No wonder five people quit this week and Erik had to send for me. Aunt Katrina is driving everyone mad!"

Already, Bridget missed the easy rapport she'd shared with the Marshalls. But she remembered Lottie's words. Mrs. Olson needed her. She looked at the list again. "You might as well show me where Room 10 is. The sooner we start, the sooner we'll finish."

Anna started for the Main House. "Follow me."

At eleven o'clock, Bridget and Anna had turned back all the beds, left pieces of fudge and lollipops in each room according to its occupants, and had completed every errand on Mrs. Olson's list including the cleaning. Bone weary, they put their brooms and carpet sweepers away and walked to their dormitory. Bridget was reaching for the door handle when someone called out, "Anna! Wait!"

Bridget turned to find a boy of about fifteen, all arms and legs, sprinting toward them.

"It's Eddie, the dish washer," Anna told Bridget.

He paused to catch his breath, wiping the sweat from his brow with the cuff of his pale blue work shirt. Pulling a piece of foolscap from his pants pocket, he told Anna, "Your aunt wants you to do these chores tonight."

Anna held the paper under the lamplight. "'Set tables for breakfast. Wash and pit cherries. Section oranges and grapefruit.'" She focused on Eddie. "These are Katie Little Bear's jobs."

"She quit."

"What about her mother? Is she still the cook?"

"Mrs. Little Bear got into a terrible row with your aunt and walked out a few minutes ago." He turned and sprinted off, disappearing in the darkness.

"No cook, no scullery maid," Anna said disgustedly. "I'd like to rip this paper to shreds."

Despite an overwhelming desire to turn in for the night, Bridget took the list from Anna. "I'll take care of this."

Anna's brows came together, her head moving slowly from side to side in frustration. "I'll go with you."

They entered the Main House through the back service door. The sound of a dish shattering in the dining room drew them there. Mrs. Olson was standing behind a big round table, her back to Bridget and Anna. In front of her was a stack of china plates. Taking one in hand, she flung it toward the picture window. It shattered into tiny splinters, cracking the sheet glass before landing on the polished oak floor where the remnants of another plate had come to rest.

"Take *that*, Mrs. Little Bear!" the enraged woman cried. She picked up another plate.

Bridget rushed forward, taking it away. "Easy now, Mrs. Olson."

The startled woman turned on her with a frightening, wild-eyed gaze. "You! Give me that!" She lunged forward.

Bridget evaded her.

Mrs. Olson picked up another plate from the stack. "I'll get you, Katie Little Bear!"

Anna rushed forward, knocking the plate from her aunt's hand. "Stop it!"

Momentarily stunned, the woman turned and swung at Anna, slapping her hard across the face. "Don't you talk to me that way!"

Anna crumpled to the floor, her face in her hands.

Bridget hurried to her side, wary of Mrs. Olson's next move, but the woman only stared blankly at them, then began to wander aimlessly about the room, mumbling to herself.

"We've got to get help," Bridget told Anna. She assisted her out of the room, closing the double doors behind them. When she turned around, Mr. and Mrs. Hackbardt were coming toward them in the hallway.

"What's the racket?" Mr. Hackbardt grumbled.

"I heard dishes breaking in there," Mrs. Hackbardt claimed haughtily. She reached for the doorknob.

"Clumsy kitchen help," Bridget said, taking Mrs. Hackbardt by the elbow and turning her toward the parlor.

"Can I get you a bedtime glass of milk or a cup of coffee? I'd be glad to bring it to your room," she offered sweetly, escorting her away from the dining room. "You're in number 23, aren't you?" She remembered Mrs. Hackbardt had requested extra pillows for that room earlier in the evening.

"Hot chocolate would be nice," the woman said.

"I'd prefer an ale," said her husband, shuffling along behind.

"I'll bring your beverages right up," Bridget promised. She returned to Anna who was leaning against the dining room door. "Are you all right?"

She rubbed her cheek, bright red and already starting to swell, then nodded. A dish crashed against the dining room door, making her flinch. "I must find Uncle Kal," she said.

Just then, Erik, his father, and grandfather came rushing in through the service door.

"I heard glass breaking," Erik said, his face flushed with concern.

"It's your mother. She's like a wild woman in there." Bridget indicated the dining room.

"I knew it! She's been working too hard," Gramps said.

"I'll talk to her," Erik's father said, reaching for the doorknob. Two plates hit the door in rapid succession. In the pause that followed, he opened it a few inches. "Katrina?" When all remained quiet, he stepped into the room.

Erik followed him, trying to step past the pile of broken china at the door. Splinters crunched beneath his feet.

His mother stared at his father, then at him. Her eyes were red and unfocused and her blond hair was all askew.

"Katrina, I love you," his father said quietly.

94

She turned away and wandered toward the cracked front window.

Erik, his father, and grandfather moved toward her. "Mother, it's getting late. Won't you come upstairs with me?"

Shoulders drooping, she mumbled and turned around. Focusing on Gramps, her eyes opened wide. "You! It's all your fault! I *hate* you, Professor Evenson!" She rushed forward, pounding her fists against his chest.

"Katrina, no," he said futilely. Slumping to the floor, he clutched his left side.

"Katrina, stop it!" Erik's father shouted, grabbing her wrists and pulling her away.

Erik stooped down. "Come on, Gramps. You've got to get out of here."

He groaned and tried to get to his feet, but slipped to the floor again, his face ashen.

CHAPTER

9

Bridget rushed to the old man's side. "Put one arm around my neck and one around Erik's," she said.

While Mrs. Olson's ranting continued, she helped Erik get his grandfather out of the dining room.

"Gramps! Are you all right?" Anna cried, closing the door behind them and kneeling at his side as Bridget and Erik lowered him to the floor. He slumped against the hallway wall.

Erik unbuttoned the old man's shirt, then turned to Anna. "You'd better send David to Sutton's Bay for Dr. Kendall."

"No," Gramps protested weakly, gasping for air. "My Revivo . . . " He fumbled for it in his shirt pocket.

"I'm getting Dr. Kendall whether you want me to, or not," Anna argued. "I don't want to lose you, Gramps!" She took off through the back exit.

Erik reached in his grandfather's pocket and pulled out the Revivo packet only to discover it was empty. "Do you have more medicine in your room, Gramps?"

He shook his head.

"The doctor will have medicine," Erik said, hoping the

physician's prescription would be more effective than the patent medicine.

Gramps moaned and struggled for breath. " . . . Don't trust . . . doctors."

"I'm afraid you'll have to this time," Erik said sympathetically. He took out his handkerchief and began mopping the sweat off the old man's brow, wishing he could somehow do the breathing for him. Through the closed doors of the dining room, he heard his mother's shrill voice. A knot formed in his gut, knowing he could do nothing to calm her, or to ease his grandfather's struggle. He silently prayed for strength, wisdom, and healing.

"I'll go after a pillow and cover," Bridget said. "I don't think we should risk moving him before the doctor comes."

Erik nodded.

Bridget had nearly reached the entrance to the parlor when she came face to face with Clarissa Hackbardt.

"Miss Richards, my parents have been waiting for quite some time for their drinks," she complained.

"I'm terribly sorry. I'll bring them right away," Bridget said.

Clarissa peered past her, trying to see down the hall. "What's going on there?"

"Please, Miss Hackbardt, go back to your room," Bridget urged.

The young woman forced her way past. "Erik, what's happened?" she asked, hurrying to his side.

Intent on fetching the pillow and cover, Bridget left the problem of Clarissa to Erik. When she returned moments later, the brewer's daughter was holding Gramps's head on her lap. Mrs. Olson's piercing voice again penetrated the thick dining room door, her words unintelligible.

Bridget caught the look of inquiry Clarissa sent Erik, but he remained silent.

"Miss Hackbardt, why don't you go upstairs now," Bridget suggested kindly. "I'll be right along with hot chocolate and ale."

Clarissa took the pillow from Bridget and placed it under Gramps's head. When she reached for the coverlet, Bridget stooped down and spread it over the patient herself, thankful to see he was breathing a little easier now.

Clarissa rose. "I'll get the hot chocolate and ale myself, Miss Richards. I know where the kitchen is." Turning to Erik, she said, "I'll send my folks down after they've had their refreshments. They'll want to help out at a time like this."

"Nothing more can be done until Dr. Kendall gets here," he said.

"Maybe not for your grandfather or your mother, but somebody's got to take care of your guests. Even if my father is supposed to be a silent partner in this business, he'd be the first one to want to lend a hand."

She was gone before Erik could protest. He sat back, leaning against the wall, remembering the embarrassing moments Hackbardt had caused his father the previous year when he had insisted on helping to build a bonfire on the beach. Erik was trying to figure a way to avoid the same problem this year when his mother's voice penetrated his thoughts. He sighed. "It's going to be a long night. Dr. Kendall won't be here for an hour or more, and no telling how long Mother will be . . . not herself."

Bridget nodded, her thoughts bouncing from Gramps, to Mrs. Olson, to wondering how— even with the help of Clarissa's folks—the guests who had come to fill every room of The Clovers Hotel would be taken care of in the manner they deserved. Thoughts came to her, ideas she wanted to discuss with Erik, but they would have to wait until a more appropriate time.

His mother and father were still sequestered in the dining room a quarter of an hour later when Mr. and Mrs. Hackbardt came down the hall.

"Clarissa told us what happened," Mr. Hackbardt said in his raspy voice. Despite his portliness, he squatted down beside Gramps, whose breaths came irregularly. "Sorry you're not feeling well, Mr. Olson. Dr. Kendall will fix you up." He patted the old man's hand.

"I just knew things weren't right when I heard all those dishes breaking," said his wife.

Mr. Hackbardt rose, and Erik with him. "I'm sorry your vacation got off to a rough start, Mr. Hackbardt," Erik said.

The brewer waved off his apology. "I'm more worried about the other folks staying here. My wife can fill in for your mother. I'll see to your father's duties." He scratched his beard. "By the way. What *are* your father's duties?"

Erik thought a moment, trying to figure a way to avoid answering. Bereft of ideas, he spoke candidly. "Papa sees to the building maintenance and supervises the farm work and groundskeeping. David takes care of the horses, milk cows, and rigs. I help out wherever I'm needed."

"Can you call a meeting of your employees in the morning?"

"Sure," Erik said, "but I'm sorry to tell you, with the problems my mother's been having lately, most of the employees have quit."

Mr. Hackbardt's heavy brows moved together. "That

99

puts us in a real predicament."

"I have an idea," Bridget said, rising to her feet. "Tomorrow, I'll go visiting. I'll find as many of the former employees as I can and tell them they won't be working for Mrs. Olson if they come back."

"I'll take you," said Erik.

Mr. Hackbardt nodded. "When you talk to the folks who quit, you're to tell them there's a five dollar bonus if they come back to work for the next two weeks."

Mrs. Hackbardt patted her husband's arm. "That's my Horace. Generous to a fault."

Mr. Hackbardt took his wife's hand in his and gazed adoringly into her eyes. "Winnie, dear, why don't we go to Katrina's office and look things over so we'll be ready to handle the front desk bright and early in the morning."

"Such a smart man you are, Horace," she said, picking invisible lint from the sleeve of his pinstripe suit.

"Mother hasn't used her office much this year," Erik said. "You'll find information on the bookings beneath the counter of the registration desk."

"Thank you. You're a dear, sweet boy. Any mother would be proud." The Hackbardts disappeared down the hall.

Bridget settled on the floor beside Gramps again and Erik sat next to her. Except for the old man's labored breathing, he seemed stable. She leaned back against the wall, shoving her hand into her skirt pocket absent-mindedly. Feeling a folded piece of paper, she pulled it out to read it. With a sigh she handed it to Erik. "Your mother's list of breakfast chores. She sent it to Anna via Eddie at about eleven o'clock. The cook had walked out and the scullery maid had quit so she enlisted Anna to do the kitchen work. We were on our way over here when we discovered your mother breaking china. I'm beginning to wonder how and where breakfast will be served."

Erik glanced at the dining room door, then focused on Bridget. "Nothing can be done until Mother and Father are out of there. Then I'll get my brother and sister to help you." He folded the note and gave it back. Uncertainty and fatigue were evident in Bridget's tired blue eyes. How he wished her first night at The Clovers had been different, but there was no time for regrets. Reaching for her hand, he gave it a reassuring squeeze. "Everything will work out, I promise."

Bridget leaned back against the hard wall and allowed her eyelids to drift shut. The sight of Mrs. Olson in a rage came to mind, then dissolved allowing exhaustion to take its course. As she began drifting off to sleep, Erik pulled her close until her head was resting on his shoulder. The nearness of him kept her awake for awhile, but she eventually dozed off. Her next awareness was of the dining room door opening. Erik stood, and helped her to her feet.

His parents emerged, his father's arm about his wife's shoulders. She looked down at Gramps. Bridget held her breath, hoping she wouldn't fly into another rage at the assumption he was Professor Evenson, but the woman seemed not to recognize him, or anyone else as she glanced about with haunting, empty eyes.

"I'm taking your mother for a ride," Mr. Olson quietly told Erik, then he kneeled down at his father's side. The old man continued sleeping fitfully.

Erik crouched beside his father. "I think Gramps is going to be all right. Dr. Kendall is on the way."

Mr. Olson nodded, then whispered something into

Erik's ear.

Mrs. Olson stared at her husband accusingly, her eyes opened so wide, Bridget thought they would pop out of their sockets. "What did you say?" she demanded loudly. "What did you tell him?"

Gramps stirred, his eyes blinking open, then drifting shut.

Mr. Olson sprang to his feet. "I said I'm taking you for a ride," he told her quietly.

"No you didn't," she accused loudly. "That's not what you said. I *know* what you said. You're taking me to the hospital. You think I'm sick. Well I'm *not* sick. I'm just fine. *You're* sick." Her wild-eyed gaze shifted to Bridget, then Erik. On the floor, Gramps came fully awake, a pained expression on his face. Oblivious to his suffering, Mrs. Olson continued. "All of you. You're all sick. I'm not sick. *You're* sick."

"Quiet, dear," Mr. Olson said, his finger to his lips. "Come with me to the hospital now so I can get well."

"What about Erik? He has to come, too. And Gramps."

"Erik isn't sick enough to go to the hospital right now, and the doctor is on his way here to treat Gramps," her husband told her. "But we'd best get going. I need to be at the hospital as soon as possible."

The blank look came into her eyes again. "Yes. As soon as possible," she said, her voice drifting off as her husband led her away.

When they had left by the service door, Erik turned reluctantly to Bridget, so full of shame he could barely speak. "He's taking her . . . to the State Mental Hospital in Traverse City."

The prospect of Erik's mother being committed there

sent a shudder through Bridget. She'd seen the massive Gothic building from a distance on the west side of the city, set off by itself with bars at the windows. "I'm sorry. I'm so sorry."

Erik shrugged. "It's the best thing Father can do. You heard her. She needs help. Maybe the doctors there can do something for her."

"I'll pray about it," Bridget said.

"Yes. Pray about it. And I'll pray you and my brother and sister can get breakfast for seventy-five guests in the morning. I'm going upstairs now to wake them and tell them what's happened. Stay with Gramps, will you?"

Bridget nodded and took her place on the floor again.

Soon after Erik returned, Dr. Kendall arrived with his wife, a nurse. After examining Gramps and administering tincture of digitalis, he was moved to his room at the back of the first floor where the Kendalls stayed to observe him.

With Anna's help, Bridget cleaned up the broken dishes in the dining room and set places for breakfast, thankful no dinner plates would be needed. They prepared the fruit, took an inventory of the provisions, and planned the remainder of the breakfast menu before turning into bed at three in the morning.

Two and half hours later, at the crack of dawn, a rooster began crowing, and despite her fatigue, Bridget dragged herself from bed. A sleepy Anna arose too. As they started down the path toward the kitchen, Bridget noticed light coming from the windows.

"Someone is already in the kitchen," Bridget said, quickening her pace. She rushed through the back door, Anna at her heels. The tempting aroma of fried cakes filled the room.

A large, middle-aged woman in a blue dress, her straight black hair tied back in a leather thong, looked up from a kettle of hot oil on the kitchen stove. At the center work table, a skinny girl in a waist dress as brown as the coffee she was grinding brushed a strand of dark hair from her eyes and stared.

"Mrs. Little Bear, Katie, you're back!" Anna exclaimed.

"Hmph," said the woman, her wide, brown face expressionless. "What you want?" she asked sourly.

"Eddie said you'd walked out. I came to cook breakfast."

"Hmph," the woman said again. After a prolonged silence, she explained, "I walk out when Mrs. Olson make me angry. Mr. Erik come see me this morning. He tell me about new boss lady. I come back." She pointed to Bridget with the handle of her wooden spoon. "Who you?"

"Bridget Richards. I hired on as a chamber maid yesterday."

The Indian woman nodded. "Mr. Erik say much good about you." She waved her spoon at both her and Anna. "Go eat. Then I give you plenty work."

Katie put several fried cakes on a platter, poured two cups of tea, and set them on a tray which Bridget carried to the staff dining room. She ate quickly, then took tea and fried cakes to Gramps's room. The old man was pleased to see her, and Dr. Kendall reported that his patient's condition was continuing to improve and that his wife would stay with him throughout the day.

Relieved at the good news, Bridget hustled back to the kitchen. Ingrid and Ole and all three of the Hackbardt daughters had already come to pitch in, and by seven o'clock, they all had received basic instructions from Mrs. Little Bear in serving breakfast and clearing tables and were ready to greet guests with a smile.

Mrs. Hackbardt hovered nervously near the door, inquiring whether guests had slept well and offering suggestions for the day's activities. Bridget, Anna, and Clarissa, took orders and served while Rachel and Polly cleared tables. Each of the Hackbardt girls moved quickly, proving they were no strangers to hard work, but Bridget was met with a glum face each time she crossed paths with Polly.

At nine o'clock Mrs. Little Bear closed the dining room and clean-up began. While Eddie washed dishes, the younger Hackbardt sisters dried. Bridget helped Mrs. Little Bear put away leftover food and clean up the kitchen while Clarissa, Ole, Ingrid, and Anna changed linens in the dining room, swept the floor, and set tables for luncheon.

At half past ten, with everything nearly back to normal, Erik and Mr. and Mrs. Hackbardt called everyone to a meeting in the dining room. The only member of the outdoor crew still employed at The Clovers was David. He and Eddie sat at one large round table while the women sat at another.

Erik stood off to the side, and Bridget couldn't help noticing the smile sent his way by Clarissa, who was seated across from her, and the one the Wisconsin girl received in return. Bridget wanted to kick her, but ignored the impulse, thankful that soon, she would be leaving with Erik to help recruit former employees.

Mr. Hackbardt, who had been pacing the floor, came to stand by the men's table. Thumbs tucked beneath his suspenders, he addressed David. "I'm taking over for Mr. Olson while he's away. I demand hard work, loyalty, and cooperation."

Erik cleared his throat and stepped forward. "Excuse me, Mr. Hackbardt. David's one of the hardest working, most loyal employees of all. He needs helpers, though. Both of his assistants quit yesterday."

"We'll get 'em back. Right, Olson?"

"Yes, sir!"

Hackbardt turned to David again. "Until then, *I'll* help you out. Now let's get to work!" Mr. Hackbardt started for the door. David reluctantly followed.

Mrs. Hackbardt directed her attention to those remaining. "The first thing I want to say is thank you for doing a fine job with breakfast. I heard many compliments. That's remarkable since we're so short-handed.

"That brings me to my next point. As soon as I'm finished here, Mr. Erik is going to see if the employees who have quit will come back to work. For now, I'd like those of you who worked breakfast, to work both the midday meal and dinner tonight. In the times between, household chores must be tended to. Anna needs all the help she can get, so when this meeting is over, I'd like everyone but Clarissa to go with her." She turned to her eldest daughter. "Clarissa, you'll go with Erik. While he sees to the hiring, you can buy provisions—and be sure to get two dozen dinner plates." She handed her daughter a long list. "You're all excused."

Bridget intercepted Mrs. Hackbardt on her way to the door. "Excuse me, ma'am, but *I'm* to go with Mr. Olson this morning. It was all decided last night with Mr. Hackbardt."

Mrs. Hackbardt offered an appeasing smile. "I'm sorry, Miss Richards. Plans have changed. I'd love to let you go, too, but Anna needs your help."

"I'm sure Clarissa would do a fine job cleaning rooms and making beds. She's a very hard worker," Bridget pointed out.

"That, she is," Mrs. Hackbardt agreed, "but I know my daughter better than you. She's an excellent negotiator, and I would be remiss in trusting the purchasing to anyone else. I'm sure you understand." She took her leave before Bridget could say more.

Across the room, Erik's and Clarissa's heads were together as they pored over the list of provisions and discussed a plan to accomplish both their tasks with maximum efficiency.

Bridget's heart sank.

As she turned to follow Anna out the door, Polly Hackbardt scooted past, taunting her with a quiet, sing-songy, "Nah, nah-nah nah, nah."

CHAPTER

10

Disappointed as Bridget was to be left behind to tend housekeeping chores and serve luncheon, she put forth her best effort, praying for Erik's success in recruiting former employees. Her prayers must have worked, for when she and Anna reported to the kitchen to begin preparations for dinner, Mrs. Little Bear said she had enough help, and she sent Bridget and Anna to see Mrs. Hackbardt about entertainment for the children that evening.

With the single exception of Polly Hackbardt, the youngsters behaved admirably and enjoyed themselves thoroughly during the ghost story-telling contest she and Anna held around the campfire on the beach. Theirs was a smaller version of the large bonfire Mr. Olson built for the adults with some of the planks from *Brede's Bargain* which had been brought from Leland.

By half-past nine, the youngsters had returned to their parents. On the way to their dormitory, Bridget and Anna checked on Gramps, whom they found recovering nicely from his heart spell, then they prepared to turn in for the night.

"I can hardly wait to get back to South Manitou tomorrow," Anna commented as she let down her dark hair and brushed it with long strokes. "I don't mind helping out here, but I never have liked the Hackbardts, especially Clarissa and Polly. Besides, Mr. Trevelyn is delivering my new organ to the island on Friday. I can't miss that!"

At mention of Nat and the island, Bridget suffered a slight twinge of envy, but it vanished quickly. She thoroughly believed the Lord wanted her here, at The Clovers. "Will you be attending the church service tomorrow? I understand Mr. Olson has invited Brother Bennard, the evangelist, to come and preach on the lawn in front of the Main House."

"I'll be here. Let's go and sit together," Anna suggested.

On Sunday morning, several guests and many of the staff attended the outdoor service. Rachel Hackbardt went forward during the altar call, and Bridget prayed the young girl would become strong in her new commitment to Christ.

Anna left for Leland soon after church to catch a boat for South Manitou. By midday, several weekend guests had checked out, and Bridget went to work changing the bed linens and giving the empty rooms a thorough cleaning. When she had finished her duties, she paid a call on Gramps, who was being tended by a widow, Frau Finkler, whom Erik had hired. The old man showed improvement despite complaints about his new nurse when she was out of earshot.

When Bridget knelt by her cot to say her evening prayers, she had much to be thankful for: she had a newfound sister in Christ; The Clovers Hotel had a full staff again; Gramps was growing stronger. But she was *most* thankful for the next two days she would have off. When she had seen Erik in the staff dining room at supper he had assured her that he would spend tomorrow showing her the Leelanau Peninsula just as they had planned. He had even requested box lunches from Mrs. Little Bear.

When Bridget's eyes closed, her vision was of riding with Erik in a surrey along the tree-lined road to Northport, sparrows chirping, a fresh breeze blowing in off the bay, the sun peeking through the canopy of hardwoods to dapple the road with its ever changing pattern—and not a soul in sight to infringe on their time together.

She was awakened by a sun patch that seeped past the muslin curtain at the dormitory window to spread a streak of light across her face. Rested and full of anticipation, she arose and held back the curtain at the screened window. Blue sky stretched to the horizon, precluding any chance that rain would dampen her day. She closed her eyes and inhaled the clear breeze off the water. When she opened them again and looked down at the bay, her breath caught in her throat. Tied fast at The Clovers Hotel dock was the *Manitou Lady*.

A knot of anxiety formed in her stomach. In twenty minutes, she was to meet Erik for breakfast in the staff dining room and discuss their plans. Now, there was Nat to contend with. As eager as she was for news of her family and friends on the Manitou Islands, she hadn't forgotten the friction between Nat and Erik the day Mrs. Olson sent her away jobless.

"Forgive me, Lord, for wishing Nat weren't here today," she prayed out loud, thankful she was alone in the room. Quickly, she washed and dressed, brushing and pinning her hair securely atop her head before stepping out into the beautiful morning.

Halfway up the drive from the dock, Nat spotted her and waved, his pace quickening. Hesitantly, she moved toward him, her apprehension tempered by his wide smile.

Nat hadn't been pleased when he'd tried to call on Bridget yesterday at the Marshalls' in Traverse City, and had learned she'd gone to Omena. Lottie had done her best to convinced him the move was in Bridget's best interests, but he still wasn't keen on her working around Erik Olson.

When he was within a few feet of her, however, he realized she looked decidedly more rested than when he'd seen her last. He made a point to smile when he greeted her. "Omena must agree with you!"

Nat's cheerful tone put Bridget at ease. "I'm getting accustomed to it," she replied casually, hoping to avoid any implication of difficulties during her short tenure there.

He stepped close, taking her hand in his and giving it a squeeze. "It's good to see you again, Bridget."

She couldn't deny the reassuring comfort of Nat's hand about hers, nor her fondness for him as if he were a part of her very own family.

"I wish Michael were here," he said. "He still talks about ya."

Michael's face came quickly to Bridget's mind, an image she had been too distracted of late to conjure up. She could see Nat's little boy running through the sand by the South Manitou Light, plopping down, and picking up a clam shell to play with. "I miss him," she admitted without aforethought, then regretted the words. She didn't want Nat getting the wrong idea. As much as she cared about him and his son, she cherished her life apart from them, too.

Nat continued. "Miss Marshall says you have today

and tomorrow off. Come with me to the Grand Traverse Light Station. I'm on my way there to deliver a load of bricks for the fog signal building they're putting up." His hazel eyes were full of hope.

Bridget released her hand from his, looked away, and took a tiny step back before focusing on him again. "I can't. I have other plans."

She watched his chest rise as he inhaled deeply, and she steeled herself for a cutting remark about Erik, but the smile that had faded now reappeared. "You're not the only one I came to see at The Clovers Hotel today, ya know."

Bridget laughed nervously. "I'm not?"

"I came to let the Olsons know I'm plannin' to make an excursion run to Buffalo Bill's Wild West Show next Tuesday, in case their guests want tickets. You're going, aren't ya? It's your day off."

Suddenly Bridget remembered her promise to Kenton McCune. She could feel her face growing warm. "I . . . I suppose I will." Ashamed of herself for hiding the full truth, she added, "Actually, I've wanted to go ever since I read the advertisement about it in the Traverse City paper."

"This excursion was your sister's idea. Charlie's got some mind when it comes to the shipping business." He shaded his eyes with his hand and scoured the grounds. "She's around here somewhere—she and Seth."

"Charlotte and Seth are here? Why didn't you say so? Let's go find them!"

"They're at the Main House, I think. They disappeared inside there just before you came out of the dormitory. Charlie could hardly wait to go make her sales pitch. She's mighty good at it, too!"

Bridget set a brisk pace toward the Main House, Nat at

her heels. "You haven't said a word about the rest of the family--Mama, your folks. Have you seen Aurora and Harrison?" she asked, referring to her older sister on North Manitou.

"Everyone's fine, except Aurora and her dyspepsia," Nat said. "To tell ya the truth, I think she's in the family way. No one's come right out and said so, but every time I bring it up with Charlie, she gets that impish gleam in her eye, as much as to say I'm right."

Eager to learn whether she would soon be an aunt, Bridget hurried up the steps and into the Main House. At the registration desk, Charlotte and Seth were concluding their discussion with Mrs. Hackbardt.

Charlotte's brown eyes lit up when she saw her older sister. "Bridget! I was just about to come looking for you!" Charlotte hurried to embrace her.

Bridget held her tight, then stepped back to take a good look. "Marriage agrees with you, little sis. You look happier than ever."

"I am!" Charlotte said, beaming. "What about you? Seth and I sure were surprised when Nat told us you'd moved off the island."

"I'm doing just fine," Bridget assured her sister.

Seth came to stand beside his wife, his lopsided smile broader than usual. "It's good to see you again, Bridget." He leaned down, brushing her cheek with a brotherly kiss, and Bridget exchanged the affection.

"How 'bout a kiss for *me*?" Nat protested.

Following a moment's hesitation, Bridget complied with his request, only to hear Erik's voice coming from behind.

"There you are, Miss Richards. I knew something

important must have come up, or you'd be at breakfast by now."

Despite his pleasant tone, Bridget detected a look of disappointment in Erik's blue eyes. "Mr. Olson, let me introduce you to my sister and brother-in-law, Mr. and Mrs. Seth Trevelyn. Charlotte, Seth, my good friend, Mr. Erik Olson." To Erik, she said, "They've come with Nat on business—to offer our guests excursion tickets to Buffalo Bill's Wild West Show in Traverse City next week."

"You're going, aren't you, Mr. Olson?" Charlotte asked. "There'll be shooting exhibitions by Annie Oakley and Johnny Baker, a reproduction of Custer's Last Battle on the Little Big Horn, and eleven hundred men and horses commanded by Colonel Cody himself!"

Erik grinned. "I don't see how anyone could pass it by, the way you describe it, Mrs. Trevelyn." He turned to Bridget. "Would you like to go?"

Nat spoke up. "I asked her first. She's going with me. It's all decided."

"No, Nat," Bridget countered. "I'm not going to the show with you."

"But you said you would, not ten minutes ago," Nat argued.

Bridget spoke calmly. "I said I'd wanted to go since I saw the advertisement in the paper about the show. I didn't exactly say I was going with you."

"Ohhh," Nat replied, his single word laden with skepticism.

Bridget turned to Erik. "To answer your question, I'd like to go with you, too, but I accepted an invitation from someone else before I came to Omena. I hope you understand."

"Of course," Erik said, but the curious look in his eyes told otherwise.

Eager to change topics, Bridget focused on Charlotte. "Nat says Aurora hasn't been feeling well."

Charlotte took Bridget by the arm. "If you fellows will excuse us, we need a few minutes for family business. We'll be right back."

When the women reached the front porch, Bridget said, "I'm dying to find out if Aurora is expecting an addition to the family."

"She is! But neither she nor Harrison want it noised around just yet. Mother knows. Seth asked me about it and I couldn't lie to him. I think Nat has figured it out, too, but no one else."

"Oh, Charlotte! We'll be aunts! When will the baby arrive?"

"January!"

"January? I certainly hope Harrison is planning to move to the mainland for the winter, unless he wants to deliver the child himself."

"That's exactly what Mama said, but you know Harrison. He'll make his own mind up about it."

Through the screen door, Bridget overheard Erik, his voice more forceful than usual. "Mr. Trevelyn, I think Miss Richards is perfectly capable of making up her own mind how to spend her days off."

"Just see to it you treat her with respect, or you'll have me to answer to," Nat warned loudly.

Bridget nudged Charlotte toward the door. "We'd better get back inside."

Charlotte linked her arm with Nat's. "Come on, brother. We've got a load of bricks to deliver."

"Charlie's right," Seth said, flanking his brother on the opposite side. Looking back over his shoulder, he added, "Nice meeting you, Mr. Olson. See you later, Bridget."

"Good bye, Sis," Charlotte added, disappearing out the door.

Bridget turned to Erik. "I'm sorry about Nat. And I didn't mean to keep you waiting at breakfast. Can we begin this day all over again, starting now?"

Erik offered a forgiving smile. Gesturing toward the hall, he said, "Come on. Mrs. Little Bear's flapjacks and bacon are just waiting for you. And the box lunches are ready, too."

When they had settled down to breakfast at the staff dining table, Bridget asked, "How far is it to Cat's Head Point? I'd love to do some sketching there."

Erik recalled several outings he'd taken the previous summer to the point of land west of the light station. "It's a little over nine miles from here. The road's good most of the way, but it ends at Mr. Taylor's farm. We'll have to walk the last three-quarters of a mile."

Bridget shrugged. "I've spent a good share of my life walking the length and breadth of South Manitou. I'm sure three-quarters of a mile to the shoreline and back won't hurt me."

"I'll take Father's camera along. While you're making pictures with a pencil and paper, I'll make mine on film."

"I didn't know you were a photographer."

Erik laughed. "I'm not. But Papa has twenty-five more pictures to take on his roll of film. Then we can send the camera in to Kodak and they'll develop all hundred of them and put in fresh film. We're still wondering how our photographs came out from last Christmas!"

"I can see we'll make a suitable pair for the day, you with your camera and me with my sketchbook and pencils," Bridget concluded.

A quarter of an hour later, Erik handed Bridget aboard his favorite carriage for two. He stopped by the kitchen to collect the box lunches and a large jar of iced tea, thinking it was odd that Polly Hackbardt came out and handed them to him before he could even climb down from the driver's seat. He put the thought from his mind as he struck out in the direction of Northport.

The road Erik traveled looked just as it had in Bridget's dream, all dappled with sunny patches and quiet enough to hear the melodies of sparrows and cardinals, and the more raucous calls of jays and gulls.

Passing an orchard and farmyard, the odor of manure stung her nose, only to be overpowered by that of a skunk. She turned to Erik, wrinkling her nose, and laughed at the exaggerated look of displeasure he offered in return.

About four miles beyond Northport, he reached a farm—the Taylor farm, he told her. Pulling up the long drive to a farmhouse set on the edge of the woods, he said, "I met the Taylors last summer when I came up this way. I'll ask if I can park the buggy here and turn the mare out to pasture."

Following a brief conversation with Mrs. Taylor at her back door, he unhitched the mare and led her through the pasture gate. When he returned to the rig, he hung his camera around his neck and draped a blanket over his shoulder.

Bridget tucked the two box lunches beneath one arm, her sketchbook beneath the other, and poked five sharp pencils through her hair. Even though she knew they were sticking out in all directions and looked ridiculous, she felt so comfortable in Erik's company, she didn't care.

Bridget's hair adornments made Erik smile. He couldn't think of another young lady in his acquaintance who would feel enough at ease with him to poke even one pencil into her topknot, let alone five.

Eager to press on to the beach, he pointed out an opening in the woods about ten feet to the north. "If we follow that path straight on, we'll be at the water's edge in about twenty minutes," he said, leading the way down the woodsy trail. He pushed ahead, wary of the leaves of three along the sides of the trail. "Be careful of the poison ivy," he cautioned. "It's everywhere."

Bridget pulled her skirt close to keep from brushing the harmful weeds, accustomed to the same dangers on South Manitou. Several minutes later, she followed Erik onto the wide beach of sand strewn with pebbles, rocks, driftwood, and logs. The breeze blew lightly from the southwest, and gentle waves spoke quietly to the waterline.

"Pick your spot and I'll clear away the stones," Erik said, scanning the shore in both directions.

She headed toward the point of land called Cat's Head, about a hundred yards away. There, she could see three miles to the northeast. Though she knew the lighthouse stood just around the tip of the peninsula, it wasn't visible to her now.

Looking across the water and slightly to the west, she could make out South Fox Island hanging near the horizon like an optical illusion. More recognizable to the west and south was North Manitou Island; in the haze beyond, South Manitou; and plying the ribbon of blue-gray waters between, a steamer headed northeast.

Gulls flew overhead while others walked the beach, picking at gravel. A moth fluttered erratically to the yellow flowers on a clump of weeds growing between the rocks, then took refuge in the woods.

When Bridget turned to Erik, his focus on her was through the lens of his father's camera.

"Say Wisconsin cheese!"

"Michigan cheese, please!"

"Got it!" he said with the snap of his shutter. "You'll look terrific, especially with those pencils in your hair."

"You joker," she accused, reaching for her topknot and nearly stabbing herself on the sharp tips of lead in her hurry to pull out the pencils. She pointed them at a somewhat clear spot on the beach. "Spread the blanket right there, Mr. Olson. I'm eager to make a sketch of you."

He chuckled. "I have a feeling it won't be as flattering as I'd like."

CHAPTER

11

Bridget had been sketching for an hour or more when she saw a rowboat with two boys and a dog heading for the point. Still several yards away, their frisky tan mongrel jumped into the lake, swam ashore, shook the water from her coat with a vengeance, and ran into the woods, barking excitedly. Erik took off his shoes and socks, rolled up his pant cuffs, and helped the youngsters—about thirteen and fifteen years of age—to pull their heavy wooden boat onto the beach. Setting aside her sketchbook, Bridget joined the others.

"Where are you fellas from?" Erik asked, taking the anchor from the bow of the dinghy and wedging it behind a couple of large rocks.

"We're from the light station," said the lanky, older boy, pushing a shock of sandy hair off his wide forehead. "I'm Jack Goodrich, and this here's my brother, Toby."

"We've been fishin'," said Toby, tossing his head to flip the dark brown hair from his hazel eyes. He shoved up the sleeves of his blue shirt, reached into the water off the stern of the boat and proudly held up a stringer of perch.

"Your mother sure will appreciate you boys bringing dinner home tonight," Bridget said. "I know what it's like, eating provisions from the Light Service. I'm Miss

Richards. My mama is the assistant keeper on South Manitou."

"You're a lightkeeper's kid, too?" Toby asked, offering a crooked-toothed smile.

"Me and my two sisters and two brothers," she replied.

"We've got seven more brothers and sisters at home," Jack said. "The baby's not even walking yet. I'm the oldest." To Erik, he said, "Is your father in the light service, too?"

"No. He's in the hotel business at Omena. I'm a friend of Miss Richards, Mr. Olson."

The boys' dog came bounding out of the woods, dashed up the beach, then circled back, coming to sniff Erik's hand.

He scratched her behind the ears. "You have a great dog, here. What's her name?"

"Taffy," said Toby.

"Taffy, can you fetch?" Erik asked, picking up a piece of driftwood and throwing it several yards down the beach.

Taffy took off, quickly becoming confused over which piece of driftwood Erik had thrown. Ignoring the search altogether, she began to track a scent she picked up on the beach.

"Taffy! Come!" Jack hollered. "Sorry, Mr. Olson. She's not very good at fetchin'."

"She's just a free spirit," Erik said. Picking up his camera, he asked, "Do you think she'll stand still for a picture? I'd like to take one of you boys with Taffy standing in between."

"I'll hold up the fish!" Toby said, scrambling to retrieve the stringer from the back of the boat.

When Erik had snapped a picture of the boys with their

dog and string of fish, he said, "I'd like to take a walk down the beach. You fellas interested?"

Taffy barked and wagged her tail in wide swipes.

"Let's go!" said Toby.

"You comin', Miss Richards?" Jack asked.

"You fellows go ahead. I'll stay here and finish my sketching," she said, returning to her spot on the blanket.

She watched them as they walked away, listening to the boys' cheerful voices, and Taffy's happy yelps until they grew faint, then she picked up her sketchbook and quickly roughed in the dinghy with the three fellows and dog in the background, strolling the beach. By the time they returned twenty minutes later, she had added several details to her sketch.

Erik gazed over her shoulder at it. "Very nice work, Miss Richards. I think you should make more sketches of the beach and put them up for sale at The Clovers. I'm sure our guests would buy them. I'll hang a cork board by the main desk with a sign over it, 'Bridget of Cat's Head Point -- Artist Extraordinaire,' and you can pin all your drawings there."

"You're joking."

"I mean it. You'll do it, won't you?"

She shrugged. "I'll think about it."

"Good. Now, I'll tell you what I'm thinking. I'm *hungry*."

"Me, too," said Toby.

"You boys are welcome to share our box lunches," Bridget offered.

"We brought our lunch pails," Jack told her, getting them out of the dinghy. He and Toby found flat rocks for seats, and settled down near the small beach blanket.

Erik sat beside Bridget, handing her one of the boxes. "I hope Mrs. Little Bear made us sandwiches out of the roast beef left over from Sunday dinner."

"I hope so, too," said Bridget, sliding the string off her box, but when she opened the lid, she discovered otherwise. "Look! Nothing but a mud pie!" She tipped her box for Erik to see.

He quickly opened his own box, finding a second mud pie. Removing the small tin, he dumped the contents on the beach in disgust. Humiliation burned his cheeks. "I know Mrs. Little Bear and her kin are fond of jokes, but I can't believe she did this."

"I can't, either," said Bridget.

Erik thought a moment. "Polly Hackbardt! She did it, I'm sure. She's been jealous of you since the moment she met you."

Bridget laughed. Jack and Toby joined in, which made Taffy bark. Erik tried to keep a straight face, but found himself laughing, too.

When all the noise had subsided, Jack said, "You can share our lunches. Here, Miss Richards. Eat half my sandwich. It's only cherry jam, but Mama just put it up last week when the new crop came in."

"And you can have half of mine," Toby told Erik.

"Thanks, fellas. We'd have a long wait for lunch, without you." He held up the jar of iced tea Polly had given him. "Do you think we can trust it?" he asked Bridget.

"*You* try it."

He unscrewed the lid, took one sip, and poured it out on the beach. "She put salt in it instead of sugar."

"We get our drinks from the lake," Jack said.

"Yeah. We drink out of our hands," Toby explained.

Erik waded out to his knees and filled the jar with lake water, then set it beside Bridget on the blanket. "I guess that's the best we can do for now. We can stop in Northport for supper on our way home."

"I think we'll be able to survive," Bridget assured him with a smile. When she had finished her half of the jam sandwich, she said, "Jack, you be sure and tell your mama for me that she makes excellent cherry jam."

"I will," he promised. "She bakes good maple nut cookies, too." He took one from his lunch bucket, split it in two, and gave her half.

Toby did likewise for Erik.

While Erik was savoring the homemade morsel, his thoughts were on Bridget. He had noticed the secretive admiring looks being sent her way by the boys, and he couldn't blame them. He was finding more to like about her with each passing minute, and his attraction for her involved far more than her pretty, round face, wide set eyes the shade of spring larkspur, and hair as golden as wheat ready for harvest.

His private thoughts ended when Jack put his pail back in the boat and whistled for Taffy. "We'd better get on home now."

"It's been a real pleasure meeting you boys," Bridget said. "You be sure and tell your folks you shared your lunch with a Richards from the South Manitou Light Station."

"We will!" Toby promised.

Erik retrieved the anchor from its perch behind the rocks and pushed the boat off the beach. Once the boys and their dog were seated in the dinghy, he gave it a mighty shove, sending it into water deep enough for rowing.

When he had dried his feet and pulled on his shoes and socks, Bridget said, "I'm ready for a walk now. How about you?"

"Sounds like a fine idea," he said, pulling her to her feet. With her hand in his, he steadied her as she picked her way across the rocks and limbs that littered the beach to the west of Cat's Head Point.

Erik remained silent for several minutes, and Bridget couldn't help noticing that his usually sparkling blue eyes now seemed pensive and sad. When they reached a large driftwood log, she brushed off the sand and invited him to sit beside her.

"Something's bothering you," she began. "I hope you're not still upset about the box lunches."

After a silent pause, he offered a half-hearted chuckle. "No, I'm not upset about the box lunches. But you can bet I'll have something to say to Miss Polly Hackbardt when we get back."

When a contemplative moment had passed, Bridget asked, "Are you worried about Gramps?"

Erik shook his head.

"The hotel?"

Again, he shook his head, then drew a long breath and let out a low sigh. "It's mother." With his admission, the mantle of shame he carried on his shoulders seemed to grow heavier.

"Your father did the only thing he could, taking her to the hospital," Bridget reasoned.

"I know. But I feel guilty. I hadn't had much time to think about Mother until today, with all the guests and the upheaval at the hotel over the weekend. Now that I've given it some thought, I know I'm to blame for her problem." He hung his head, unable to meet Bridget's eyes.

"But why?"

"I never should have asked her to work for Professor Evenson," he admitted glumly.

"I don't think you're being fair to yourself," Bridget contended. "You couldn't have known things would turn out this way when she started the drawings for his book two years ago."

"I should have seen it coming. She's a perfectionist. She worked day and night drawing one dinosaur bone after another. Then she'd rip them up and do them all over again. I should have known she was expecting too much of herself and made her stop."

"She wouldn't have listened," Bridget told him flatly.

"I should have *made* her listen," Erik maintained. He rose from the log and paced agitatedly along the water's edge, picked up half a dozen stones, and one by one, angrily hurled them into the lake, wishing he could so easily rid himself of the black mood inside.

He turned toward Bridget again, feeling even more guilty that her day was being ruined by his foul disposition. Sitting beside her again, he tried to clear his mind of unhappy thoughts.

The next few minutes passed in uneasy silence, and Bridget could tell Erik was still in anguish over his mother. Gently, she touched his arm. "Would you mind if I said a prayer?" When he shook his head, she spoke quietly. "Heavenly Father, please help Erik to forgive himself, and please touch his mother's heart with your healing hand, so that she can be restored to health and home. In Jesus' name, Amen."

Erik reached for her hand. Taking it in both of his, he looked deep into her lovely eyes. "Thank you. I feel better. And I apologize for being such poor company today. I hope you'll forgive me. Can we start this day all over again for the third time?"

"I'm sure we can," she replied instantly.

Erik consulted his timepiece. "It's going to take us awhile to get back to the rig and drive to Northport. What do you say we make a start for supper?"

"Let's go!" She took him by the hand and pulled him up, almost stumbling on the shifting pebbles.

Erik caught her with his arm about her waist, hugging her securely to his side. "Careful! We don't need another disaster today."

The unexpected closeness, the press of his lean form against her, sent a warmth coursing through Bridget. She was certain her cheeks were the color of Indian paintbrush, but she ignored the thought and slipped her arm about Erik's waist. "You're right. I'd better hang onto you so I don't break an ankle."

With Bridget clamped tight beside him, Erik took his time, in no hurry for this walk—and their hold on one another—to end. Every few steps, she would glance up at him with a tender look that made words unnecessary, and though his feet were walking on solid ground, his heart seemed to soar with the gulls overhead. For now, the shackles of worry and guilt were broken, and his thoughts were filled with the gentle woman by his side.

Bridget cherished the careful manner in which Erik was escorting her over the rough beach—his steps so small she was sure even a toddler could keep pace. But when she smiled up at him, the contentment on his face offered assurance that he was at last enjoying himself, and she gave silent thanks for these pleasant moments.

At the Taylor farm, Erik quickly hitched up the buggy and turned onto the road to Northport. "I'm really looking forward to dinner at the Porter House," he said as he urged his mare into a trot. "After all that fresh air, and only meager portions at lunch, I've developed quite an appetite. I hope you're hungry."

Bridget chuckled. "A proper lady shouldn't admit this, but I'm so hungry, I think I could eat a two-inch steak and still have room for a baked potato and a piece of pie."

They both laughed, and Erik realized how completely beguiling he found Bridget's honesty. "I can guarantee you'll get one of the very best steaks you've ever tasted at the Porter House. They have a chef who comes up from Chicago every summer. He really knows his beef. The dining room is pleasant, too. They have candles on each table, and fresh flowers. I think you'll like it."

"I'm *sure* I'll like it," Bridget said, knowing that, aside from tasty food, the only ingredient she needed to make her meal special was Erik.

He pulled into Northport at six o'clock, pleased with the perfect timing of his arrival. He'd been to the Porter House several times last summer with the Hackbardts and knew from past experience that, although the dining room opened at five, neither the service nor the food was as good then as at six, when the chef and the evening waitresses were operating at peak efficiency. It was best to come early in the week, also, when the dining room was less crowded.

He brought his rig to a halt by the board walk on Waukazoo Street and was helping Bridget down when a familiar surrey pulled alongside him. His heart plummeted when he recognized Mr. Hackbardt and his three daughters.

"Mr. Olson! Miss Richards! Fancy meeting you here!" the brewer said in his gravelly voice.

Erik muttered under his breath, thinking how Hackbardt had been causing all manner of trouble in his life. After two days of redoing every chore the man had set his hand to, Erik didn't need the overstuffed brewer barging in on his evening with Bridget. But he forced himself to remain pleasant.

"Good evening, Mr. Hackbardt."

"Why don't you and Miss Richards join us for dinner?" he said, helping his daughters down.

Bridget looked directly at Polly, who stuck her tongue out when her father wasn't watching. Rachel mumbled a scolding and headed toward the restaurant. Clarissa offered a friendly smile. Bridget returned it as she slipped her arm through Erik's.

"Thanks for your offer, Mr. Hackbardt," Erik said, "but I couldn't accept."

"I insist!" said the portly man, resting his heavy hand on Erik's shoulder. "We're always too busy at The Clovers to sit down together. Besides, I'll be insulted if you refuse."

Seeing the helpless look on Erik's face, Bridget spoke up. "Mr. Hackbardt has a point. It would be bad form to turn him down. And maybe this *would* be a good time for all of us to talk."

Despite sharp disappointment, Erik said, "Then we accept."

Inside, Mr. Hackbardt requested a table for six. Bridget was seated next to the wall, beside Erik and across from

Rachel. Clarissa took the place on Erik's left, directly across from her little sister.

While Mr. Hackbardt ordered steaks for everyone and monopolized Erik with talk of his day at The Clovers, Bridget took note of the pleasing decor, rich in its use of native Michigan hardwoods. The random wood floor, all done in maple, oak, and walnut, reminded her of the patchwork quilt on her bed at South Manitou, an artful combination of scraps too lovely and useful to be discarded.

The lower half of the walls consisted of alternating maple and walnut boards, creating an interesting striped pattern. Above the chair rail, ivory wallpaper silk-screened in scarlet depicted Chinese pagodas and cherry trees in bloom. A painting hung beside their table, and though it was somewhat primitive in nature, Bridget recognized Carrying Point, the finger of land protecting Northport's harbor, and the main dock where the steamers *Emma E. Thompson, Columbia,* and *Alice M. Gill* were tied up. On shore beside the pier, fishnets hung on driers.

Though Bridget liked fish, she was glad tonight's meal would be steak. Moments later, hers was set before her, still sizzling. The aroma of the seared beef and the tenderness when she cut into it, made her ravenously hungry.

She was about to pop the first juicy morsel into her mouth when Mr. Hackbardt turned his attention to her and said, "Tell us what you did on your day off, Miss Richards. Did you enjoy yourself?" Stuffing an oversized piece of his own steak into his mouth, he continued to gaze at her, awaiting an answer.

Reluctantly, she set down her fork. "As a matter of fact, I did. All but the box lunch, that is. Someone substituted mud pies for Mrs. Little Bear's sandwiches."

Polly giggled.

Mr. Hackbardt swallowed with a gulp and sternly addressed his youngest daughter. "Polly, do you know anything about this?"

Her eyes opened wide, and Bridget believed the girl was truly surprised by the accusation—or that she was an exceptional actress.

"No, Papa," Polly answered firmly.

Mr. Hackbardt shook his fork at her. "Don't lie to me, now. I'll take you over my knee if you're not telling the truth."

"Honest! I don't know anything about the mud pies!" Polly insisted, her face growing scarlet.

Though Erik had been certain Polly was to blame, he was beginning to have his doubts. He couldn't help noticing that Rachel shifted in her seat. And when he glanced at Clarissa, a satisfied little smile was on her lips. No matter how the prank had been carried out, Clarissa would naturally be pleased by it.

Mr. Hackbardt focused on Erik. "Mr. Olson, as soon as we get back to The Clovers, you and I must have a talk with Mrs. Little Bear. This type of shenanigan is completely unacceptable. We'll have to let her go."

Though Erik was appalled by the prospect of losing Mrs. Little Bear, he assumed this must be Mr. Hackbardt's way of finessing the truth from his daughter. "We'll have to hire a replacement right away. Do you know of anyone?"

Mr. Hackbardt's brow furrowed, then a smile tilted the corners of his mustache. "Of course! My cook, Mrs. Ziegler! I'll send a telegram in the morning. She can be here in three days."

Polly gasped.

Rachel moaned.

Clarissa spoke up. "You can't mean it, Papa. Mrs. Ziegler?"

"Why not?"

"She's a *terrible* cook! Mother's been trying to find a replacement for months."

"I *like* her cooking," Mr. Hackbardt insisted.

"That's because you like wiener schnitzel. At least once a week, she cooks wiener schnitzel. All her recipes are from the Old Country—dumplings and potatoes and sausages. A body can stand only so much of that heavy fare. The guests won't like it."

"Mrs. Ziegler is the perfect replacement and I won't hear another word about it," Mr. Hackbardt stated, shoving another large piece of steak into his mouth.

Though the conversation moved to other topics, Erik had all but lost his appetite over the problem that awaited him on his return to The Clovers. He couldn't help noticing that Bridget, too, only picked at her food.

His restiveness continued throughout dinner and on the drive to Omena. He couldn't help wishing his father were there to deal with the Hackbardt problem, but he was still in Traverse City seeing to his mother's care.

Erik stopped to let Bridget out near her dormitory, then drove to the barn, pulling up behind Hackbardt. Polly and Clarissa disappeared as soon as they climbed out of the surrey, but Rachel lingered behind.

Mr. Hackbardt stepped up to Erik the moment he climbed down from his rig. "Son, let's go directly to the kitchen. You let me do the talking. I've got a speech all planned for Mrs. Little Bear."

"Don't you think—"

"Papa, Mr. Olson, I've got something to tell you," Rachel interrupted.

"Not now, child," Hackbardt said gruffly. "Go see your mother. Tell her we're back."

"No, Papa! You've got to listen to me!" Rachel insisted, her eyes welling with tears. "As the Lord is my witness, I promise you, I'm telling the truth. Clarissa made the mud pies. I saw her!"

CHAPTER

12

Bridget was almost to the dormitory door when Clarissa's voice came from behind.

"Miss Richards, wait up! I need to talk to you!"

Bridget faced Clarissa, certain from her smug expression that she was about to tell on Polly for the mud pie incident.

"Miss Richards, don't be too flattered by the attention Erik pays you," she warned. "I've known him all my life. He'll soon tire of your company. I expect he'll have any number of lady friends before this summer is through. But when September comes, he'll return to Wisconsin and me. Of that, you can be sure!" Turning on her heel, she strode off.

Bridget went inside to wash her face and collect a handful of sharp pencils. Clarissa's words were still echoing in her ears ten minutes later when she stepped outdoors again. To her dismay, she noticed Erik arm in arm with the haughty girl, strolling toward the croquet lawn, behind the Main House.

Disheartened, Bridget moved off in the opposite direction. Making herself comfortable on a patch of grass near the dock, she commenced sketching the sailboats on the bay. Perhaps Erik was right. Her drawings might hold appeal as mementos for guests. If not, at least concentrating on artistic endeavors would serve to shut out further thoughts of the disagreeable Wisconsin girl and the possible truth of her claim.

"I just knew you wanted to be alone with me. I wanted to be alone with you, too," Clarissa cooed.

Erik kept his silence until they neared the bench at the far end of the croquet lawn, away from the other guests. "Have a seat, Clarissa," he said, his congenial tone masking his frustration.

She did as he suggested, leaving ample room for him beside her, but he had no intention of sitting down. Instead, he paced the lawn in front of her. "That was a shameful, childish prank, putting mud pies in our box lunches and letting the blame fall on Mrs. Little Bear."

She put on a look of surprise. "What makes you think I had a part in it?"

He regarded her sternly. "Don't play the innocent with me, Clarissa Hackbardt. I've known you too long. Now what do you have to say for yourself?"

Clarissa stiffened. "I'm not the least bit sorry. I don't know why you waste your time with that South Manitou Island girl, anyway. She's already got two other beaus."

The truth stung. Erik tried to ignore it. "I'll tell you why I spend time with Miss Richards. She's kind, interesting, and a pleasure to look at. I'm not surprised other gentlemen have noticed."

"She's not nearly as pretty as me," Clarissa said smugly. "She's positively plump! Probably from all the fudge she ate at the candy shop!"

"Watch your tongue! I'm already angry with you," Erik

warned, struggling to keep his own tongue in check.

A silent moment passed before Clarissa spoke. "I'm sorry I upset you. Please don't stay angry with me. I've got a surprise for you." She took two small pieces of chipboard from her skirt pocket. "Tickets to Buffalo Bill's Wild West Show. You'll go with me, won't you?"

The thought of attending the show with Clarissa held no appeal, but an idea came to him. "I'll go under one condition. That you come with me now and apologize to Miss Richards for the mud pies, and that you promise me right here and now, never to pull a prank like that again. You're an adult. It's time you act like one."

Clarissa shifted her gaze from Erik to the tickets in her hand. After a long silence, she looked up, a tear dampening her cheek. "I'm sorry. I promise to behave myself from now on. I'll tell Miss Richards I'm sorry, too."

Though Bridget kept her focus on the bay and her nearly-completed sketch, she could see from the corner of her eye that Erik and Clarissa were approaching.

Erik spoke first. "Miss Richards, Miss Hackbardt has something to say to you."

Bridget added several pencil lines to her drawing before looking up at Clarissa. Her expression was contrite. Bridget offered a smile and asked in the sweetest tone she could muster, "What did you want to tell me, Miss Hackbardt?"

"I probably should have said this earlier," she began. "I'm very sorry about your lunch today. I know my little sister gave the boxes to Erik this morning, but I have *no idea* how the mud pies got in them. I'm going right now to have a talk with Polly. I'll make sure she gets properly reprimanded. Nothing like this will ever happen again, I promise!" With a swish of her skirt, she departed up the drive to the Main House.

Erik sighed, watching her go, then sat down beside Bridget. "It's always something with the Hackbardt girls. I've known them all their lives, but I still can't tell what to expect from one minute to another."

A grin spread across Bridget's face, then laughter bubbled forth. "I'm sorry. I just keep thinking of the way you looked when we opened our boxes today."

Erik smiled, then joined in with a chuckle. "I'm glad you took it so well."

Bridget shrugged. "When faced with a choice, I try to choose laughter over anger." She closed her sketchbook. "If you don't mind an abrupt change of topic, I was just thinking about Gramps. Do you suppose he'd mind if I called on him? He'd probably enjoy hearing what happened today."

Erik got to his feet and helped Bridget up. "Excellent idea. I was planning to stop in and see him myself, anyway. He's been complaining about the nurse I hired."

Brede Olson was watching the activity on the croquet lawn through the sitting room window by his daybed, wishing for some way to rid himself of his overbearing nurse, when he saw his grandson and the girl who reminded him of his Freya approaching.

"I have visitors. Open the door," he demanded of Frau Finkler before his guests even knocked. "Then take yourself on a walk. I want to see my company alone." Now that his strength was returning, he was determined to out-boss the domineering woman who was forcing his life into

137

a pattern of rest, meals, and medicine. The routine defied his spontaneous nature, and he balked at every opportunity.

The gray haired woman took off her spectacles and set them on the table along with her German Bible. "*Bei mir, bist du nicht shöen.* I vill tell your grandson he must raise my salary, or find someone else to put up with you." Brushing the wrinkles from her dark skirt, the stocky woman opened the door.

"Good evening, Frau Finkler," Erik said. "How is Gramps doing?"

"He must needs a slave. Always, something. Do this. Do that. Never a moment's peace," she informed him.

Bridget laughed, then stepped inside. "Glad to hear you're feeling strong enough to be scrappy, Gramps."

The old man's spirits lifted the moment he saw her. "My, but you're a pretty sight."

"We thought maybe you'd like some company, if you're not too tired," Erik said.

"Tired? I'm only weary of Frau Finkler's bossiness. I don't need a nurse. You should let her go." To the hired woman he said, "Now you go on and take a nice walk and don't hurry back. I want to enjoy some young company for a spell."

"With pleasure," the woman said, retrieving her Bible and her glasses from the table on her way out.

Pushing himself up from the day bed, Gramps moved to the chair Frau Finkler normally occupied. "The two of you sit on my bed," he said, settling against the overstuffed chair back. "Now tell me what you've done with your day."

"We've been up to Cat's Head Point, just west of the light station," Erik told him.

"And you've had a mighty fine time," Gramps said. "I can see it in your faces."

The girl's cheeks colored, reminding him even more of his Freya. He hadn't meant to embarrass her. He would have regretted it, except that his grandson noticed the pretty blush, and slipped his hand over hers.

"Not a perfect day, Gramps," Erik said, "but we had fun. You won't believe what happened when it came time to eat our box lunches."

As the old man listened to Erik and Bridget take turns telling of the joke played on them by the Hackbardt sisters, he couldn't help thinking that, even if this young couple didn't yet know it, they were meant for each other. Bridget, with her easy laugh and bright smile, tempered Erik's more formal approach to life.

His sincere appreciation of her congenial nature, and his recognition of her natural artistic talents had given her the confidence to trade the security of her island community for experience in a broader world. Indeed, she reminded Gramps of his beloved Freya, and he took pure pleasure in her company.

" . . . So when I opened *my* box, I found a mud pie, too," Erik was saying.

Gramps laughed as heartily as he was able, and soon the room was filled with the sound of three happy voices. When silence fell, Erik said, "Now it's your turn, Gramps. Tell us a story. Tell Miss Richards about the Norwegian Regiment, and Colonel Heg."

He gazed out the window, envisioning himself as a young man at the time when the nation was divided. "I went off to Madison to train as a soldier 'way back in 1861," he said, recalling the difficult parting from his

139

beloved Freya. He could still remember the bittersweet farewell—sadness mingled with the excitement of going off to war.

"Nine hundred of us assembled at Camp Randall in Madison. We formed The Fifteenth Wisconsin Regiment. Governor Randall appointed Hans Heg as our Colonel. A good share of us, Heg included, were from the Old Country. We divided up into three units—the Scandinavian Mountaineers, Odin's Rifles, and the Norway Bear Hunters. I was in the Norway Bear Hunters along with one fella who'd only been in America for four months—Private Nelson. He could barely understand English. But I taught him the meaning of the different commands, and all winter long, we drilled.

"Then it came time to leave Wisconsin. It was March of 1862. I remember to this day how cold the wind blew—cold, and damp enough to send a chill to the bone. The sky was heavy with clouds. Beneath my feet, the snow was trampled with mud from a recent thaw. I looked down at my boots. The toes were shiny, but the soles were caked with dirt. I wondered then if I would ever stand on Wisconsin soil again.

"Then I looked up and saw my beloved Freya. She had promised to come bid me good-bye, and your father—he was but eight years old then—came to see me off, too. He was a brave young man. He hugged me and tried to keep the tears from his eyes. He told me not to worry, and he promised to take care of his mama while I was at war. I said I knew he would do a fine job as man of the house.

"Then I took Freya in my embrace. She wrapped her arms tight about my neck as if she never would let go. The scent of her lemon verbena and the softness of her golden hair against my cheek I never will forget. I looked into her watery, blue eyes and promised I would come back to her. She said she would pray for me. And those were the last words we shared before I left Wisconsin.

"I had trained hard to fight for my country. I knew I was a good soldier, but nothing could have prepared me for my first battle.

"I lay in a meadow, head down. The enemy advanced. Musket balls screamed past me. The stench of sulfur hung heavy in the air. I lifted my head just a little. A bullet grazed my scalp. Blood trickled down my cheek and onto my collar, and I pressed my handkerchief to the wound with a trembling hand. The ground shook with canon fire. I lifted my head a second time and raised my musket. I had a Confederate in my site when a ball struck my left hand, spoiling my shot. Then a piece of shell hit my right foot. The thunder of the enemy's artillery increased tenfold. All around me, men were shouting. I prayed I'd make it through this battle, that I would live to see my beloved Freya again. Somehow, I survived.

"When the day's fighting ended, one out of ten of our men had been killed. For every man who died, three were too badly wounded to fight. I was one of the lucky ones. With a bandage on my head and another on my hand, I returned to battle the next day.

"The weeks went by. Sometimes we fought. Other times, we marched until we thought we could march no more. Our leader, Colonel Heg, was the bravest man of all. Once, he was shot in the leg and fell from his horse. I helped him take cover and stayed by him. He wasn't badly hurt—not until the following year.

"I'll never forget the day he fell—September nineteenth

of 1863. The day before, we had taken a position along a winding creek called Chickamauga. That's Indian talk for 'river of death.' The fighting started at eight in the morning. By noon, the fallen soldiers were piled up like cordwood. Our forces broke and ran, but by nightfall, both lines held.

"The next day, Rosecrans ordered our troops to close a gap in the line. That's when Colonel Heg took a gut shot from a sharpshooter's rifle. We all knew this was a mortal wound. We carried him to a hospital tent. I wanted to stay with him but he wouldn't hear of it. He told me I was needed in battle.

"I went back to the fighting. The confederates stormed us. The Union forces retreated—all except George Henry Thomas. He held onto the Rock of Chickamauga.

"Men were falling all around me. Again, I prayed the Lord would keep me safe, that He would bring me home to my beloved Freya. Somehow, I survived. The next day, I learned Colonel Heg had died.

"We limped back into Chattanooga. It was cold then. Hardly any supplies made it through, and those that did were crawling with rats. We took little solace knowing the Confederates were in just as bad shape.

"Then, in October, Grant came to Chattanooga. Bragg held Lookout Mountain, south of town, and Grant was determined to defeat him there. On the twenty-fourth of November, we stormed the mountain. Bragg withdrew, and for weeks after, we all posed for pictures on Lookout Mountain.

"For two more years, the fighting continued. When the war ended, one of every three men in my regiment had died. Most of us had suffered injuries.

"In the spring of 1865 I started for home. My right arm was in a sling. My head was again bandaged and my uniform was ragged and dirty. Even my boots had holes. I took the train as far as Racine, and when I got off, I thanked the Lord for putting my feet on Wisconsin soil.

"Then I set out for Waterford, where I had bought the mill and general store from Hans Heg in 1860. I walked all day, and all day I wondered whether my Freya would be waiting for me. I wondered whether my Kal would recognize me. I wondered if I would recognize him.

"At last, I reached the edge of town. From a distance I could see the mill wheel turning. I started down the busy street, past the smithy. Black smoke rose from its chimney and stung my nose. The ringing of the hammer against the anvil sounded like chimes to my ears. Old friends spoke to me. I nodded and kept walking toward the mill. Traffic parted to let me pass.

"Soon, I could see the millwheel turning, and hear the water splashing over it, laughing and tumbling into the millstream. Customers came out of the mercantile and whispered to one another when they recognized me. I stopped in the road and stared at the storefront, afraid to go in.

"Then the door opened and out came a boy of eleven. He reminded me of myself at that age and I was sure it was my Kal. I smiled at him. He stared at me, almost in pity, and went back inside.

"I waited and watched. Seconds passed like hours. My heart pounded so loud I could hear it in my ears. Memories of the war came back, of artillery and canon fire booming. I could see the explosions of battle around me. I almost dropped to the ground.

"I closed my eyes and told myself I was no longer at war. When I opened them again, my Freya was standing on the boardwalk in front of the store. Kal was beside her.

"She was more beautiful than I had remembered. Her cheeks were stained pink. Her hair, fine as spun gold, was drawn gently back from her face. Her eyes, the color of forget-me-nots, gazed wonderingly at me.

"'Brede?' she asked, stepping off the boardwalk.

"I took a step toward her. 'Freya, I've come home,' I said.

"Then, she was in my arms, the scent of her lemon verbena filling my senses, the softness of her hair against my cheek. The years of our parting melted away in the warmth of her embrace. Silently, I thanked the Lord for bringing me home to my beloved Freya."

Following a moment of quiet reflection, Gramps said, "Five happy years we shared, then in 1870, my Freya took sick with a fever and went to be with the Lord." Pulling his handkerchief from his pocket, he wiped the moisture from his eyes, noticing that both Bridget's and Erik's eyes were also sparkling with the mists of sentimentality.

He was stuffing the damp cloth into his pocket when Frau Finkler barged through the door. "Time for bed, Herr Olson!" She set her thick Bible on the table by his chair, then shooed Erik and Bridget off the daybed. "Good night. *Grossvater* must sleep."

Bridget couldn't help noticing the swift change in Gramps's expression, from serene to disgruntled the moment the nurse reappeared. "Frau Finkler, how would you like the day off tomorrow?" she asked. "I'd be happy to stay with Gramps, if he'll have me."

"Bless you, Miss Richards!" the old man said. "What a

144

joy that would be."

"And I'll stay with him tonight," Erik offered. "You can go home right now, if you want, Frau Finkler. I'll get David to drive you." He reached for the doorknob.

Frau Finkler put up a staying hand. "Wait!" She disappeared into the bedroom next to the sitting room. A moment later, she reappeared with her satchel. Stuffing her Bible into the bulging carpet bag, she said, "You stay. I find David. *Guten abendt!*"

When the door had closed behind her wide bustle, Bridget noticed Gramps's smile had returned, though a hint of fatigue shadowed his eyes. "It's getting late. I'd better go."

Gramps pointed a crooked finger at Erik. "Son, see your lady friend home. I'll be fine for the few minutes it will take you to walk to the dormitory and back."

"Are you sure?"

"Go on," he said with a wave of his hand. "I'll be angry if you don't."

Erik took Bridget by the hand as he walked her to the dormitory, his touch sending a pleasant tingle through her. When they arrived at the door, she turned to him, finding a tender look in his eyes that made her wish the evening weren't about to end. But his grandfather's need of him remained foremost in her mind. "You'd better get back. I'll see you in the morning. Should I bring breakfast for Gramps?"

Erik gazed down at the young woman whose kindness made her beautiful beyond definition. "Bring breakfast for the three of us. Mrs. Little Bear will put it all on trays. Katie and Eddie will help carry it."

"Until morning, then."

"Until morning." Reluctant to release her hand, he brushed it with a kiss, and slowly backed away.

As Bridget turned to go inside, she caught a glimpse of Clarissa in the distance, headed swiftly toward them. Whirling around, she yanked open the screen door and hurried inside, letting it close with a bang. What were her chances with Erik, she wondered, as long as the cunning, conniving Clarissa remained at The Clovers?

CHAPTER

13

One last time Nat tightened the ropes holding the crated organ in the wagon, then climbed aboard beside Charlotte and Seth and drove off the dock and onto the road to the Steffens's cottage. Nearly two weeks had passed since he'd last seen Anna—that Sunday in the cemetery when he'd so shamelessly poured out his heart. He'd thought of her several times since he'd loaded her organ onto the *Manitou Lady* early this morning.

Despite the lateness of the hour—already it was nearly seven and neither he nor Seth nor Charlotte had eaten supper—he was determined to offload the instrument and take it to her tonight. The rest of his cargo could wait until tomorrow.

With Seth's and Charlotte's approval he'd decided not to charge freight from Traverse City to South Manitou even though the Steffenses could easily afford it. It was the least he could do in return for Anna's sympathetic ear, listening to him go on and on about Meta.

No sooner had he pulled to a halt by Anna's front porch than she came bursting through the screen door, her face bright with anticipation. "You've brought my organ!" she cried. Before Nat could even respond, she whirled around and ran back inside shouting, "Tom, Papa, come quick!"

Nat chuckled and turned to his brother. "I'm guessin' we won't be able to get the thing uncrated quick enough to please her."

Within moments, Mr. Steffens and Tom came to lend a hand, and Nat knew from the first moment he saw them where Anna had come by her brown eyes and dark hair. Her tiny figure must have been inherited from her mother, he concluded, for the Steffens men were both six feet in height and brawny enough to manage one end of the instrument while he and Seth lifted the other.

Inside the cottage, Anna enlisted the help of her mother and Mrs. Nolan, their sturdy, redheaded housekeeper, in pushing aside the gramophone and curios cabinet. Several minutes later, her father, brother, and the two Trevelyns eased the organ into place against the parlor wall.

Anna set the music she had bought in Traverse City on the music rack, pulled out several of the stops, and ran her hand over the walnut key cover, too impressed for words. When she looked up, Nat was watching her, arms crossed on his chest, his mouth curved in a half-smile.

"The least you can do is let us hear ya play, now that we've finally brought the thing all the way from Traverse City," he said.

"This had better sound good, for the price they're charging," Mr. Steffens warned.

"You won't owe a penny if you don't like it," Anna said, "but I'm sure you're going to love it." She slid back the key cover, then looked down and gasped. "Where's the stool?"

"Right here," Charlotte answered, carrying it through

the parlor door and setting it in place.

Anna sat down, opened the knee swells, pumped the pedals, and lit into a vigorous rendition of *The Band Played On.*

Nat couldn't keep from smiling as he listened to Anna's confident performance. Her music was filling more than the cottage with cheerfulness—it was filling his heart as well.

When she reached the chorus, she shouted, "Everybody sing!"

Her mother, father, brother, and even the hired lady joined in lusty voices. Too self-conscious to sing out loud, Nat hummed while Seth and Charlotte stood back and listened.

> Casey would waltz with a strawberry blonde
> And the Band played on
> He'd glide 'cross the floor with the girl he ador'd
> And the Band played on . . .

When Anna finished the second verse, she looked back, her gaze on Nat. "This time, I want to hear all the Trevelyns on the chorus!"

Nat knew his baritone voice would be badly off key, but he belted out the words. Seth and Charlotte joined in robust tones, seemingly trying to drown him out.

When the third verse and chorus had ended, Mr. Steffens said, "How about a chorus of *A Hot Time in the Old Town?*"

"*After* dinner," Mrs. Steffens insisted.

"I think we should invite the Trevelyns to dinner," Anna said.

"Can you stay?" asked Mrs. Steffens. "We'd love to have you."

Nat wanted to accept, but he looked to Seth, who looked to Charlotte, who simply shrugged. "We'd best be on our way," Nat decided.

Mr. Steffens pulled his pipe from his pocket, hung it in his mouth, and focused on Nat. "I make it a rule never make payment on an empty stomach, so if you want to collect for shipping, you'd best stay and eat."

Nat grinned broadly. "I don't intend to charge you for shipping."

Before her father could argue the point, Anna said, "All the more reason to accept our hospitality. Now, you've *got* to stay!"

"Besides, we've got an ice house full of fish," Tom said. "A couple more man-sized appetites at the table will be a welcome sight to Mrs. Nolan."

"Mr. Tom's right about that," Mrs. Nolan said. "It won't take me but a minute to throw more fish into the skillet." She started for the kitchen.

"I'll unhitch your team," Tom offered, heading out the door.

"It's all settled, then. I'll add a leaf to the dining table and set out three more places," Anna said.

"I'll help you," said Charlotte.

"And I'll see what I can do in the kitchen," said Mrs. Steffens. "You fellows might as well make yourselves comfortable on the porch for the next few minutes. It's the best place in the house to contemplate an appetite."

Though the meal was by no means a hurried affair, Nat thought it ended all too soon. When Anna invited him, his brother, and Charlotte to stay for more singing, he was in no mood to refuse.

Anna started with her father's favorite, *A Hot time in the Old Town,* followed by *Hello! Ma Baby* and *In the Baggage Coach Ahead.* As she had hoped, the strains of the only cottage organ on the island drew several neighbors who willingly lent their voices to the Steffens and Trevelyn chorus. Confidently, she continued through her repertoire --*Ta-Ra-Ra-Boom De Ay!, Who Threw the Overalls in Mistress Murphy's Chowder?, The Cat Came Back, Daisy Bell,* and *Down Went McGinty.*

Despite Nat's off-key singing, he was enjoying himself too much to leave until Anna had played through her song book. As she bid the last of her neighbors good bye at the front door, he and Seth and Charlotte thanked Mrs. Steffens for a fine meal. They were saying good-night to Anna when her father interrupted.

"Wait up, Mr. Trevelyn. I haven't paid you yet. I'll go make out a bank draft." Turning to Tom, he said, "You'd better go hitch up Mr. Trevelyn's team."

Nat was about to protest payment when Seth distracted him. "Charlotte and I have decided to walk home. We'll see you tomorrow."

"I'll drive ya. It won't take but a few minutes to bring the team around," Nat insisted. To Anna, he said, "Tell your father I won't accept payment, and that's that." He followed Seth and Charlotte out the front door.

Anna hurried after Nat, catching him by the sleeve before he stepped off the porch. When Charlotte and Seth were out of earshot, she quietly scolded him. "Let your brother and his wife go. Can't you see they want to be alone?"

Nat watched as Seth claimed a small bag from the

wagon with one hand, pulled his wife close to his side with the other, and strolled off into the moonlight, pausing to press a kiss into her hair. The couple had behaved so businesslike while working with him aboard the *Manitou Lady*, he had forgotten they were also newlyweds entitled to their privacy.

He turned to Anna. Her essence of spring violets bespoke sweetness, and the soft yellow of the porch lamp subtly defined the contours of her cheeks. From within rose an urge to reach for her. He could almost feel her in his arms. How he longed for an embrace.

Then a powerful sense of guilt flooded over him. He was being unfaithful to Meta, disloyal to the memory of her, thinking such thoughts about another woman so soon after her death. Still, he couldn't ignore his manly desires.

Anna saw the unmistakable look of longing in Nat's eyes, the sadness that quickly replaced it, and sensed the anxiety in the air, so thick it was almost tangible. She wanted to say something—anything—to ease the tension, but no words seemed to come.

Then her father stepped out the front door. "This ought to cover the charges," he told Nat, stuffing a folded draft into his breast pocket.

Nat tried to recover himself enough to mount an argument but the words that came out instead were, "Thank you, sir."

Mr. Steffens disappeared inside the house, and Nat's attention returned to Anna. The spell that had seemingly caught him in a web of desire was disturbed, but not completely broken. Though he could hear Tom hitching up his team and he knew he should go help, his feet wouldn't move. He kept his eyes on the pretty brown ones that gazed up at him, trying to find the words to say good night.

He waved off a mosquito about to land on her shoulder and slapped at another on his arm. "You should get back inside. Thanks . . . " he said, a catch in his voice forcing a pause before he added, "for a mighty nice time."

Not trusting her own voice, Anna only nodded, then went inside. As she headed for her bedroom, she passed by her new organ, pausing to again run her hand over the satin walnut finish. Already, the instrument was worth more than her father would pay for it. Tonight, Mr. Nat Trevelyn had enjoyed himself, and times like this couldn't be bought at any price.

CHAPTER

14

Despite the throng at the dock when the *Manitou Lady* arrived in Traverse City on the day of Buffalo Bill's Wild West Show, Bridget had no trouble finding Kenton McCune. She was glad she had written him a note telling the exact time and place of her arrival, for he was waiting on the pier. She hadn't expected to see him all decked out as if he were a part of the show, in a plaid cowboy shirt, denim breeches, and spurred boots. He wore a Stetson hat, and the red kerchief about his neck fluttered in the breeze.

He only seemed to be missing the sixshooters, she thought, as she waved to him from the deck of the *Manitou Lady*, where Charlotte, Aurora, and her sister's husband, Harrison, were pressed in beside her. "There's my friend, Mr. McCune. The one with the cowboy hat," she told her sisters, who were eager to meet him.

"Oh, my! What a fine-looking fellow he is!" said Charlotte, nudging Bridget with her elbow.

"So he was the first of the three to make a bid for your company today," Aurora mused, her gaze on Kenton. "For some reason, I never would have put you with an attorney who looks like a cowboy. But then, your life has changed so since we were last together at Charlotte's wedding, I can't seem to keep up. You have enough gentlemen friends for three young women." She rested a hand on her stomach, and a radiance came over her countenance. "Perhaps by the time my little lightkeeper is born, you'll have picked out a new uncle for him," she said, talking openly of her condition for the first time.

"Speaking of uncle," Harrison said, "did you mention my brother has sent word he's riding with the show?" As the passengers began to exit, he guided his wife carefully along the rail toward the gangway.

"With all the catching up we've had to do, it slipped my mind," Aurora said.

"Jake was always a wild one," Harrison told Bridget and Charlotte. "Never much for planting roots. I'm not surprised he left Montana to travel with Buffalo Bill. He said he'd leave reserved seat tickets for all of us at the ticket office."

"How long has it been since you've seen your brother?" Bridget asked.

"More than ten years."

"There'll be hundreds of men dressed like cowboys. Are you sure you'll recognize him?" Charlotte asked.

"I'm wondering that myself. But one thing I know. Jake will find us before the day is over, if he really wants to. He makes a habit of getting what he wants. Besides, he'll know which seats we'll be in." Putting his arm about Aurora, he helped her down the gangway.

Bridget followed, making introductions of her sisters and brother-in-law to Mr. McCune the moment she stepped onto the dock. Hat in hand, he bowed with a flourish. "I didn't know your sisters were as fair of face as you, Miss Richards." Smiling at Charlotte and Aurora, he said, "Fair as though they'd looked on Paradise, and caught its early beauty, if Shakespeare will forgive the paraphrase."

Charlotte smiled. "You just keep talking, and don't

worry about Shakespeare, Mr. McCune."

He chuckled. "I'm afraid my next words are not nearly so eloquent. I was going to suggest we go immediately to Front Street. Mr. Cody will be starting his parade soon. We won't want to miss it."

Bridget turned to Charlotte. "Shouldn't you wait for Seth?"

"He and Nat said we should go ahead. Harrison will leave their tickets at the office. They'll join us at the arena after they've finished here at the boat."

"That's right," Harrison said. To McCune, he explained. "My brother is part of the show. I'm sure there'll be enough tickets for us all. You and Bridget will sit with us, won't you?"

"Your brother is generous as a lord," McCune replied. "I'm honored to be part of your company."

"Let's go, then," Bridget said.

Kenton linked her arm with his and they set off with Harrison, Aurora, and Charlotte. On their way up to Front Street, she couldn't help noticing Erik, Clarissa, and her sisters in the crowd nearby. Clarissa took one look at Kenton, and above the din, Bridget could hear her derisive laugh. Erik seemed displeased by her, and refrained from looking in Bridget's direction.

Determined to enjoy her day, and her company, Bridget drew closer to Kenton—close enough to smell his sandalwood essence. The heady scent, and other thoughts pushed aside those of the Wisconsin girl. "Are the Marshalls coming to the parade?" she asked. "I've often recalled how much I enjoyed working for them."

"I invited them along," Kenton said, "but Ben wouldn't hear of closing the shop on a day when so many people are coming to town. We can stop in and say hello to them after the parade, though."

They soon reached Front Street, finding a place at the curb to view the parade. Within minutes, the music of the cowboy band could be heard in the distance.

Charlotte stepped off the curb for a better look, then turned to her sisters excitedly. "There he is! There's Buffalo Bill!"

Within moments, cheers rippled through the crowd, then the famous scout came into view. Astride a magnificent horse laden with silver trappings, the bearded frontiersman led his band. Strutting from one side of the street to the other, his shoulder-length hair blown back by the breeze, he came within a few feet of Bridget and Kenton.

"Mr. Cody!" Kenton shouted, waving his hat. The legendary man tipped his hat in acknowledgement, and rode on. Kenton turned to Bridget, beaming with excitement. "When I was a kid, he was my hero. I can't believe I've finally seen him in person!"

Bridget smiled. She never would have guessed his childhood hero was so distantly removed from the intellectual pursuits of his adult life. Like Kenton, she continued to watch Cody until he rode out of sight. Though she would never admit it to anyone, she concluded he was one of the most attractive specimens of manhood she'd ever seen.

Behind him, the cowboy band on horseback struck up a march, their mounts prancing and dancing in rhythm to the tune. In their wake came a man and a woman on separate horses, each holding a rifle high.

"Look! It's Johnny Baker and Miss Annie Oakley!" Charlotte exclaimed.

"The premier lady wing shot of the world," Bridget added, recalling the words of the newspaper advertisement.

Next, came squads of cowboys and women of the west on horseback, including one dude in a ten-gallon hat who wore a huge blue neckerchief. He rode a star-blazed mount and showcased his roping skills by dropping a lasso over one of the women riding near him.

"Do you see your brother anywhere?" Aurora asked Harrison.

Lifting the brim of his straw hat for a better look, he scrutinized the cowboys passing by. "I don't recognize Jake, but that's not surprising after all this time."

In formation behind the cowboys and western women were Cuban heroes, squadrons of Russian Cossacks, cavalry men from the United States and Germany, and military men from the Royal Irish Lancers and the English Army. They were followed by Arab, Magyar, Gaucho, Chico, and Vaquero horsemen. Then came chiefs and warriors of the Sioux Nation, the Deadwood Stage, and several covered wagons. When the last wagon had passed, most of the parade-watchers spilled into the street and headed toward the arena.

"I've never been one to follow the crowd," Kenton said to Bridget, her sisters, and Harrison, "but today, I think it's our best choice if we want to get to the arena in plenty of time to see the show."

"Don't forget, our stop at the Marshalls' candy shop," Bridget said.

"I, for one, am looking forward to it," Aurora said. "I'm certain the Marshalls can help satisfy my craving for a huge piece of creamy, vanilla fudge."

Within minutes, they reached the candy store, only to

discover the shop so jammed with customers, a line had formed on the sidewalk. Taking advantage of her previous experience with the Marshalls, Bridget went around to the back door and let herself in. Neither Ben nor Lottie seemed the least bit surprised when she stepped behind the counter and put up a box of vanilla fudge, leaving payment in the cash register. With a promise to the Marshalls to visit again when they would have time to talk, she returned to Kenton and the others.

The crowd waiting at the ticket office was massive. Following Bridget's example, Harrison went to the back door of the office, returning shortly with the tickets his brother had promised. Their seats couldn't have been better, adjacent to the grandstand in the center of the first row under the canvas tent surrounding the arena. Twenty minutes later, Nat and Seth, along with Anna and Tom Steffens, joined them there.

Nat was polite but cool when Bridget introduced him to Kenton McCune. He sat with the Steffenses, separated from Bridget and Kenton by Harrison, Charlotte, and Aurora. Though Bridget concentrated most of her attention on Kenton, telling him how much she and Gramps had enjoyed the *Tales of Unrest* when she had read to him on her day off, she noticed Nat casting glances their way from time to time.

Anna must have noticed, too, for she began teasing Nat, diverting his attention, allowing Bridget to better concentrate on Kenton as he told of his efforts, thus far unsuccessful, to locate a publisher for Mrs. Olson's diagrams of dinosaurs. He had just finished relaying this news when Bridget spotted Erik and the Hackbardt sisters taking seats a few rows back of her.

A moment later, Buffalo Bill rode into the arena, tipping his hat as the audience greeted him with thunderous applause. For Bridget, thoughts of all but the showman and his announcement took flight.

"Ladies and Gentlemen," he began in a clear, resounding voice, "permit me to introduce to you a Congress of the Rough Riders of the World."

Hooves pounded, raising thick dust as the company entered the arena whooping and hollering. Guns fired in the air as the cowboys, western women, military squads, sharpshooters, Indian, the stagecoach, and wagons appeared in turn.

When all had passed in review, Mr. Cody described the first performance. "The Pony Express was established long before the Union Pacific railroad was built across the continent, or even before the telegraph poles were set, and when Abraham Lincoln was elected President of the United States, it was important that the election returns from California should be brought across the mountains as quickly as possible. Mr. William Russell first proposed the Pony Express. He was told it would take too long—seventeen or eighteen days. A wager was made that the time could be made in less than ten days. The trip was completed in nine days and seventeen hours. Mr. Billy Johnson will illustrate the mode of riding the Pony Express, mounting, dismounting, and changing the mail to fresh horses."

A cowboy led a pony into the arena and held it still in front of the grandstand. At the sound of a brass fanfare, a hush fell over the crowd. Bridget watched in amazement as a rider raced into the stadium, stopped almost in front of her, and unhitched his mail pouches in a few fleeting seconds.

"Go, Mr. Johnson!" Kenton hollered when the fellow switched his bags and hopped aboard the fresh pony. He tore out of the stadium like a streak of wind.

The next two acts kept Bridget equally as enthralled. An Indian on foot raced an Indian on a pony. A cowboy, Mustang Jack, claiming to be the best standing high-jumper in the world, jumped over a burro. Then, he jumped over a Mustang pony, and afterward, he cleared a white horse sixteen and a half hands high. The audience went wild with applause.

Music played, and an announcer said, "I now have the pleasure of introducing Mr. Johnny Baker, of North Platte, Nebraska, expert in rifle and revolver shooting. Mr. Baker will give an exhibition of his skill, holding his rifle in various positions."

"Watch close," Kenton told Bridget. "Mr. Baker was a champion when he was only sixteen. He's been traveling with Mr. Cody's show from the start, back in '83."

Holding his rifle sideways, Mr. Baker blew up his first target, a composition ball resting in a scoop-like holder. Then he put his rifle to his shoulder and smashed the second target. He performed variations of the same trick: holding his rifle on top of his head; standing with his back to the target, bending forward, and shooting between his knees; and leaning backward over a support and shooting over his head. Then, an assistant picked up Baker's feet and raised them in the air until the champion was standing on his head. Again, he shot accurately.

When Johnny Baker had left the arena, Charlotte nudged Bridget's elbow and pointed to the entrance at the end of the stadium. A woman on horseback was waiting to ride out. "Look! Annie Oakley! She's as good as Mr.

Baker. Just you watch."

When Buffalo Bill had announced her, she rode across the turf to resounding cheers and applause. Then a handsome, darkhaired cowboy loaded a clay pigeon into a trap, and Kenton said, "That's Frank Butler, her husband. When Miss Oakley was only fifteen, she beat him in a shooting contest. He courted her for a year, then married her and gave up his shooting career to manage hers. Wait till you see his part in her act!"

At first, she performed similar tricks to Johnny Baker. Using a shotgun, she hit a clay pigeon sprung from a trap. Then her husband released two clay pigeons in rapid succession and she hit them both. She laid her gun on the ground, and after the trap was sprung, she hit first one clay pigeon, then two of them released in close succession. Then Mr. Butler took a position fifty yards down the field from Annie Oakley.

Kenton squeezed Bridget's wrist. "Watch closely."

Mr. Butler lit a cigarette and put it in his mouth. Miss Oakley set aside her shotgun and picked up a rifle, then turned her back to him. Holding a mirror, she took aim over her shoulder. Charlotte gasped. Bridget held her breath.

Taking her time, Miss Oakley adjusted the angle of her shot. Deathly silence reigned.

Bang!

Miss Oakley's bullet shortened Mr. Butler's cigarette to a stub.

The audience erupted with cheers and applause. The band lit into a rousing tune while Miss Oakley took a turn around the ring to acknowledge the ovation.

Bridget clapped her hands so hard, they stung. A few

seats away, Anna jumped to her feet in excitement. Charlotte let out a cheer, then reminded Bridget, "See! I told you she was just as good as Mr. Baker!"

When all was quiet, the announcer spoke again. "Next on our program, a re-enactment of an attack on the Deadwood Stagecoach, plying between Deadwood and Cheyenne. This coach has an immortal place in American history, having been baptized many times by fire and blood. The gentleman holding the reins is Mr. Higby, an old stage driver, and formerly the companion of Hank Monk, of whom you have all probably read. Seated beside him is Mr. John Hancock, known in the West as the Wizard Hunter of the Platte Valley. Bronco Bill will act as out rider, a position he has occupied in earnest many times with credit. Upon the roof of the coach is seated Mr. Con Croner, the Cowboy Sheriff of the platte, to whose intrepid administration of that office, Lincoln County, Nebraska and its vicinity are indebted for the peace and quiet that now reigns. Mr. Croner's efforts drove out the notorious Middleton gang.

"The coach will start upon its journey, be attacked from an ambush by a band of fierce and warlike Indians, who in their turn will be repulsed by a party of scouts and cowboys, under Mr. Cody's command. Will two or three ladies and gentlemen volunteer to ride as passengers?"

Kenton leaped off his seat and waved his hat in the air. "We'll ride!" He drew Bridget up beside him.

The announcer nodded.

As they headed for the coach, she heard Anna saying, "I want to go, too!" When Bridget glanced back, she saw Nat holding her by the elbow, arguing for her to sit down again.

Bridget stepped up into the coach and settled on the

leather seat beside Kenton, unable to believe they were becoming part of the show. When Mr. Hancock had closed the door, she peered out the window, listening as the announcer continued his description.

"It is customary to deliver parting instructions to the driver before he starts on his perilous journey. Mr. Higby, you are entrusted with valuable lives and property. Should you meet with Indians or other dangers en route, put on the whip, and if possible, save the lives of your passengers. If you are all ready, go!"

The coach rolled comfortably toward the end of the arena. Just as it began to make its turn, a band of Indians came charging alongside, whooping and hollering.

The coach swerved hard, pressing Bridget firmly against Kenton. He put his arm about her, steadying her as the coach swung in the opposite direction.

"Passengers, get down!" she heard Mr. Hancock shout.

Kenton grinned broadly and slid closer to the window, pulling Bridget with him. "I wouldn't miss this for the world!"

Gunshots filled the air. Fierce, painted Indians kept up their pursuit. One young brave rode so close Bridget could see pale scars on his coppery chest.

Within moments, the coach circled past the grandstand. Mr. Cody and a band of cowboys set out after the fierce Indians.

Hooves pounded. Dust flew. The sound of gunfire and the essence of spent gunpowder filled the air. The coach swerved several more times. Kenton held Bridget tight to keep her from falling off the seat. The cowboys rode hard, driving off the enemy.

The coach came to a stop by the grandstand, and

Kenton helped Bridget out. Slightly dizzy from the zig-zag ride, she stumbled. Kenton caught her, his strong arm about her waist. He held her steady by his side as they headed toward their seats.

Bridget couldn't resist glancing in Nat's direction. While others in the audience applauded, he scowled. Several rows back, Erik smiled broadly at her and pointed to his camera. Beside him, Clarissa showed genuine lassitude.

When Bridget and Kenton had taken their seats again, he took her hand in his and spoke quietly in her ear. "Thank you for coming to the show with me. I'm having the best time of my life!"

She squeezed his hand and smiled. "I'm glad! So am I!"

Throughout the next several acts, Bridget's hand remained in Kenton's. They watched military demonstrations on a platform set in the center of the arena. Squads moving in circles like hands on a clock marched with precision timing. Bill Cody showed how he earned his name, "Buffalo Bill," shooting off blanks as he chased after three monstrous buffalo let loose in the arena. Pawnee and Wichita Indians put on a display of their native sports and pastimes, then danced the War dance, Grass dance and Scalp dance. Afterward, Buffalo Bill led troops in a re-enactment of Custer's Last Stand.

When the battle ended, Kenton told Bridget, "If Buffalo Bill had been there, it wouldn't have been the last stand."

She laughed. "He *is* almost as good as his legend."

When the battlefield had cleared, the announcer addressed the audience again. "Now for our final demonstration, we will show you the attack upon a settler's cabin by a

165

band of plundering Indians, and their repulse by Mr. Cody's party of scouts and cowboys. After our entertainment you are invited to visit the Wild West camp. We thank you for your polite attention, and bid you all good afternoon."

"Did you hear that?" Kenton asked excitedly. "We're invited to visit the Wild West camp. You'll go with me, won't you?"

"I wouldn't miss it!" Bridget replied.

Within a few minutes, a settler's cabin had been constructed in front of the grandstand and the "settlers" tended their chores: a mother and daughter cooking over an outdoor fire; a father and son chopping and stacking wood. Then, two dozen Indians charged onto the scene.

The women screamed and ran inside. The men followed, closing the door and aiming rifles out the unshuttered windows.

Buffalo Bill burst into the arena followed by twenty hard-riding men. One of them was knocked from his horse by an Indian in front of Bridget and Kenton. Another cowboy came up on a star-blazed mount—the fellow Bridget had seen in the parade wearing the ten-gallon hat, the big blue neckerchief, and twirling the lasso. He shouted to Kenton and Bridget.

"That man's off his horse. Go help him!"

Kenton sprang from his seat, taking Bridget with him. Together, they pulled the man to his feet. When he had climbed onto his mount and ridden off, another man fell from his horse a few yards away. Again and again, Bridget and Kenton, along with other members of the audience, helped fallen cowboys back into their saddles, always careful to stay clear of the path of hard-riding

Indians.

When the battle ended, Bridget and Kenton were several yards from their seats and started walking back to where Charlotte, Seth, and the others were waiting for them. The Cowboys and Indians were clearing off the field, and the dude on the star-blazed horse pulled up in front of Bridget. He tipped his huge hat and smiled broadly, his tanned face looking more handsome than she had remembered.

"You're Miss Richards, aren't ya?" His words were more a statement than a question. Before Bridget could reply, he said, "I'm Jake Stone, Harrison's big brother."

"*You're* Harrison's brother?" she asked, unable to see the resemblance.

"That's right, miss."

Kenton extended his hand to Jake. "Then our thanks to you, Mr. Stone, for a most memorable afternoon, one I shall never forget."

"My pleasure," Jake said, turning again to Bridget. "Seein' as how you've been a real enthusiastic participant in Mr. Cody's Wild West show today, I was wonderin' if ya might like to ride with me on Star, here. There's not many young ladies can say they had a ride with a real cowboy from Mr. Cody's Wild West Show."

"I . . . " Bridget glanced at Kenton, struggling to find the words to tactfully decline.

"Go on!" Kenton said. "It will be a ride you'll never forget. I'll help you up."

Not wanting to appear ungrateful, she resigned herself to the ride aboard Jake's tall horse. With his strong arm pulling her up, and Kenton's hand beneath her feet, she was soon situated sideways in front of Jake. Feeling cramped and uneasy at being held in place by the arms of a near stranger, she reminded herself she would soon be on solid ground once again.

"We'll catch up with ya at the Wild West Camp in a bit," Jake told Kenton.

"See you there!"

As soon as Star began moving, Bridget was certain she'd slip off the saddle.

Jake must have sensed her anxiety for he tightened his arms about her. "Don't worry, Miss Richards. I ain't about to let ya fall off," he said soothingly, and she recognized in his voice the same bass timbre that characterized Harrison's.

Cutting to the end of the arena, he exited near the Wild West camp, but instead of turning right, toward the tents, he turned left onto Front Street.

The back of her neck prickled with apprehension. "I thought you were taking me to the camp."

"I am," Jake said reassuringly, "*my* camp. I got me a ranch and a real wild west camp out in Montana. All's I need now is a woman. You'd look right pretty sittin' there on my front porch. I'd be real happy comin' home after a hard day's ride, knowin' you'd be there a-waitin' to greet me."

Desperate to hide her panic, Bridget laughed nervously. "I know you're joking, Mr. Stone, but the fun's up. Let me off your horse. *Now!*"

Jake tightened his hold about her and urged his horse into a canter. "This ain't no joke," he said solemnly. "I got me a good woman—a *Richards* woman—now we're gonna *ride!*" Digging his spurs into Star's flanks, the horse galloped off.

CHAPTER

15

With all the activity at the arena, Front Street was nearly deserted, allowing Jake easy passage. Desperate for a plan of escape, and equally fearful of falling off Star, Bridget clutched the arms of the man who had taken her hostage and shouted above the noise of the horse's hooves.

"We need a preacher to marry us. I know one who'll do the job in Glen Arbor. That's about twenty miles west of here."

Jake slowed up a bit. "Good thinkin', Miss Richards. The sooner we're hitched up legal-like, the better. Now all I gotta do is find the right road." Reaching the end of Front Street, he stopped to holler at an old man rocking on his front porch. "Which way to Glen Arbor, sir?"

The old gentleman pointed toward the water. "Go left up by the bay. You'll see the sign."

"Much obliged!" Jake tipped his hat, then urged Star into a canter. The thought he'd soon be married put a smile on his face. This plan he'd been hatching for weeks was falling into place much easier than he'd expected, and the one unattached sister Harrison had described to him in his last letter was much prettier than he'd expected, too. He liked a woman with some meat on her bones. She'd take well to the hearty life in the West.

Bridget kept her silence as Star carried her and her unwanted suitor away from the city and her sisters and friends. Surely, they had missed her by now and were making plans to find her. With every second that passed, she fought the desire to try an escape on her own. When they had gone about a mile down the road toward Glen Arbor, she said, "I'd like to get down and walk a spell."

Jake stared at her, one eye squinting. "You wouldn't be thinkin' of runnin' off, now, would ya? 'Cause that'd do ya about as much good as kickin' a hog barefoot."

"I'm not aiming to run away," Bridget said.

"Good. 'Cause I got my lasso right here." He reached for the rope hanging from his saddle. "I'd catch ya quicker 'n an auctioneer can say 'jack rabbit.'"

"I know you would. I saw you in the parade. You're very handy with a rope. Now, would you *please* let me down?"

Jake climbed off Star and reached for Bridget. She started to slide off the saddle, then fell solidly against him. He held her tight a few inches off the ground. The belt of his holster dug into her, reminding her of the two guns he carried and the bullets that circled his waist.

"I'm gonna like holdin' ya close when we're married," he said innocently. "O' course, it ain't proper till then. Nothin' wrong with a little hand-holdin' 'fore we're married, though." He set her gently on the ground, took her hand firmly in his, and began leading Star down the road.

Bridget kept her silence, resenting every step that took

her farther from those she loved. A few minutes later, they came upon a farmhouse and small barn. Standing in the drive was a buggy hitched to a roan mare. Diapers hung on a line in the side yard near a well pump.

"I'm thirsty," she said. "Would you ask those folks if they'd let me have a nice, cold drink from their well?"

"We'll just go an' help ourselves, darlin'. I'm sure they won't object. An' if anybody comes out, don't you say one word. I'll do all the talkin'. Understand?"

Irritated by his lack of trust, she began to argue. "I don't know why—"

Quicker than a flash he pulled his six-shooter from his holster, shot the knob off the top of one clothespin, then twirled his gun about his finger and slid it back into his holster. "Like I said. I'll do all the talkin'," Jake solemnly reminded her. "Now go on an' get your drink."

Bridget had taken but a few steps toward the well when a young farmer in a wide-brimmed straw hat came hurrying out of the barn. Jake pulled his gun and began twirling it about his finger, a broad smile on his face. "Howdy, pardner. My woman's in need of some refreshment. Didn't think you'd mind sharin' some o' your water with us." He took aim at the young man.

The farmer put up his hands and backed away. "Help yourself. Take all you need."

"Thank ya kindly," Jake said. Sending off a shot that blew straight through the crown of the farmer's hat, he continued. "We need to borrow that horse 'n buggy o' yours for a spell, too. I'll see ya get 'em back."

The farmer nodded his head vigorously. "Take them."

At the well, Bridget took her time pumping the handle. When the cold water gushed out, she filled the dipper that was hanging by the spout and sipped slowly. Jake was tying Star to the back of the buggy. Intuition told her to turn her back to him and put her other hand in her pocket. Still sipping from the ladle, she pulled out the handkerchief embroidered with her initials and dropped it on the ground, then she refilled the dipper and turned to Jake with a sweet smile. "Care for a cold drink, Mr.—"

Jake cut her off with a pistol shot in the air then offered a smile that appeared forced. "You're forgettin' your promise to keep quiet, darlin'. Now bring that drink here, and we'll be on our way."

Though Bridget's hand was shaking so badly she spilled half the water from it, she managed to carry the other half to him, all the while praying he wouldn't notice the little white square she had left by the well.

Gun in one hand, ladle in the other, he took two swallows then tossed the dipper in the direction of the pump. Under his breath he said, "Now get in the buggy and don't try nothin' else or I'll gag ya and hogtie ya till we get where we're goin'."

Bridget nodded and did as he said. He climbed aboard beside her, turned the buggy around, and headed out. When they'd gone a quarter of a mile toward Glen Arbor, he said, "That wasn't smart, tryin' to drop my name to that farmer back there after ya promised me ya'd keep still."

"Drop your . . . I wasn't doing any such thing!" Bridget protested. Then she laughed nervously. "I guess I'm not accustomed to someone else ruling my tongue. I'll do better from now on."

"That's my girl," Jake said putting his hand on her knee.

Bridget wanted to jump off the rig, but instead, gritted

her teeth, silently saying a prayer of thanks when Jake's hand returned to the reins.

She sat as far from him as possible on the narrow buggy seat and prayed for a peaceful end to her dilemma once they reached Preacher Mulder's parsonage. Jake remained quiet, setting the mare at a brisk trot, the only conversation that between the creaking rig and the clip-clopping hooves. After a long while, he slowed the pace to a walk.

"It's mighty peaceful-like here," he said, drawing a deep breath. "Smells clean, too. Like water instead of dust. I've been away from the big lakes so long, I'd forgotten what it was like in this part of the world."

"I've never known anything but the lakes," Bridget said.

"You will soon enough," Jake promised. "I ain't anything like my brother, Harrison, stayin' on an island. What kinda life is that? I've been all over with Buffalo Bill and his show. When my chance came to see the world, I grabbed it without a second thought," he said with a snap of his fingers. "I sunk most of my earnings into a copper mine. It paid off big. Now I've got more money than I can spend in a lifetime. Bought my sheep ranch with some of it. You'll like it there. I promise," he said, laying his hand on her knee again.

The contact made her squirm, but she forced herself to keep up with the conversation. "I don't know the first thing about sheep. I don't know much about Montana, either, but surely there must be some young lady there who would be eager to take you for her husband."

Jake pulled his hand away, forming a fist, and scowled. His gaze burned into her with such fierce anger, she thought he would hit her. Then the fire faded from his

173

blue-gray eyes and he put his arm about her and pulled her tight against him. "Ain't no lady in Montana for me. *You're* my lady, Miss Bridget. I've known it for weeks."

"How could that be?" Bridget challenged. "You never saw me before today."

"Blame it all on my brother. Harrison told me 'bout the superior quality o' Michigan women. Said I oughta come back here. He told me all 'bout his wife. Then he said a little about each of his wife's sisters. I knew the youngest was gettin' hitched. I knew there weren't no claims on you."

"But there *are!* Nat Trevelyn claims he's going to marry me when the summer's through."

"Is he that city cowboy you was sittin' with?" Jake threw his head back and chortled. "What would ya want with him, when ya can have a *real* cowboy? Now answer me that, Miss Bridget!"

Jake's grip tightened on her shoulder to the point of pain, and she kept her silence. Several minutes later, when he had released her to put both hands on the reins once again, she said, "Mr. Stone, you can't steal a bride. You can't make someone want you. Please stop the rig and let me go."

You can't make someone want you. The words echoed in Jake's mind, making him deaf to the plea that had followed. He recalled an earlier time, another place, the spark of love found, anguish of love rejected. The torment had rent him in two. Angry fire had burned in his heart thereafter, hot enough to turn the broken pieces into molten steel and forge them back together. When the heat had dissipated, he had discovered a steel-like strength within. Sometimes, his heart was cold as his name. At others, it flashed hot as the hinges of Satan's door. He seemed to have little control. He only knew that what he'd once wanted more than anything else in the world, he'd been denied, and he would not be denied any want again.

In the several moments while Bridget waited for Jake to reply, she recognized anger, heartache, and fierce determination in the depths of his smoky eyes. But what frightened her most of all was the tone of utter ruthlessness when he spoke again.

"*I* want *you,* Miss Bridget. And what I want, I get."

Bridget gave up talking and began praying in earnest. She prayed for God's grace and protection. She prayed Jake's dark thoughts, black mood, and desperation would pass. She prayed Preacher Mulder would be able to talk sense into him. She prayed to be reunited with her sisters and friends. And most of all, she prayed Jake would come into fellowship with the one who could replace his hurts with happiness.

Bridget was still praying some time later when Jake drove into Glen Arbor. The town seemed too quiet. He parked the buggy in front of the parsonage and helped Bridget down. His arm about her waist, he led her back to his horse, unhooked his lasso, and slipped it over his shoulder. When she started toward the house, he stopped her. With his free hand, he tipped her chin up, forcing her to meet his gaze. The tenderness and vulnerability in his smile tugged at her heart.

"You're one beautiful bride, Miss Bridget. I'm mighty proud to be takin' ya to the altar."

As Bridget gazed into his rugged, handsome face, she couldn't help thinking for a brief instant how thrilling this moment should be for an innocent young lady about to become the bride of a western romantic hero. But her nightmarish reality swiftly eclipsed the daydream. She forced the corners of her mouth upward and searched for an appropriate response. "I . . . I'm flattered that you think I'm beautiful, Mr. Stone. Truly, I am."

Jake placed her hand in the crook of his arm and escorted her onto the porch of the modest two-story house, knocking boldly on the front door. While they waited for a response, Bridget recalled her last visit there, when Nat and Meta had eloped. How she wished Nat were here now to help get her out of this mess!

Shifting his weight impatiently, Jake knocked again and waited. Bridget prayed for Preacher Mulder to answer, to bring an end to this charade she'd been forced into.

Jake tried the door. It was unlocked. He opened it several inches and hollered. "Anybody home? Preacher, are ya there?"

A voice came from behind. "You folks lookin' for Preacher Mulder?"

Bridget turned to find a stooped-over woman in a blue calico dress and matching sunbonnet. "Yes, ma'am. Do you know where we can find him?"

"He's gone to that Wild West Show. He'll be back this evenin'."

Jake tipped his hat. "Thank ya kindly, ma'am. We'll wait inside." Gripping Bridget painfully by the elbow, he ushered her inside, quickly shut the door, then yanked her toward him, his smoky eyes sparking with anger. "I told ya to let me do all the talkin'. Now don't you forget it!" He cast her aside so roughly she landed on the floor. Her heart pounding, her stomach churning, Bridget lay paralyzed by fear as Jake set his ten-gallon hat on the hall tree. When he turned to her again, she quickly brushed the moisture from her eye.

Jake stooped beside Bridget, his anger forgotten, sympathy swelling within for the woman who was quivering like a frightened fawn. Gently, he lifted her to her feet and held her by the shoulders. "I'm mighty sorry, Miss Bridget. Guess I just don't know my own strength. Forgive me?"

She could barely stand to look at him, but managed a furtive glance upward and a quick nod.

He released her. "Go on in the kitchen. I got me an appetite. I sure hope ya can cook."

He followed her through the parlor to the kitchen that overlooked the backyard, unbuckled his holster, laid it across the small table, then sat down, propping his foot on his knee. Using a pistol as a pointer, he aimed at the oak ice box. "Open 'er up. See if there's vittals enough to make me a man-sized supper."

Bridget prayed for ample provisions, fearing Jake's reaction if the ice box proved empty. She opened the door a crack to peek inside. Finding her prayer answered, she swung it wide for Jake to see.

"Eggs 'n bacon. That'll make a fine supper. I like mine scrambled. And fry the bacon real crisp. How are ya at biscuits?"

Bridget wanted to say she'd known how to make tender biscuits since she'd been a girl of ten, but she was too afraid to talk, and simply shrugged.

Jake rose, a broad grin on his face. "I'm a real ace at biscuits. I'll fire up the oven, then tell ya how it's done." He put down his pistol and began crumpling up sheets of old newspaper that had been stacked on the box of kindling. While he laid his kindling and the larger sticks in place, Bridget eased nearer the table and started to reach for his pistols.

He turned and slapped her hand away so hard and quick, she could feel the welt rising. "Don't touch what ain't yours, woman!" Strapping the holster on again, he said, "Why didn't ya just ask me to move 'em so ya could set the table?"

Deep fear returning, she shrugged again.

"What's the matter? Got a twitch in your shoulders?" He laughed derisively. "You can talk, so long as it's just the two of us. I'm gettin' kinda tired of hearin' my own voice. Speak up from now on. Understand?"

"Yes, sir," Bridget replied, her voice little more than a whisper.

Jake struck a match to light the fire, shut the stove door, then sat down again. "You get on with the cookin'. I'll supervise. Do ya know any songs? My ma used to sing while she was workin' in the kitchen. I'll bet ya have a good singin' voice. Sing me a tune while y'r makin' my supper. Will ya do that, darlin'?"

Bridget started immediately to sing *What a Friend We Have in Jesus*. To her surprise, Jake began to hum along, then she remembered Harrison's singing ability and realized his older brother shared his musical talent. Though she remained fearful of Jake and his brittle temperament, the words of the song offered solace. "Have we trials and temptations? Is there trouble anywhere? We should never be discouraged. Take it to the Lord in prayer."

Somehow, she managed to sing all the while she rolled out and baked the biscuits and fried the eggs and bacon. Jake made coffee, adding his voice to each tune, sometimes even singing the words. The music seemed to sweeten his disposition.

When supper was ready and she sat across the table from him to eat, he said, "I'll ask the blessing. Heavenly father, bless this food to our use, and bring Preacher Mulder home soon as we're done eatin'. I'm too hungry to share this here meal with 'im, but I'm a-hankerin' to get hitched to this woman you done give me. Amen."

Throughout the meal Bridget worried for the safety of Preacher Mulder and his wife when they returned. Under Jake's watchful eye, she cleaned up the dishes and set the kitchen in order. He dogged her when she visited the outhouse, then tied her to a kitchen chair and went out to use the facility himself, and feed the horses.

Moments after he left, the calico-clad woman who had said the Mulders were at the Wild West Show, came in through the rear door. "I knew something was amiss here." She started to untie Bridget.

"Don't!" Bridget warned. "He'll be back any moment and he could kill us both! Listen carefully. I'm Bridget Richards. Send someone to Traverse City to find Preacher Mulder, Harrison Stone, and the Trevelyn Brothers. Tell them Jake Stone plans to make Preacher Mulder wed us as soon as he gets here."

She started to open the back door, then shut it quickly. "He's coming!"

"Go out the front! Hurry!"

With a thump, thump, thump of her cane, she made haste to the front door. Bridget heard it latch just as Jake entered the kitchen, whistling. He started to untied her.

"Sorry I had to put ya through this. Couldn't take the chance my pretty bride might get weddin' night jitters and run off." He coiled the lasso and slipped it over his shoulder. "Let's set in the parlor awhile, darlin'. Ya could read to me a spell."

Bridget picked up the Bible from the center table and started toward Mrs. Mulder's rocker.

With his hand on her shoulder, Jake redirected her to the sofa, took the Bible from her, handed her a bound copy of *Munsey's Magazine* instead, and sat close beside her. "Find me a nice story in here. I heard all them Bible tales when I was a kid."

Quietly, she began to read, thankful for the cooling breeze that flowed in through the open parlor window. An hour passed, then another. At half past nine, he lit lamps and paced the floor, pulling back the curtains to look down the road. He sat beside her again and she read some more. Bridget noticed his eyelids were getting heavy, now. When they had remained closed for several seconds, she began to reach for one of his guns.

At that exact moment, a voice boomed from the darkness. Bridget recognized it as the pulpit voice of the evangelist, George Bennard, who had conducted the outdoor service at The Clovers on her first Sunday there. His words floated in through the open window, loud and clear.

"Brother Stone, the breath of Satan is hot on your neck! Let that woman go, or you'll surely burn in hell for your sins!"

CHAPTER

16

Jake awoke with a start and grabbed Bridget. Keeping her in front of him, he drew his pistol and held it near her head, then forced her to the open window. With the barrel of his six-gun, he pushed back the curtain.

In the deep shadows of dusk, Bridget caught a glimpse of the evangelist wiping his forehead and mouth with his white handkerchief. He stood alone, but wagons and carriages lined the road, and rifle barrels were aimed at the parsonage.

Bennard raised his hands, a Bible in one, his handkerchief in the other. "I'm not armed, Brother Stone. My only weapon is Jesus. The son is mightier than the gun. Let go of that innocent, Christian woman and get down on your knees. Only a prayer for forgiveness can save you now!"

"She's mine! I love her! I won't let her go! I know Preacher Mulder is out there somewhere. Send him in. I'm takin' me a wife!" He leveled his gun at the evangelist and sent off a shot, knocking the Bible from his hand.

Bridget gasped. Jabbing her elbow into Jake's stomach, she twisted hard, determined to free herself.

He groaned and tightened his grip, laying his gun alongside her ear. "That ain't smart, Miss Bridget."

"Let me go! Let me out of here, and I'll see that no one harms you."

"Oh, no. Nothin' doin'. You're gonna marry me like ya said ya would. It was you, suggested we come here to Preacher Mulder's to get hitched. Now y'r gonna keep that promise."

Bridget tried to think of some new argument, but no thought came to her.

Brother Bennard hollered out again. "Brother Stone, hold your fire. Brother Mulder is coming in the front door. He'll marry you. Then you and your bride can ride out of here in peace, as long as you don't fire any shots."

Bridget's thoughts raced. She wouldn't marry this outlaw. She wouldn't! Maybe Preacher Mulder was coming in to try to talk Jake out of his demands. She prayed it was so.

Jake pushed back the curtain and hollered, "Come in slow, Preacher Mulder, and nobody gets hurt." Turning away from the window, he forced Bridget to the center of the parlor. Gaining a view of the front hallway and door, he pointed his gun toward the entrance.

At the sound of the front door unlatching, Bridget prayed God would surround Preacher Mulder and her in a cloak of divine protection. Ever so slowly, the door swung open. When Bridget saw the man before her, she couldn't believe her eyes. Standing in front of her was Erik, dressed in a cleric's collar! She drew a quick breath and nearly said his name, but the warning look in his eyes stopped her.

Jake gestured to him with his gun. "Come in slow, now, preacher. Stop right here, in the middle of this parlor."

"I'll need my church discipline," Erik said, cautiously

indicating a book on the center table that stood beside Jake. "It contains the wedding ceremony." His voice held a pious quality, and Bridget thanked God that Erik sounded convincing in his role as the minister.

Jake nodded. "Move slow. Don't try nothin'. And keep it short. I don't want no long ceremony."

"I understand, Mr. Stone. I promise you, this won't take long."

Jake kept his aim on Erik while he picked up the book and leafed through the pages. Opening to a point near the center of the book, Erik looked up, directly into Jake's eyes. "Mr. Stone, there's only one small matter before I begin."

"Don't stall on me, now, preacher," Jake warned.

"No, Mr. Stone. I won't stall on you. I think you ought to know I can't marry you while you're pointing a gun at me. That would constitute a marriage performed under duress. It wouldn't be legal. If you'll just set your pistol on the table, I'll begin."

Bridget prayed Jake would cooperate. After a moment's deliberation, he said, "You wouldn't try nothin' funny on me now, would ya, Preach?"

"As a man of God, I give you my word, I will do no such thing."

Jake relaxed his hold on Bridget and slowly laid his gun on the white doily covering the table.

No sooner had his hand come away from the weapon, than Erik launched himself at Jake, letting out a mighty shout!

The force of Erik's assault knocked Bridget down too, but she scrambled away. The center table fell over, sending the pistol sliding across the floor toward Jake. Before

Bridget could get it, the room filled with men.

Nat grabbed the pistol. Kenton McCune helped Bridget up. Harrison fell on his brother, helping Erik divest him of the gun still in his holster and force him face down, wrenching his arms behind his back. Seth used Jake's lasso to tie his hands and feet.

When the cowboy lay helpless on the floor, Harrison said, "Brother, you've done some mighty wild things in your life, but this time, you've gone too far."

Jake twisted his neck to look up at Harrison. "Little Harry, you always was a good boy. And one thing's certain. Ya know a good woman when ya see one. I'm just sorry we ain't both gonna be married to Richards ladies."

Pulling the preacher's collar from about his neck, Erik came to where Bridget and Kenton were standing. "Are you all right, Miss Richards?"

She gazed up at the cut on his cheek and the bruise on his forehead, and thought of the risk he had taken to free her. With a silent prayer of thanks, she offered a modest smile. "I'm fine, thanks to you, Preacher Mulder." Rising on tiptoe, she kissed his damaged cheek.

He put his arm about her shoulder and ushered her out the front door. There, on the front yard, Charlotte, Aurora, and Anna surrounded her and smothered her with hugs.

"Are you all right?" Charlotte asked.

"I can't believe Harrison's brother stole you!" Aurora said.

"You're the bravest woman in Michigan!" Anna told her. "I'd have fainted on the spot if some cowboy had run off with me."

Bridget laughed from nervous exhaustion. "I'm fine. All I need now is some peace and quiet."

From the shadows, Clarissa stepped forward. "If it weren't for Erik, you'd be the prize of that wild west hooligan right now. And your reputation would be sullied for life."

Bridget looked for Erik, thinking he would still be nearby, but he was several yards away, in conversation with Brother Bennard, Preacher Mulder, Kenton, and the lady in calico. She met Clarissa's gaze directly. "You're absolutely right, Miss Hackbardt. And I intend to see that Mr. Olson receives all the credit he's due for saving me from a fate worse than death." Turning on her heel, she set off in Erik's direction.

Clarissa followed close behind. Erik and Kenton saw them coming, and broke away from the others.

Kenton approached Clarissa. "Miss Hackbardt, I was wondering if I might have a word with you?" To Erik and Bridget, he said, "Excuse us, if you will. We'll only be a moment." He took Clarissa by the elbow and led her away.

Alone with Erik, Bridget held out her hand to him, words unnecessary as their fingers intertwined and they left the folks still lingering on Preacher Mulder's lawn for the solace of the beach only half a block away.

Erik paused a few yards from the water's edge. The sound of waves lazily lapping sand played harmony to the anthem of thankfulness in his heart. He turned to Bridget, taking up her other hand, and held them both to his chest. In the wan light of the moon, he saw weariness and strain in the pretty eyes that in days past, had sparkled with innocent enthusiasm.

Bridget gazed at the man who had faced grave peril for her sake. His face, handsome as a Norse god at any other time, was now careworn, distraught, and beginning to swell where Jake had punched him.

They both spoke at once.

"I was afraid he'd kill you—"

"I was sure he'd force himself on you—"

In the silent moment that followed, Bridget imagined Jake turning his gun on Erik, hearing the explosion, watching Erik slump to the floor. Agony, like a bolt of lightning, struck deep in her heart, and in that instant she realized she cared far more for Erik than she had ever suspected.

In his mind's eye Erik envisioned Jake Stone pushing Bridget to the floor, pinning her there by the force of his weight, pressing his mouth over hers. He glimpsed himself strangling the man who had stolen her innocence— grabbing onto the ends of his blue neckerchief and pulling on them until he could pull no more. In that moment he understood that he cared so deeply for this pretty, vulnerable young woman from South Manitou, he would stop at nothing to protect her.

The strong hands that had offered Bridget comfort now gripped tightly, as if they never would let go. Tears began to well in her eyes—tears of thankfulness for tragedy spared.

At the glimpse of moisture on Bridget's cheek, Erik pulled her against him, overtaken by a sense of never wanting to let go.

Bridget felt the smooth cotton of Erik's shirt against her cheek, the dampness of her tears soaking through its fabric, and couldn't stop the flow. She searched her skirt pocket for her handkerchief, then remembered she had dropped it by the farmer's well, hoping to leave a clue to her whereabouts.

Erik held her tightly, savoring the anointing of his shirt

by her precious tears. When several moments had passed and her sobs quieted, he released his embrace, pulling a folded square of white linen from his pants pocket and offering it to her.

She shook it open expecting to see his initials embroidered in the corner, stared at it a moment, then gazed up, finding a pleased look on his face. "My handkerchief! I never thought . . . " Her tears began to flow again, happy ones this time, and Erik took her in his arms once more, swaying gently from side to side.

He spoke quietly. "You had nearly every living soul in two counties tracking you down. But no one was more intent on finding you than me. I was bound and determined to return that little piece of fabric to you, the quicker, the better."

When her spate of tears had subsided, she blew her nose and dried her cheeks. "The Lord knew I surely would have need of this . . . and you. I thank God for bringing you to me." She folded the damp cloth and tucked it into her pocket, then reached out to him once more. Hand in hand they turned toward the parsonage, their newfound kinship making words unnecessary.

CHAPTER

17

As Erik and his father approached the Traverse City State Hospital on the second Monday in August, he repeated the silent prayer he'd been saying on each visit since his first one five weeks ago. He thanked God for the attractive Gothic facility with its church-like spires reaching toward the sky, and the natural beauty of the grounds, abundant with flower gardens, trees, and lawns. He was thankful, too, for the excellent care his mother was receiving. She hadn't complained even once about the food which was produced by hospital employees and inmates on the adjoining farmland. His own mother had helped with the vegetable-growing as part of her treatment. He thanked the Lord for her excellent medical care, considered among the best in the country. And as his father brought the rig to a halt near the door of the Center Building, he prayed that his mother would respond well to Kenton McCune, who had proposed this special meeting with her.

The attorney, nattily dressed in a morning suit and carrying a leather porfolio beneath his arm, greeted Erik and his father the moment they entered the hospital. "Thank you for coming, both of you," he said extending his hand to the elder Olson, then to Erik. "Shall we go right up to Mrs. Olson's room?"

"By all means," said Erik's father, heading for the stone steps to the seond floor.

Erik was the first to enter her room. Her back was to him as she stared out her barred window. Erik spoke as cheerfully as possible. "Mother, I bring good news!"

She turned toward him. Her face, pale as the sallow beige on the plaster walls, began to show a hint of color. For the first time since she had been committed five weeks earlier, her mouth curved in a smile. "You've come to take me home! Thank God!" She paced agitatedly alongside her narrow iron cot. "I knew this would be the day! I just knew it! When I saw you coming, I knew something was different. I knew I'd be going home. Oh, thank God! You're taking me home!" She clasped her hands to her cheeks, tears glistening in her dark-rimmed eyes.

Erik's father took her hands in his. "Calm yourself, Katrina. I want you to meet someone. This is Mr. Mc-Cune. He's an attorney. Mr. McCune, my wife."

"Pleased to make your acquaintance, Mrs. Olson." Kenton set his portfolio on her stool and opened it. "Do you remember the diagrams you made of the dinosaur skeletons?"

She stared at him as if looking through him.

Kenton continued. "Your son brought them to me and I've arranged for them to be published. I have payment here for the rights to your artwork." He took a check from his case and offered it to her.

Her face flushed crimson. She wrenched her hands free from her husband and swatted at the check. It drifted to the floor. "You liar! You nasty, malicious, cruel liar! You and Professor Evenson! You'll both burn in a firey inferno for your deception!" She shook her fist at Kenton.

Erik's face grew hot with embarrassment. He stooped to retrieve the check, then spoke calmly, but firmly. "Mother, it's true."

"Don't call me Mother! I'm not your mother! Who are you, anyway?"

Familiar with such lapses from several previous visits, Erik ignored her remarks. "Your drawings, and Professor Evenson's writings, will be published about six months from now."

"I don't draw. I don't know what you're talking about. You're impossible! All of you! Now get out!" She turned again to the window, her back to her visitors.

"Katrina, *please*," her husband pleaded, coming to stand beside her. "Don't be like this. Mr. McCune has done us all a great favor, finding another publisher after the first one went bankrupt."

The woman faced her husband. "You're talking like a mad man! I threw out all those drawings weeks ago, when we opened The Clovers. They've long since been burned."

Kenton spoke quietly. "Your son very wisely pulled them out of your trash basket. They are one-of-a-kind, Mrs. Olson. They will stand as the most definitive, comprehensive work of this century concerning prehistoric life on the North American continent."

Several silent moments passed. She glanced over her shoulder at Kenton, a calmness replacing her previously stormy mood. Then her gaze settled on her husband. "Take me home," she quietly demanded.

"I love you, Katrina, but you can't come home today."

Her eyes widened. "You *don't* love me!" She raised her

fists to strike his chest.

He caught her hands tightly in his. "Yes, I *do* love you. Now we must go." He released her and started toward the door.

She collapsed on her cot, face in hands, sobbing.

Erik had grown accustomed to the hystrionics that took place at each parting and ignored them. "Good bye, Mother. We'll come again soon. I'll deposit your check in the bank."

Her sobbing instantly subsided and she looked up accusingly. "If you really loved me, you wouldn't leave me here! You wouldn't take my money!"

"Good day, Mrs. Olson," said Kenton, following the others into the hallway.

Mr. Olson closed his wife's door behind them. "Thank you for coming, Mr. McCune. I'm sorry for what she put you through. I thought maybe she would improve when she heard your news. I guess I was wrong."

"Perhaps in time, she'll see things as they are," Kenton suggested.

"I pray you're right," said Erik, following his father and Kenton down the stone steps and out the main entrance.

Kenton offered his hand to each of the Olsons. "I'll be in touch with you the minute the books come off the press. I'll want Mrs. Olson's autograph on a copy for myself."

"I hope by then, she'll be sane enough to give it to you," Mr. Olson said skeptically.

"I share that hope. Good day!" Kenton stepped into his fancy buggy, trimmed in velvet and silk and sporting sterling silver scrolls. Donning his top hat and gloves, he released the brake and slapped the reins against his gray gelding.

Erik couldn't suppress the stirrings of jealousy within as he watched Kenton drive away, the epitome of stylishness, the picture of success. He headed toward the weathered hack his father had rented at the livery when they'd arrived on the boat from Omena.

As they drove off the hospital grounds, his father said, "Did you tell me the other day that Miss Richards has accepted a post as nanny in Traverse City at summer's end?"

Erik sighed. "Mr. McCune saw the listing in the newspaper and sent it to her. She'll be working for the same family she had applied to by letter before she left South Manitou. She'd sought an interview with them the day after Mother turned her away from The Clovers, but she was told the position had been filled. Evidently, it came open again, and they've accepted her. She'll be living with the Ferrises on Washington Street—the same man who runs the European Horse Hotel, where we rented this old rig."

Following a quiet interval, Mr. Olson said, "You're more than a little fond of her, aren't you, son?"

"Yes, sir." The next moments were filled with the rattling and creaking of the buggy while Erik contemplated his true regards for the South Manitou Island miss, then he spoke of a discovery he had made in recent days. "You know, Papa, ever since I rescued Miss Richards from that crazy Stone fellow, my outlook on things has changed."

"How's that?" Mr. Olson asked thoughtfully.

"I don't take life for granted anymore. And the fondness I had for her is much keener now than ever. I really hate to think of leaving Michigan at the end of the summer season. You know what I mean?"

Mr. Olson chuckled. "I know *exactly* what you mean, especially after meeting Mr. McCune today." Moments later, he said, "If Miss Richards really cares for you, no fancy lawyer will be able to steal her away."

"You sound just like Gramps," Erik said with a laugh.

"He's wise." Mr. Olson turned left, toward the bay, then continued on the subject of his father. "Thank goodness he's been growing stronger each day. The problems with your mother have taken the lion's share of my time this summer. I'd don't know what I'd have done if Papa—"

"Don't even say it," Erik interrupted. "He's going to keep on getting better, and live a very long life."

Mr. Olson grinned. "No one can accuse you of talking grim." His smile faded and he became contemplative.

Erik, too, had thoughts of his own on a situation he'd been wanting to discuss with his father for quite a while. "Papa, I know the Hackbardts have been good friends."

"The best. Fine business partners, too. Without them, we couldn't have kept things running at The Clovers this season." Mr. Olson slapped the reins, putting the mare into a trot along an empty stretch of the street.

"But Papa, what should I do about Clarissa? She's much fonder of me than I am of her. I keep trying to make her understand we'll never be more than friends, but she pays no attention. Sometimes she gets my Irish up so, I want to have it out with her! But I know it would only make things worse."

"That is at tough one. I'm afraid you'll have to work it out on your own. Like you said, it won't pay to burn your bridges with anyone, especially a Hackbardt."

CHAPTER
18

Bridget awoke with a start. Heart pounding, breath coming in short gasps, she shook her head, trying to vanquish the nightmare. Memories of Jake Stone haunted her, of his pushing her so roughly she began to fall. But instead of hitting the hardwood floor, Erik appeared out of nowhere to catch her in his waiting arms. She inhaled deeply in an effort to calm her jangled nerves, then checked her bedside clock. Though she hadn't planned to get up quite so early, there was no point in staying in bed. She was too disturbed to fall back to sleep.

Besides, this being the last Monday in August, she and Erik had planned an early start for an all-day outing, their last before season's end and the close of The Clovers that was scheduled eight days hence, on the Tuesday following Labor Day. Outside her dormitory window, the sky was starting to take on salmon streaks of first daylight. With a silent prayer of thanks for fair weather, she dressed quickly, donning the woolen cloak her mother had sent via Nat last week when northern Michigan temperatures had taken a sudden downward turn. Grabbing the blanket from her cot and the cloth bag containing her sketchbook and pencils, she headed for the staff dining room, taking a circuitous route to the dock and back, delighting in the exquisite sunrise over the bay.

As she entered the Main House from behind, she overheard a familiar voice in the lobby. Proceeding quietly down the hall, she saw that Clarissa was speaking to one of the guests—a finely dressed, bespectacled lady who was studying the board where Erik had posted her artwork for sale.

"The artist who drew these was abducted a short while ago by a ruffian from Buffalo Bill's Wild West Show," Clarissa informed the gray haired woman.

She peered over the top of her glasses. "You don't say."

"Oh, yes. He was a genuine outlaw. He carried her off to Glen Arbor, and the two of them were holed up there alone for hours before the sheriff's posse found them." Clarissa moved closer to the woman and spoke in a hushed voice. "Of course, I've known her for some time. She secretly admitted that she didn't really want to be rescued. She said she didn't even mind that he took liberties with her. In fact, she even plans to visit him in prison! Now I ask you, would you want to own a piece of artwork by a woman such as this?"

Bridget's face grew hot. Her grip on her cloth bag and blanket turned to steel.

Quickly, the older woman stepped back from the board, a horrified look on her face. "No! Of course not! Thank you for telling me." Swiftly, she strode away.

The triumphant smirk on Clarissa's face made Bridget want to scream. She marched into the lobby, stopping within an inch of the Wisconsin girl's nose. "Clarissa Hackbardt, you're the most despicable liar I've ever known!"

Clarissa took a faltering step back, her cheeks pale. "Miss Richards . . ."

Following a moment's pause, Bridget spoke in measured words. "I pray to God that He forgives you your lies about me, because I certainly do not." Turning on her heel, she headed for the staff dining room, praying all the way that God would help her to find the forgiveness she could not yet claim.

Erik's friendly smile and the tempting aroma of fresh, hot coffee welcomed her. "Good morning!" he said cheerfully.

His greeting offered a pleasant contrast to Clarissa's lies. Bridget determined then and there to put thoughts of the troublesome woman out of her mind for the rest of the day, but she couldn't seem to muster a response.

Erik continued. "Mrs. Little Bear's porridge does wonders to ward off the morning's chill." He removed the overturned saucer that was covering Bridget's bowl of cereal as she poured herself a cup of coffee from the pot on the sideboard. She sat across from him at the plank table and began stirring cream and brown sugar into her oatmeal.

"You're awfully quiet this morning," he observed. "Are you experiencing a case of the mulligrubs?"

His use of the ridiculous sounding word made her smile in spite of her dour mood—and served as a reminder that his congeniality would be sorely missed when he returned to Wisconsin. "Maybe I do have the mulligrubs," she said contemplatively. "This *is* our last outing before you sail off to the other side of Lake Michigan."

He sighed and wiped imaginary sweat from his brow. "Thank goodness."

"Thank goodness?! You mean you can't wait to get away from me?"

He put palms out. "No, no, no! I'm not eager to get

away. I'm simply glad you're not bothered by something serious."

"But this *is* serious. I'll . . . miss you."

Erik smiled ruefully. "And I'll miss you, living in Traverse City, near neighbors with Mr. McCune."

She smiled slyly. "He *is* a rather nice gentleman to have for a neighbor. On the other hand, you'll be near neighbors with—" Clarissa's name was on the tip of her tongue, and she determined once again to banish thoughts and words of the annoying woman from her day. Taking an abrupt turn in the conversation, she continued. "What do you say we finish breakfast and get on our way to the light station as quickly as possible? No point in discussing unpleasant topics when we could be out enjoying ourselves."

Erik sipped his coffee, then gazed directly into her cornflower-blue eyes, thinking they would be even more lovely beneath the blue Leelanau sky. Placing his hand on hers, he said, "You're absolutely right." Eagerly, he tucked into his porridge again.

When they had finished their cereal, they stopped by the kitchen for their box lunches—checking inside to make certain no mud pies had been substituted for their sandwiches—then set off for the light station in the buggy David had hitched to Erik's favorite mare.

Bridget pulled her blanket tight about her shoulders and arranged the heavy woolen lap robe about her legs, settling in for the long drive. From the two previous outings she and Erik had made to the lighthouse earlier this month, she knew they would spend two hours on the road each way, but she cherished every moment in Erik's company, especially times away from The Clovers when she didn't have to share him with the guests who naturally deserved his utmost attention. And she looked forward to seeing the Goodrich children again—all nine of them—and to finishing several more sketches to put up for sale at The Clovers over the Labor Day weekend when the hotel would be full. The extra money her artwork had brought in over the summer had been a welcome addition to her meager wages, but the compliments from the guests were the real reason she kept turning out new drawings.

By mid-morning, after traversing long stretches of aromatic, woodsy road, stopping in Northport to rest and water the horse, and listening to various sonatinas by jays, sparrows, and sea gulls, Erik pulled onto the drive leading to the light complex. The Goodrich's dog, Taffy, came bounding down the lane to greet them. Her noisy welcome was expected, only this time, she seemed particularly agitated, her behavior bordering on frantic.

"We seem to have really set her off today," Erik observed.

"She acts as if something's amiss." Bridget peered down the lane, expecting to see Jack and Toby, the oldest boys, or eleven-year-old Sarah and nine-year-old Ross coming to greet them. "I wonder where the children are. With all Taffy's noise, surely they know someone's coming by now."

Erik stopped by the barn and helped Bridget down, then glanced toward the keeper's quarters, expecting to find some sign of the children. "Maybe the whole family's gone on a picnic."

"And left Taffy behind?" Bridget asked skeptically.

They had started toward the house when Jack came stumbling out, clutching his side and moaning. He made a wavering path toward the outhouse.

"Jack!" Erik rushed to the boy's side, wrapping his arm about the fifteen-year-old's spindly waist. "What's the matter?"

Bridget hurried to support the sick boy on the opposite side.

"Food poisoning," Jack said weakly, his face white as chalk. "I've got to . . . " he gestured toward the outhouse, "hurry!"

They hustled him to the privy. Erik helped him inside while Bridget waited but a few feet away, her own stomach churning at the sound of Jack's violent retching.

A few minutes later Erik and Jack emerged, the boy's shirt untucked, his suspenders dangling at his sides. Bridget put her hand to the boy's forehead, finding it hot, then helped Erik walk him toward the house. "Are your folks sick, too?"

Jack nodded. "We're all sick, 'cept for baby Zaneta. She's didn't eat the corned beef last night."

Before they reached the door, Toby came staggering out with Ross, Upton, and Yancy, his nine-, seven-, and four-year-old brothers. Behind them were eleven-year-old Sarah, six-year-old Vera, and five-year-old Willow, the younger two each clutching a small basin.

Bridget turned to Erik. "You help the fellows, I'll help the girls."

While the boys went into the woods, Bridget assisted the girls in using the latrine. When their bouts of diarrhea and vomiting had subsided, she took them inside, finding little Zaneta in the back hall whimpering. The odor of her diaper demanded immediate attention. "You need changing, don't you, Zaneta?" Bridget picked up the little tot.

"Mama's too sick to do it," Sarah said. "I was gonna do it, but I had to go to the outhouse first."

"I'll take care of her," Bridget said, "you girls go lie down."

From the front sitting room, she heard Mrs. Goodrich's frail voice. "Miss Richards, is that you?"

"Yes, ma'am." Bridget carried Zaneta to the front of the house. Mrs. Goodrich lay on the sofa, pale as the white sheet which covered her. Keeper Goodrich was stretched out on the floor nearby, gaunt and haggard. Sarah, Vera, and Willow lay down on the floor near their mother.

Keeper Goodrich propped himself unsteadily on one elbow. "The light . . . " He spoke with considerable effort. "It burned out. I couldn't . . . "

Zaneta began to whine. "Don't worry, Keeper Goodrich. I've had plenty of experience cleaning the lamp chimneys and lens on South Manitou, and replenishing the oil. I'll put the tower in order as soon as I change Zaneta." She thought a moment, then asked, "Where's your assistant, Keeper Wilson?"

"Sick," he said in a half-whisper. Then he began to heave. Throwing off his blanket, he unsteadily gained his feet and stumbled out the front door.

By the time Bridget had changed Zaneta, Erik and the boys had returned. The front sitting room looked like an infirmary, with the furniture pushed back and nine of the Goodriches lying on the floor. Zaneta's playpen stood in the corner.

Bridget carried Zaneta to Erik. "Could you watch her while I take care of the light in the tower?"

"Sure," he said, reaching for the youngster, but the moment he touched her, she turned away, burying her head against Bridget's shoulder. He spoke soothingly, rubbing her back. "You needn't be afraid of me, little one. I won't hurt you."

When Zaneta showed no sign of going to him, Bridget carried her to her playpen. The little girl started crying the moment Bridget set her down.

"Hush, Zaneta," her mother said in a frail voice, but the little girl kept up her wailing.

To Erik, Bridget said, "If I leave, she'll probably let you pick her up just to get out of the playpen." Quickly, she climbed the stairs. The bawling stopped before she reached the supply closet on the second floor.

There, she donned the special linen apron to prevent damage to the Fresnel lens, gathered together the rag, buff skin, and feather brush, then climbed up into the light tower. Immediately, she hung the lantern curtains at the windows, pausing for a moment to look down on the progress that had been made on the new fog signal building. It was nearly complete, and she would have expected a crew to be busy finishing the project. Today, not a soul was in sight. Knowing that workmen customarily take meals with the lightkeeper's family, she didn't have to wonder why no one was on the job.

Turning to the task at hand, she took up the feather brush and carefully dusted every piece of glass on the Fourth Order Lens. The process took much less time than on South Manitou, where the larger Third Order Lens was in use. Next, she wiped the lens carefully with a soft cloth and polished it with the buff skin.

Her work on the lens complete, she carried the lantern down to the supply room and began cleaning its chimney with a soft rag. Since the light had burned itself out rather than being turned off, it was considerably more sooty than it otherwise would have been, but she soon had it clear and sparkling again. Carefully, she rubbed off the light ash remaining on the wick, then filled the reservoir with oil, leaving room for expansion.

Hanging up her apron, she closed the tower room door behind her and quickly descended to the first floor to see how the patients were faring. All but the youngest Goodrich was resting quietly, the only sound on the first floor, that of Erik's singing. She followed his voice to the kitchen.

There, she found him making chicken broth, and a medicinal infusion of blue gentian and chamomile tea while entertaining Zaneta who sat in her high chair munching on a sugar cookie. Bridget joined in singing the Mother Goose melody.

"Little Robin Redbreast sat upon a tree. Up went the pussy cat and down went he. Down came Pussy Cat, away Robin ran. Says little Robin Redbreast, 'Catch me if you can.' Little Robin Redbreast jumped upon a spade. Pussy Cat jumped after him, and then he was afraid. Little Robin chirped and sung, and what did Pussy say? Pussy Cat said, 'Mew, mew, mew,' and Robin flew away."

Zaneta giggled and clapped her hands. Bridget couldn't help noticing how perfectly at ease Erik was at the stove and with the small child.

Together, they served the warm liquids to their patients. Many times throughout the day, Bridget silently thanked God for Erik's helpful ways—always ready to go to the outhouse with a suffering child, fetch a cup of tea or broth and hold it to a little one's lips, or change Zaneta's diapers.

By late afternoon, Bridget was exhausted. She could

see by the way Erik was stretched out in Keeper Goodrich's easy chair, he was equally tired. Zaneta lay beside her father, fast asleep, and all the other Goodriches were resting peacefully, at last. She took satisfaction in knowing the symptoms of diarrhea and vomiting had disappeared for all the family except Jack, who had eaten more corned beef than anyone, but was nevertheless improving.

With the day coming to a close, Bridget took Erik by the hand and led him into the kitchen where she could speak with him in private. "I know we need to start for Omena now, if we're going to get there before dark, but Keeper Goodrich is in no condition to tend the light. I think it's best if I stay and do it. I'll find some way to get back to The Clovers tomorrow."

Erik's head moved slowly from side to side, a tender smile curving his mouth. He gently embraced her shoulders. "I won't leave you here. I'll stay and drive you back myself. Tonight, you can teach me what it's like to tend a light."

Bridget chuckled. "You? But you can't climb a tower without turning white and—"

Erik put a finger to her lips. "Don't say it. I've seen enough stomach upset for one day. I promise you I won't get sick if I go up in the tower with you. After all, it's built into the top of the house, and it's nowhere near as tall as the light on South Manitou."

Bridget gave him a skeptical look.

He continued. "If I can rescue you from a cowboy gone loco, surely I can climb to the top of this house without getting sick."

Bridget drew a deep breath. "You'd better be right. The last thing I need is one more person who can't keep his stomach right side up. For now, we'd better see to some supper."

By the time they had finished their evening meal and cleaned up the dishes, it was time to tend the light. Bridget led Erik up to the supply closet, fetched the lamp and special matches provided by the light service, then began her climb up the steep steps to the tower.

Erik paused at the base of the stairs, watching Bridget ascend the winding, narrow treads. Taking a deep breath, he gripped the railing and placed his foot on the first tread. A warmth shot through him. He took two more steps. The rhythm of his heart accelerated to a gallop, and an inescapable sense of panic brought beads of sweat to his upper lip.

When Bridget emerged in the tower, she pushed aside one of the curtains to let in some light. After setting the lamp in the lens, she gazed down at Erik. He was stalled near the bottom of the open tower stairway, a stricken expression on his pallid face. "Go down. There's no point making yourself miserable."

Anger swelled within Erik, and disappointment in himself for letting panic rule him. He surged up the stairs.

"Duck!" Bridget hollered when he reached the place where the steps made a tight turn, but her warning came too late.

The blow to his head sent a sharp pain through his skull. He clamped his hand to the spot, hoping pressure would lessen the agony. Still determined, he crept up the remaining stairs, emerging in the light tower to sit on the floor.

Bridget knelt beside him to inspect the bump on his head. "You poor soul." She pried his hand away from the injury and carefully parted his hair, running her finger gently over the sore spot. "You'll have a goose egg, but at least you didn't cut your scalp. You'd better go back downstairs and put ice on it."

He shook his head and slowly got to his feet. "Now that I've come this far, I'm not leaving until you've shown me how you tend the light."

She began to take down the curtains, revealing the scene of the lake and the islands offshore. He tried to ignore the eagle's nest view and the increasing queasiness it caused in his stomach by concentrating on helping Bridget, taking each curtain from her and laying it neatly aside.

Bridget sensed Erik's increasing discomfort. When the curtains were all down, she took the matches from her pocket and handed them to him. "You light the flame," she said, lifting the chimney of the lantern.

He struck the match, and with a shaky hand, touched it to the oil-soaked wick.

Bridget turned down the flame. "I'll have to keep adjusting the lamp for the next half hour, or so, until the light is burning at full brightness. I wish you'd go down now. I think I hear Zaneta crying."

Erik cocked his ear toward the stairs and heard nothing, but with the throbbing of his head increasing with every minute, he was more than ready for an ice pack. Gripping the stair rail again, he began his descent.

"Don't forget to duck this time!" Bridget reminded him.

He tucked his chin, making it to the floor below without incident, then descending to the first floor. Zaneta and the rest of the family were asleep. In the kitchen, he chipped himself some ice, wrapped it in a towel and held it to his head, then went outdoors for a stroll along the beach.

From the tower, Bridget gazed at the early evening view of the islands in the distance—South Fox barely visible in the increasing haze of an August evening, and North and South Manitou, with their sandy dunes and forest-green stretches of shoreline distinct.

She watched Erik strolling the beach with the ice pack held to his head, and wished she had her sketchbook in the tower with her to put the image to paper. He waved to her and she waved back. Later, when the evening sky had turned to dusk and the tower light was burning efficiently, she went to join him.

Erik smiled when he saw her coming. His headache gone, he tossed away the ice and spread the towel out on a rock to dry, then held out his hand to the young woman who, despite the shadows of fatigue beneath her eyes, was the prettiest miss he had ever known.

The secure feeling of Erik's hand about hers as they walked by the water, the lakeshore lullaby of waves licking the beach while crickets and locusts sang sonnets, made Bridget wish the summer could linger on and on. But she must face the fact that tonight was one of her last in his company.

She thought back to their first meeting at Anna's, and certain truths about their friendship spoke to her heart, begging to be shared. She paused to face Erik. The light of the Leelanau moon illuminated the rugged, yet pleasing lines of his countenance, making him more handsome than ever. "I believe God puts us at the right place at the right time, if we let Him. I warrant He wanted me here today, to help the Goodriches, and I thank Him for sending you with me. You're a great blessing to me, Erik Olson, in more ways than you know, and I mean it with all my heart."

Bridget's words stirred yearnings deep within, and he brought her nearer, wrapping his arms loosely about her waist. The stars shown down on her lovely, round face, making her blue eyes glisten. He pulled her close, his forehead touching hers. "Bridget Richards, you're the most beautiful woman I've ever known," he half-whispered. "I thank God for bringing us together. And I believe He had one more reason for sending us to this place." Ever so gently, his lips tasted hers, their sweetness surpassing nectar, or honey, or even the fudge at the Marshalls' candy shop.

Erik's kiss sent Bridget's heart soaring. Wrapping her arms about his neck, she gave herself up to the pleasures of his affection, thanking God for this innocent romance in the light of the Leelanau moon. She couldn't help wishing it never had to end.

CHAPTER

19

Tired but satisfied after her first day as nanny for the Ferris children, Bridget went outdoors to tidy up their playhouse—the converted bell tower from the old Traverse City High School which their father had installed as an attractive addition to the side yard of the new gabled home he had built last year. When she had collected the rag doll, rubber ball, and plush dog, she paused to sit awhile on the playhouse step. Turning her face to the evening sun, she closed her eyes, soaking in its warmth. The soft breeze off the bay, and the solo of a nearby robin comforted her. When she opened her eyes again, much to her surprise, a familiar figure was cutting across the lawn toward her.

Nat smiled and pulled off his captain's cap. "You're a tough one to keep up with. This isn't the first time I've come lookin' for ya and discovered you'd moved."

She patted the step and he sat beside her. "Nice of you to come, Nat," she said with sincerity, thinking his protectiveness toward her, so troubling on past occasions, had been tempered by time.

"I stopped at The Clovers dock at dawn this morning thinkin' you'd be done workin' there, yesterday bein' Labor Day. David told me where to find you." He cast a backward glance at the house. "Nice place."

"It was a blessing to be hired on here."

He regarded her through a half-squinted eye. "You're tired, but I can see it's a good tired."

She grinned broadly. "The Ferris children are a real joy. Their folks are some of the nicest people I've ever met." She half-turned, looking at the rambling home. "And of course, the location is absolutely lovely." After a moment's pause, she asked, "How's Michael?"

Nat beamed proudly. "Fine. Just fine. Talkin' up a storm, and gettin' into everything. At least that's what Miss Stef—that's what I'm told whenever I get home to see him." His smile faded. He took up his hat, running the bottom edge between his fingers.

"Tell me what's on your mind, Nat," Bridget gently urged, realizing they hadn't spoken at length since the day he'd invited her to attend the Wild West Show, then turned hostile with Erik.

Nat set his cap on his knee again, his expression complacent when his hazel eyes met hers. "You were right, back at the start of the summer, when ya said it was best not to rush into marriage. I didn't want to admit it, but now I know I was wrong to press ya then, and I'd be wrong to press ya now."

Bridget sensed much more in Nat's words than a simple admission to an error in judgment. Unwittingly, he had already admitted the real reason for his change of heart toward her. She began to put it in her own words. "When I think back to the party I attended at Anna's, I realize none of us anticipated the outcome. Especially not where your friendship with her is concerned."

Nat laid his hand over hers. "Now don't go jumpin' to conclusions. Yes, she's my friend. She offered to take care of Michael sometimes, to help take the burden off my Ma.

That's how we've gotten to know each other better."

Bridget remembered her jealous reactions to Anna the day after her party, when they all had come to the Leelanau Peninsula on the *Manitou Lady*. Things had changed considerably in the interim. "I'm pleased for you, Nat, and for Michael and Anna. I hope your friendship with her will flourish. I mean that."

He gazed deep into her eyes. "And yours with Mr. Olson," he said sincerely, squeezing her hand. She squeezed his in return. Then Nat's gaze shifted to the street, and a carriage coming to a stop by the walk. "Speakin' of Mr. Olson . . . "

Erik alighted and strode purposefully toward them. Nat and Bridget met him midway across the side yard. Erik nodded at Bridget, his expression troubled, then he focused on Nat. "Mr. Trevelyn, I've just been to your boat and spoken with your brother. He said I'd find you here."

"Right enough. What's on your mind?"

Erik hesitated. Indicating the step near the playhouse, he said, "I think it's best if we sit down." When the others had settled on the concrete, he took a place alongside Bridget.

She could see from the dark look in his eyes, and the way he lowered them to stare at his hands, he was reluctant to speak his mind. She spoke softly, dispensing with formality. "What is it, Erik? Please tell me."

He swiped at the moisture in his eyes that was threatening to embarrass him by spilling down his cheeks. Forcing words past the croquet ball in his throat, he said, "Early this morning, Gramps was feeling poorly. I sent for Dr. Kendall, then I went in and sat by his bed. His eyes were closed, and I wasn't sure if he was awake or asleep. I heard him say, 'Freya, my beloved Freya, you've come for me, just like I knew you would.' After that, he just went limp, and I knew he'd . . . passed on."

"I'm so sorry!" Bridget lamented.

"My condolences," Nat offered.

Unable to maintain his composure, Erik rose and walked away. When he had blown his nose and dried his eyes, he sat down again, this time beside Nat. "Gramps's wish was to be cremated and to have his ashes scattered in Green Bay. Father and I were wondering if you would take us, and the Steffenses aboard the *Manitou Lady* so we could lay him to rest the way he wanted."

Nat nodded without hesitation. "Seth's probably told ya we're headed to Wisconsin with our next load anyway. Can you leave Omena tomorrow mornin'?"

Erik nodded.

Nat rose, his gaze on Bridget. "I'd better be on my way." To Erik, he said, "Would you mind givin' me a lift back to my boat?"

"Not at all." To Bridget, Erik said, "I'll write."

"Give my sympathies to the rest of your family," she told him.

He nodded and turned away. She watched the two men as they walked toward the carriage, and was touched by the sight of Nat's hand resting compassionately against Erik's back.

Beneath a sky as gloomy as her own heart, Anna stood with her family and that of her cousin, Erik, at the stern of the *Manitou Lady*. The odor of coal smoke, intensified by the dampness, hung in the air, and the vibration of the engine pulsed through her. Cold, drizzly rain, so typical of the first week of September, augmented her tears over Gramps's passing as they neared the city of Green Bay, some two miles distant.

Uncle Kal, emptying the urn containing his father's ashes over the rail of the steamer, spoke solemnly. "Ashes to ashes, dust to dust. May he rest in peace."

As Anna watched the fine, gray particles scatter over the water in the steady breeze, memories of another heart-breaking loss came flooding back. Sobbing quietly, she sought refuge alone on the upper deck.

From his position in the pilothouse, Nat saw Anna's shoulders shaking as she wept. He had never known her to be sad, only quietly reverent during her visits with him and Michael to Meta's grave several times this past summer. Seeing her so distraught now sent a pang through his heart. He wanted to go to her, put a hand on her shoulder, offer consolation, but he couldn't leave the wheel of his boat. Within a few minutes, he would be approaching the city of Green Bay, and maneuvering in the Fox River in the stiff afternoon wind would be tricky. He pulled the lever to tell his brother, below, to reduce speed, and told himself to be patient a couple more hours, until he and Seth would join the Steffenses in their home on Monroe Avenue for dinner.

Anna began counting the number of times the signal bell rang, trying to take her mind off her sorrow, but with little success. Her summer on South Manitou, her organ concerts, the few hours of pleasure she'd been able to bring to Nat whenever he'd stopped at the island to visit his son, were but happy interludes and joyful remembrances now veiled by renewed pain. For three months she had put aside the greatest sadness of her young life and busied herself with new endeavors and friendships in hopes she could overcome the loss of the previous November. But with her return to Green Bay, the memories and the woe came back in a deluge.

She tried to ignore them, and concentrate on the sights she hadn't seen since the end of spring—the Chicago and Northwestern railroad yards on the west side of the river; the sprawling, brick Hoberg Paper Mill with its tall stacks coughing up sulfurous clouds that dimmed the already dull day; a trolley car heading up Main Street, its bells clanging.

Within minutes, a hack was carrying her along Monroe Avenue toward the Italianate residence she called home. She couldn't help thinking of the towered brick building to the south on Webster Avenue, where she had spent many happy hours.

It called to her heart, and as the carriage parked by her home, she longed to take a drive in that direction, but she could not visit there now. She must see to unpacking her trunks before the Trevelyn brothers joined them for the evening meal. Thoughts of Nat brought an idea to mind. She said little during the solemn dinner of roast beef with all the fixings and fresh-baked apple pie served with sharp cheddar cheese. But when conversation among the men broke up and the Trevelyns headed for the door, Anna seized the opportunity to speak quietly with Nat in the foyer.

"I know you're eager to get back to your boat, but I was wondering if you would come with me to a very special place? It's not too far from here."

Nat sensed an underlying importance in Anna's request. He glanced at Seth.

"Go on, brother. I don't mind going back to the boat alone. I'll see you later." Seth pulled his jacket collar up

213

and let himself out.

Nat took Anna's cloak from the hall tree and held it for her. "What is this place we're goin' to?"

She fastened the hooks and pulled up the hood, stepping out onto the front porch. "It's the St. Joseph's Orphan Asylum." Nat's forehead wrinkled, and she quickly added, "I was once very . . . good friends with someone who grew up there." Swiftly, she descended the porch steps.

Within minutes, her father's runabout was rigged, and she drove Nat south along Monroe to Porlier Street, turning at the mansion of her neighbor, Arthur Neville, and again at Webster where she headed south once more. Her throat was too clogged with sentiment for conversation, and became tighter as the fortress-like landmark came into full view. She managed to clear away the lump in her throat and smile when the front door of the orphanage was opened by one of the nuns.

St. Joseph's Orphan Asylum

214

The stiff white fabric of the cornet framing Sister Mary-Margaret's face didn't diminish the customary joy in her smile. "Miss Steffens! Come in, child! I see you've brought a friend."

The warm greeting caused Anna to smile in return, tempering her maudlin mood. "Sister Mary-Margaret, this is Mr. Nat Trevelyn, from South Manitou Island. Mr. Trevelyn, Sister Mary-Margaret."

"My pleasure, Sister," Nat said, shaking her hand.

"Let me take your wraps," the nun offered. "Billy is in the front playroom. He'll be delighted to see you. He's grown considerably over the summer." She hung their coats on the tree, then turned to Anna, a query on her brow. "I expected your grandfather to be with you. Is he with your cousin's family in Two Rivers?"

Anna shook her head and forced words past the clot that threatened to cut off her speech. "He recently passed on."

Sister Mary-Margaret inhaled sharply. "I'm so sorry."

Anna pressed her lips together, struggling not to cry. Sister Mary-Margaret put her arms about Anna's shoulders. When she had regained control, she released herself from the comforting embrace and dabbed the moisture from her eyes. "Sister, what should I tell Billy about Gramps? He was with me every time I visited the orphanage last winter and spring. The two of them became quite good friends. The little fellow's sure to ask about him. I hate to tell him the bad news. It wasn't long ago that Johnny was taken from him, and you know how that broke his heart."

Sister Mary-Margaret nodded thoughtfully. "It's always a temptation to shield a five-year-old from bad news, but it's best to be honest. Tell Billy that Gramps has gone to heaven, just like Johnny."

Anna nodded. Forcing the corners of her mouth higher, she led Nat up a winding flight of stairs and down a long hall toward the playroom on the north end of the second floor. Its transomed door stood open. The familiar dovetailed floor, polished hardwood wainscotting, and pressed tin ceiling were exactly as they had been months ago on her previous visit—plain, but welcoming in their own functional way. And like before, a hint of paste wax tinged the air.

Two nuns were tending several children, two to six years old, as they played with rag dolls and rubber balls. Billy was sitting beneath the far window, his straight, dark hair falling over his forehead as he amused himself with the most unique toy in the room, a tugboat on wheels that Johnny had made. The moment he spotted Anna, he left the toy behind and came running to her with open arms.

"Miss Anna!"

Anna scooped him up and hugged him tight, certain he'd grown two inches and gained five pounds since she'd last held him. "I've missed you, Billy!"

He clamped his arms so tightly about her neck, she couldn't breathe. "I love you, Miss Anna."

When he relaxed his firm hold on her, she kissed his cheek. "And I love *you*, Billy. You're getting to be such a big boy!" She kissed his other cheek, then set him down, turning him toward Nat. "Billy, I want you to meet a friend of mine, Mr. Trevelyn." To Nat, she said, "This is a very special friend of mine, Billy Berg."

"Pleased to meet you, Billy," Nat said, offering his hand. Billy extended his small one, and Nat couldn't help liking the little fellow whose round face and bright eyes reminded him of his own son.

"Billy, Mr. Trevelyn works on a steamer, like Johnny

did," Anna said.

His eyes opened wide. "Can I come on your boat?" Turning quickly to Anna, he tugged on her sleeve. "Will you take me on his boat? *Please!*"

Anna smiled. "Perhaps some day, if Mr. Trevelyn and Sister Mary-Margaret say it's all right."

Billy's gaze shifted to Nat, then back to Anna. "Where's Gramps?"

When Nat saw Anna's eyes filling with moisture, he knelt down, taking the boy's hands in his. "Gramps has been sick, Billy."

"Will he come see me when he's better?"

Nat shook his head. "Sorry, Billy. Gramps went up to heaven like your friend, Johnny."

The boy's forehead wrinkled. "But . . . now I can't tell him I remember."

Finding her voice, Anna quietly asked, "Remember what, Billy?"

"*Hvordan står det til?* How are you?"

Anna bent down and hugged the little fellow for repeating perfectly the Norwegian phrase Gramps had taught him on his last visit. Brushing moisture from her eye, she released him. "I believe Gramps heard you, and he's saying, 'Good boy, Billy.'"

The child smiled, then focused on Nat. "Mister, will you take me home with you? Johnny was gonna take me home with him soon as he married Miss Anna. But God took him to heaven. Can I go home with you, instead?"

Anna caressed the boy's cheek, gently turning him to face her. "Billy, who would be your mama? Mr. Trevelyn has no wife—no mama at home to take care of you."

After a moment's thought, he said, "Then you could

217

marry him and be my mama."

Nat chuckled and rose to his feet. "That's an idea, son, but it's not quite that simple."

Billy's chin sank almost to his chest. "My best friend, Bobby, was adopted last week," he said with a pout. "Now he's got a mama and a daddy and a brother, and a sister all his own. I want to get adopted real bad. I want a family all my own."

"These things take time, Billy," Anna explained. "Some day, you'll have a good family and a nice home. Just keep praying about it."

A thoughtful moment passed, then a glimmer of excitement lit Billy's eyes. "I'm gonna pray you marry Mr. Trevelyn!"

Anna's face grew warm.

Nat laughed quietly and tousled Billy's hair. "Better be sure that's what you want, before ya go prayin' for it."

Billy grinned. "I'm sure, Mr. Trevelyn. I'm *real* sure."

Anna leaned down and kissed the boy's forehead. "We have to say good bye, now. It's nearly your bedtime. Be a good boy, Billy. I'll be back to visit you soon."

The child focused on Nat. "Will you come, too, Mr. Trevelyn?"

Reluctantly, Nat shook his head. "Sorry. I'll be away on my boat. But the next time I'm in Green Bay, I'll come see ya. I promise. So 'long, Billy."

On the walk home, Anna's thoughts were so occupied by the things Billy had said and her own feelings about Nat, she barely noticed the rain had stopped and breaks in the clouds were offering an attractive view of an orange ball in the western sky.

Anna's rare quiet mood allowed Nat time to assess

what he had learned about her past through Billy's conversation. Thoughts and questions came to him, and he knew he couldn't leave Wisconsin until they were shared. As he climbed the steps to the Steffens's front porch, he said, "Miss Steffens, I have some things to say to you. Would you sit and listen awhile?" He indicated the wicker settee that offered ample room for them both.

"Surely," Anna answered, taking a place on the cushioned seat.

Nat sat at an angle, his gaze direct. "Back when Meta died, I wanted to deny the hurt by marryin' right away again. I thought God's answer to my problems was Bridget, and I was mighty put out when she insisted I was wrong.

"Then, little by little, you slipped into my life. When I didn't want a friend, ya befriended me. When I didn't want to smile, ya made me laugh. When I had no song in my heart, ya made me bellow out a melody that was so off-key, even my own brother was embarrassed."

In the silent moment that followed, Anna yearned to say she was glad for his friendship but a knot the size of a monkey fist had formed in her throat.

Nat continued. "That friend of yours, little Billy, he's somethin' else. He told me things about ya I didn't know, and now it all adds up. The reason ya knew how to be my friend is because you'd been hurt bad, too. Now I gotta ask ya somethin', and I want ya to tell me the truth. Do ya still love Johnny?"

Anna wanted to cry, but she held her tears in check and swallowed the lump of emotion that had kept her silent. "I still love Johnny, and you still love Meta."

Nat's gaze shifted from Anna to the muted pattern of

cabbage roses on the seat cushion. Anna reached out, resting her hand lightly on his arm. "I have something to confess. After Johnny died, I promised myself I'd never have anything to do with a lakes man again. Then I met you. You were so miserable after Meta died, I couldn't keep from trying to help you. I saw myself in your pain, the way I had been last November, and I knew you needed to think of something else, to have some relief from the tough times. Yes, I still love Johnny, but there's room in my heart for someone else—for a really good friend, like you."

His gaze met hers again, and for the first time since Gramps's death, she offered a hint of a smile. Taking her hand in both of his, he said, "Ya know somethin', Miss Anna? I can't help thinkin' our friendship is headin' for deeper waters."

CHAPTER

20

Despite the familiar comfort of his bed at the Two Rivers, Wisconsin home of his parents, sleep eluded Erik. Sitting with Gramps while his life slipped away, the sight of his ashes floating in the breeze over Green Bay, the distressing nature of Erik's last encounter with Bridget, returned to him again and again.

More troubling than these was the advice the old man had offered the night before he died. Gramps had seemingly known his death was imminent, and had shared one last bit of wisdom.

Unable to procrastinate longer concerning his grandfather's suggestion, Erik threw off his covers, kindled the light above his writing desk, and took pen in hand.

> *Dear Miss Richards,*
>
> *On the last night Gramps was alive, he spoke with me about you, and impressed upon me the importance of expressing my feelings for you. I only regret that he died before I could put on paper the words I am about to*

write.

I would ask you now to marry me, but to do so in a letter seems a coward's way. I want to be standing right in front of you, looking into your beautiful blue eyes, and see your response when I speak of this love I have for you, this constant desire to be with you, this insatiable urge to care for you, to provide for you, and to protect you. Most of all, I want to see your lovely face when I tell you I cherish you beyond words.

My precious Bridget, my love for you is a God-given love of a man for a woman, a love that cannot be denied, a love that must be shared; a love that knows no bounds; a love pure and true and strong enough to last a lifetime.

Now I have poured out my heart to you, and some would say I am a fool, but I believe the foolishness would lie in my keeping these feelings secret still longer; that cowardliness lies in waiting for the object of one's love to be the first to commit.

My dear, I hope and pray you love me even one-tenth as much as I love you. Search your heart and if you find you do, we can work on the other nine-tenths together, and I will come to you in October to propose marriage in person, and hear your acceptance.

Please write to me and tell me what is in your heart concerning me. If you can honestly say you do not care for me, I will never contact you again. But our summer seems to indicate otherwise, and God has given me peace about my feelings for you, and yours for me.

I look forward to your reply.

Affectionately,

Erik

*   *   *

Bridget had been saving the letter from Erik until the children were asleep. She sat at the writing table in her room, adjoining theirs, and took up her letter opener, carefully slitting the heavy, foil-lined envelope.

Time seemed to stand still while she read his precious words. A tear trickled down her cheek before she finished, then she pressed the letter to her bosom, gazing blurry-eyed out the window at the playhouse and cement step where she had last seen him before he had returned to his native Wisconsin.

Dabbing the moisture from her cheek, she took out paper and pen and wrote feverishly from her heart.

> *My beloved Erik,*
>
> *I love you dearly and I will be the proudest woman in Michigan to accept your proposal of marriage, when one is offered.*
>
> *I am sorry for the brevity of this description concerning my feelings. God has not granted me the gift of words the way He has you. But He has given me an abundance of faith and love, and I believe they will stand the test of time.*
>
> *Though you haven't yet asked for my hand in marriage, I am praying we can be married in the spring or summer. My sister, Aurora, who is an accomplished seamstress, will be wintering over here in Traverse City with the Doyles, about a block away. She can sew my wedding gown and those of the attendants.*
>
> *I hope you won't mind being married on South Manitou Island at the keeper's quarters. I promise you will not be asked to climb the light tower!*
>
> *Erik, my darling, I can hardly wait to see you in*

*October. I love my work and my home here with the
Ferrises, but an important part of my life has been
missing since the day I left The Clovers. I have felt a
void only you can fill. I long for our reunion.*

*Looking forward to your visit, I remain your faithful
and loving—*

Bridget

"Get along, Thor. Get along, Odin," Erik said, urging
the team onto the dock this last Friday in September. In
one more week, he would not be coming to the pier in his
uncle's wagon to pick up deliveries. Rather, he would
board the steamer for Michigan and the woman he loved.
He touched his hand to his breast. Beneath it, tucked into
the inside pocket, was Bridget's letter. He carried it with
him always, taking it out to read whenever privacy and
time permitted.

But now, he must fetch the goods for his uncle's store.
Fall merchandise was arriving by the barrelful, and customers would come from miles around tomorrow to see his
latest wares.

The arm of the steam derrick swung from dock to cargo
deck, filling the air with black puffs of coal smoke, an acrid
odor, and the *chug-chug-chug* of its engine. Erik set the
brake and hopped down into the bed of his uncle's wagon.
When the dock worker gave the signal, the mighty mechan-
ical arm lifted a barrel high and swung it overhead, toward
Erik.

With work-gloved hands he reached up, preparing to
guide the load into place as it gradually moved closer.

A *snap* rent the air.

Pain shot through his head. The world went black.

*　　*　　*

"We thank thee, Lord, for the bounty you have set before us this Thanksgiving Day . . . "

Bridget's mind wandered while Harrison asked the blessing over the dinner she was about to share with her sister and brother-in-law, her friend, Kenton McCune, and the Doyle sisters at the home of the elderly ladies only a block from the Ferrises.

She had much to be thankful for on this day of family gatherings. A fire crackled softly in the fireplace behind her, keeping her back side toasty warm despite a precipitous drop in temperature. The golden brown turkey stuffed with sage dressing added a pleasant herbal fragrance to the small dining room, all cozy and bright with the sun filtering through ivory lace curtains.

Though her life seemed rich in blessings—a position she loved in the Ferris household; her rekindled friendship with Kenton McCune; the companionship of Aurora while she awaited the birth of her baby in January—Bridget couldn't completely shake the melancholy she had been suffering since early October when Erik had failed to visit her as promised.

She would have understood a postponement of his trip, but his complete silence left her baffled, sometimes angry, and continually frustrated, especially since she had written the week after he had failed to show, inquiring of his well-being. If she hadn't kept the letter he'd written professing his love, she'd have thought she had imagined it. The letdown since its arrival sometimes made her wish he'd never written at all.

" . . . and I ask a special blessing on our unborn child, that the infant be safely delivered when the time comes.

All this we ask in the name of our Lord and Savior, Jesus Christ. Amen."

"Amen," echoed around the table.

Harrison picked up the carving knife and meat fork. "Who wants white meat? Bridget?"

She nodded, but couldn't help wondering whether Erik preferred white, or dark.

Stop it! a voice inside scolded. *He's probably dining with Clarissa Hackbardt this very minute. Forget him and open your heart to the friends and family here with you right now!*

Kenton passed her a dinner plate bearing a succulent slab of thinly sliced white meat. "Would you care for some potatoes with that?" he asked, reaching for a bowl mounded with the white fluffy stuff. Butter had melted into a pool in an indentation on top.

"Thank you," she said, really noticing him for the first time today. His beige striped tie and brown cashmere jacket complimented his hair, a near match with the color of the vanilla caramels he'd bought on the day they first met in Marshalls' candy shop. And the sandalwood essence that clung to his neat mustache and goatee mingled pleasantly with the aromas of the Doyle sisters' dinner.

Bridget realized anew that she was truly blessed by Kenton's companionship. Despite his knowledge of her fondness for Erik, his friendship had remained steadfast yet irreproachable. Though she could not soon transcend the bounds of innocent friendship with any man, she could take pleasure in the poetry Kenton often quoted, and the literary pursuits he frequently discussed.

As afternoon wore on, however, she knew she wasn't quite keeping up her end of the conversations, and at times, her mind was adrift on silent seas of curiosity about Erik and his own family gathering.

When the last crumb of pumpkin pie had been savored, the last dinner dish replaced in the cupboard, and the last piece of silver set in its velvet-lined chest, Kenton helped her into her woolen cloak, intent on walking her home to the Ferrises.

The nippy air bit her nose and stung her cheeks, and she pulled her scarf more snugly about her neck, thankful she needn't be exposed to the chill for more than a few minutes. When they arrived at the Ferrises door, Kenton turned to her, a thoughtful wrinkle on his brow.

"I know you're troubled by lack of word from Mr. Olson. I'm planning to write to him with news that his mother's book has gone to the printer. If you wouldn't consider it out of place, I could mention your concern for him when he didn't visit here as you had expected."

"Would you? I'd be so grateful." Bridget's heart lifted, knowing the mystery surrounding Erik would soon be unraveled.

"I'll let you know the minute I learn something," Kenton promised. As he gazed into Bridget's blue-gray eyes, he kept hidden his anger over Erik's treatment of her, knowing he never could neglect her, if *he* were the object of her affection. For now, he would content himself with her friendship. Taking her hands briefly in his, he gave a little squeeze, then stepped off the porch, already composing his letter in his mind.

The city looked like a winter wonderland, Kenton thought, now that December was nine days old and a white carpet had arrived to hide the mud of fall. The beauty of the still night and the peacefulness of gently falling snow contrasted sharply with the unpleasant task of delivering Erik Olson's news to Miss Richards.

Tinkling bells fell silent as he parked his sleigh in front of the Ferris home and walked the shoveled path to the wreathed front door. The maid showed him to the small parlor where he waited patiently for Bridget, admiring the pine roping draped across the mantel and the holly sprigs encircling its brass candlesticks. The gay voices of the Ferris dinner party in the adjoining room seeped past the closed pocket doors, grating on his nerves. If only Miss Richards had the evening off, he could take her somewhere more appropriate, but she obviously could not leave the care of small children to another member of the household on a busy night such as this.

He rose the moment Bridget entered the room, failing for once to come up with a single poetic word to offer in greeting. "I'm sorry to be the bearer of bad tidings," he said, pulling the missive from his inside pocket. "You'd better sit down to read this."

Bridget's hands trembled as she took the letter from Kenton, slipped it from its envelope, and unfolded the typed page.

Dear Mr. McCune:
    Thank you for the news regarding the publication
of Mother's diagrams. I had planned to write with
word of her steady recovery, but circumstances
prevented me. She is nearly back to her old self,
having again taken up her favorite pastime of
rosemaling, an art she had practiced regularly
before Professor Evenson prevailed upon her to provide the diagrams for his study on dinosaurs some
two years ago.
    As for me, a bit of bad luck befell me, literal-
ly, on the last day of September. I had driven to
the dock to fetch merchandise for my uncle's mercan-

228

tile here in Two Rivers. The steam derrick was
lowering a barrel of china onto the bed of the wagon
when the manila hemp rope snapped, sending it
crashing down on top of me. Among my injuries were
a concussion, several cracked ribs, an injured hand,
and a broken foot. I have been recovering slowly
ever since.

The ordeal would have been much more trying, had
it not been for the constant nursing and companionship of Clarissa Hackbardt. Day and night she has
tended me, making unnecessary the hiring of a regu-
lar nurse. Though I am not yet fully recovered, her
gentle, caring ways have sped my healing, and won my
heart.

Now, for some good news. Congratulations are in
order for me. I have asked for Clarissa's hand in
marriage, and she has been good enough to accept me.
My proposal came not out of gratitude for her help,
but from my sincere fondness and affection. I
realize now, my true love of her had lain dormant
for years. Perhaps the crisis stripped away the
layers to reveal my innermost feelings and allow
them to come to the surface. I can honestly say
that, despite my unfortunate accident, I am the
luckiest man alive.

Now I have a favor to ask of you. I have not
shared news of either my accident or my betrothal
with Miss Richards. I have considered typing a
letter to her, now that I am able, but I believe a
better, kinder method would be for you to speak with
her and give her this letter, and let her read for
herself what has occurred over the past two months.
You have been a friend of hers nearly as long as I
have, and I know she holds you in high regard.

May God bless you as richly as He has me, this
holiday season!

Erik Olson

P.S. Please forgive me for not signing this by
hand. My writing hand is still recovering.

Slowly, Bridget folded the paper. Numbed by all she
had read, she fumbled as she tucked it back into its envelope. Her gaze met Kenton's. So full of compassion was
the look in his eyes, she could barely keep back her tears.

"Do you mind if I keep this?" she asked, her voice barely above a whisper.

"Of course not," he said quietly.

She ran out of the parlor, through the hall, and up the back stairs, collapsing in a sobbing heap on her bed.

CHAPTER

21

Darkness had set in by the time Erik had limped out of the Traverse City depot and hired a hack driver to take him to Washington Street. The reverent peacefulness of this Christmas Eve, and the calming voices of carolers raising *Silent Night* in song as the buggy passed along Front Street, should have soothed his troubled heart, but apprehension over the truth about Bridget tied knots in muscles already sore from the long train ride from Two Rivers.

When the driver stopped in front of the Ferrises, Erik's fragile hopes nearly shattered. Parked by the curb was a carriage he recognized, with sterling silver scrolls and upholstery of the finest silk and velvet—Kenton McCune's.

Erik paid his driver the fare, then pressed a half-dollar into his palm. "Wait right here for fifteen minutes. If I'm not back, you may be on your way." Cane in hand, he hobbled up the front walk, leaned heavily on the railing to climb the porch steps, then faced the front door. *Lord, be with me, no matter what,* he prayed silently as he cranked the doorbell. While waiting for an answer, he slipped his hand into his coat pocket for the hundredth time since leaving Wisconsin, making sure the letter and his special present were still there.

A slender maid in a black dress, white apron, and white

cap opened the door, her questioning look enhanced by her long, thin nose. He touched the brim of his tall hat. "Mr. Erik Olson for Miss Bridget Richards." He presented his calling card.

She ignored it. "I'm sorry. She has company. Come another time."

She started to close the door, but Erik prevented her, wedging his cane and his good foot through the narrow opening. "I've not come all the way from Wisconsin to have the door shut before I'm even announced," he stated adamantly. "You tell her I'm here, or I'll tell her myself."

With a sigh, the maid opened the door wide. "Follow me."

Erik could barely keep up. His nearly healed foot, now swollen from the long trip, ached badly, but he followed the ill-natured woman through the hall to the back of the house and up two long flights of stairs, despite the pain that shot through him with every step.

She paused at the top of the stairs, indicating an open door on his left. "She's in there." Abruptly, the maid left him and returned downstairs.

Voices floated to him in the hall, Bridget's and Kenton's, in harmony singing *Lo, How a Rose E'er Blooming*. Erik limped to the open door and watched as Bridget handed an ornament to Kenton who was perched on a ladder beside a perfectly shaped spruce tree. Kenton saw him first.

"We have a visitor," he told her.

Then she turned to him, the beautiful round face he remembered from their last parting now thinner than before, with hints of fatigue casting small shadows beneath her blue-as-cornflower eyes.

Bridget's heart stopped, then raced wildly. The man she had tried to forget—the broad, tall one who'd appeared handsome and strong even when mourning the death of his grandfather, now looked vulnerable and uncertain, taking one faltering step toward her, then leaning heavily on his cane.

"Erik." Her voice barely broke a whisper.

"Bridget, I've come to learn the truth about you and Mr. McCune. Have you promised yourself to him?"

Kenton descended the ladder, coming to stand beside Bridget. "Miss Richards and I are friends, nothing more. You broke her heart badly when you said you were planning to wed Miss Hackbardt—"

"Miss Hackbardt?" Erik asked incredulously. "I have made no plans with her."

"What about your letter?" Bridget asked. "The one telling how she nursed you through your recovery and the two of you have made plans to marry this spring?"

"I never wrote any such letter," Erik stated adamantly. "I came to find out the truth about *your* letter." He pulled the envelope from his pocket. "This says you've had a change of heart, that you're certain Mr. McCune will propose soon, and you plan to accept."

"That's an outright lie," Bridget claimed, taking the missive from him, hurriedly reading.

Dear Mr. Olson,
    Forgive me for my tardiness in answering your many letters. I am truly sorry to hear of your accident. I pray daily for your recovery. Because of your condition, I have delayed writing, knowing I must be completely honest with you. What I have to tell you, I did not want to say until I knew you were well on the way to restored health.
    Since my last letter to you, I have often had the pleasure of Mr. McCune's company. Our friend-

233

ship has deepened over these past several weeks.
Without any plan on our part, we find ourselves
deeply in love with one another. I am certain Mr.
McCune will soon propose marriage, and I plan to
accept. In fact, I am typing this letter in his
office while I wait for him to finish his work and
take me to dinner.
 I cannot explain my change of heart. When I
last wrote to you professing my love for you, I
expected my feelings to remain steadfast. Now, I
realize God has other plans for me. He has shown me
that the love I felt for you was only meant to last
the summer, and He has granted me the wisdom to
understand that your longtime friend, Clarissa
Hackbardt, is a far better match for you than am I.
I pray you will open your heart to the possibility
of a future with her, since the two of you are so
well suited.
 Good bye forever,
 Bridget Richards

"I don't know where this letter came from, but I surely
didn't type it, nor did I sign it," Bridget claimed. "I wrote
one letter in my own hand when you didn't come in October, but I've never even been in Mr. McCune's office. Nor
have I received any letters from you except the one you
mailed before your accident." For one fleeting, horrible
moment, the possibility struck her that Kenton could have
made up the letter, but she immediately dismissed the
notion. He'd never been dishonest, nor had he pressed her
to be more than a friend.

Taking the letter from her to study it more closely,
Kenton's thoughts leaped ahead. "Miss Richards, do you
still have the letter that came to me from Mr. Olson earlier
this month?"

Bridget nodded, hurrying out of the nursery to retrieve
it from the bottom of her bureau drawer.

In her absence, Erik regarded Kenton skeptically. "I
haven't sent you any letters since I left Michigan in Sep-

tember."

Kenton shrugged. "Perhaps not, but someone has, just like someone has written this letter attributed to Miss Richards."

Bridget returned, and Erik quickly read his supposed letter, his head moving slowly from side to side. "This part about Clarissa is highly distorted. She didn't nurse me. She *did* visit every day, but her purpose, it appears, was not only to ingratiate herself with me, but to interfere with the mail between us. I wrote you at least ten letters using my left hand, begging you to write back. Clarissa must have thrown away every one of them." To Kenton, he said, "I'd *never* ask you to tell Miss Richards I'd changed my mind about her." He rattled the page. "This is the most cowardly, ridiculous thing I've ever read."

"May I see it?" Kenton asked. Holding it beside the forgery from Bridget, he said, "Look at the g's on these two sheets. They're exactly alike— filled in and missing part of the tail. These letters were typed on the same machine."

Bridget's gaze locked on Erik.

Erik's gaze locked on Bridget.

"Clarissa!" they concluded in unison.

"She would seem to be the logical beneficiary of all this deception," Kenton observed.

"And to think it almost worked," Erik lamented. Leaning his cane against a chair, he took Bridget's hands in his and held them tightly. "I wasn't going to be convinced you'd changed your mind about me until you'd told me so yourself."

"I've never been more miserable than these last two weeks when I was certain you'd—"

Erik released her hands and quieted her with a finger to her lips. "Shhh. I have something very important to ask you." He reached into his pocket for the present he'd carried with him from Wisconsin, thankful that Kenton McCune was quietly slipping out the nursery door. Keeping the tiny ring hidden in his palm, he looked into the most beautiful round face and blue eyes he'd ever seen. "Bridget, I love you with all my heart. Will you marry me?"

Erik's question filled her with so much joy, she wanted to shout her answer from the rooftop, but managed to temper her excitement, and speak in a near normal tone, "Yes, I'll marry you!"

Reaching for her right hand, he said, "When Gramps asked Grandma to marry her, he followed the old European custom of placing a gold band on her right hand. The day they were married, the ring was switched to her left hand. Gramps gave me that ring before he died. He said you should have it, you reminded him so much of his Freya. Would you wear it the way she did until we say our wedding vows?"

Bridget smiled, tears of happiness welling in her eyes. "Nothing could honor me more."

Somehow Erik managed to keep the ring hidden while he slipped it onto her finger.

She admired the narrow gold circlet embedded with tiny sapphire chips, impressed by the beauty of its simplicity as she turned it this way and that beneath the overhead electric light. She reached for Erik, her arms circling his neck while his circled her waist. The strong line of his jaw, the contour of his cheek, contrasted with the compassion in his eyes, reminding her of the wise old man. "I hope our love and our marriage will grow as strong the one shared by your grandmother and grandfather."

Erik bent close. "With God's grace, it will be so."

His lips touched hers, and she knew without a doubt this Christmas would be her happiest, merriest, loveliest Christmas of all.

CHAPTER

22

June, 1900

Bridget couldn't believe Erik was standing beside her at the rail on the parapet of the South Manitou light tower, and was showing no sign of his old fear of heights. A hundred feet below, a gull dove for fish in the sparkling waters of the crescent bay, then rose on an updraft. The steady but mild wind teased at the silk lace of her bridal veil, rustled the satin of her creamy white gown, and enhanced the subtle fragrance of rose sachet still clinging to the delicate fabrics.

On the light station grounds below, Seth was helping Mr. Trevelyn, the head keep', take down the canopy where the reception had ended only minutes ago, and put away the chairs where guests had been seated for the outdoor wedding ceremony. Bridget gazed at Erik, who was observing the scene through binoculars. In her heart, she had Divine assurance that she had followed God's true plan for her in becoming his wife. And she was still saying silent prayers of thanks for this loving fellow, stronger and more handsome than a Viking god, whose very presence by her side sent thrills through her.

She leaned close to Erik, putting her arm about his waist. "This is the best wedding gift you could ever give me, standing way up here beside me, as calm as if you were on solid ground. How do you suppose you got over your fear of heights?"

Erik lowered the binoculars and put his arms loosely about his wife, kissing her briefly. He was sorely tempted to follow the innocent kiss with a longer, deeper one, but restrained himself, knowing they would soon be in the solitude of the Steffens island summer home, which Anna's folks had generously offered as a honeymoon cottage. With an effort, he pushed anticipation of his wedding night aside to answer his wife's question. "The only thing I can figure is that the barrel of china that hit my head last September must have knocked the fear right out of me." His thoughts turning again to the bride in his arms, he said, "You're just as beautiful a hundred feet above Lake Michigan as you were at the altar when Preacher Mulder introduced us as Mr. and Mrs. Erik Olson." Caressing her cheek, he asked, "Are you sure you didn't mind sharing your wedding day with Anna? It was just like her, coming up with a wild scheme to have her first wedding in Wisconsin, then to bring Billy here for a second wedding on South Manitou on account of Nat's folks and their lightkeeping duties."

"I wouldn't have changed a thing," Bridget assured her new husband. "It was so touching, seeing Billy with his new brother, Michael. And did you notice how they both took to baby Harry? I can't believe Aurora's son is only six months old. He certainly is growing fast."

"And so is your sister, Charlotte. It won't be long before Harry has a new baby cousin."

A steamer whistle blew, drawing Bridget's attention to the bay. "Look! The *Manitou Lady* is leaving." Borrowing the binoculars from Erik, she adjusted the lenses. "There's Billy, waving like mad. Anna and her mama and papa, and your parents are with him. I hope Mr. and Mrs. Steffens don't mind staying at The Clovers with your folks while we're using their cottage."

"They won't mind a bit. In fact, they'll be staying in our cottage while we're staying in theirs."

Lowering the binoculars, Bridget turned to Erik. "What do you mean? We haven't any cottage. We're moving into Gramps's apartment after our honeymoon."

Erik smiled broadly. "I wasn't planning to tell you this until we got to Omena, but I'm not much on keeping secrets. We'll have our very own brand new cottage at The Clovers overlooking the croquet lawn behind the Main House. Papa and I built it this spring. It's a grand sight roomier than that cramped, two-room apartment Gramps was in, but it's still plenty cozy."

"Our very own place?" Bridget said wonderingly, then leaned up and quickly kissed Erik's chin. "You're always giving me the nicest surprises."

Again, the steam whistle of the *Manitou Lady* sounded, and she raised the binoculars. "I can see your mother now. She looks truly happy. She's like a different person, now that she's recovered. I really believe she and I are going to be good friends."

A moment later, she said, "Speaking of friends, there's Clarissa Hackbardt and Mr. McCune." Bridget had long since forgiven the Wisconsin girl for besmirching her reputation and for writing deceitful letters, even though Clarissa had shown no cause to deserve it.

"Let me see." Gazing through the glasses at the departing steamer, Erik said, "I can't tell you how reassuring it is, knowing Clarissa Hackbardt won't be anywhere near this island while we're on our honeymoon."

Bridget laughed, then spoke contemplatively. "I couldn't help noticing how well Mr. McCune was getting along with her today. He spent the entire afternoon in close company with her. I think he's trying to reform her. Do you suppose he'll have any success?"

"If he's half as effective with Clarissa Hackbardt as he was with my mother's publisher, I think there's a good chance he just might be able to make a change—providing God has a hand in it."

"Amen. According to Harrison, even his brother, Jake, has made a remarkable change since he invited God back into his life. Too bad he had to go to prison to get reacquainted with Jesus."

Lowering the binoculars, Erik took his new wife by the hand. "What do you say we climb down from here and get started on our honeymoon. I've been thinking . . . "

Bridget couldn't miss the twinkle in her new husband's eyes. "Yes?"

"Maybe little Harry wants more than one new cousin to play with."

Squeezing Erik's hand, Bridget replied, "I think he'd like that."

HISTORIC NOTES

The Clovers Hotel operated from 1898 to 1955. In 1980, it was condemned and intentionally burned.

Buffalo Bill's Wild West Show actually came to Traverse City on July 19, 1898. The introduction to the re-enactment of an attack on the Deadwood Stagecoach was paraphrased from an 1883 transcript, but the author was unable to ascertain whether Hank Monk, Mr. Higby, John Hancock, Bronco Bill, and Con Croner were still alive and riding with the show in 1899.

George Bennard spent many years as an evangelist in the United States and Canada. Although he wrote more than three hundred gospel songs, he is best remembered for the words and music to *The Old Rugged Cross* written in 1913. He died at the age of eighty-five in Reed City, Michigan, on October 10, 1958.

Gramps's story about Civil War hero Hans Heg parallels the actual facts regarding Heg's involvement in the conflict, his death, and the conditions at Chickamauga.

The Victorians knew much about dinosaurs by 1899. Mrs. Olson's involvement in a publication about the subject was primarily based on *The Dinosaurs of North America* by Othniel Charles Marsh, copyright 1896.

A Personal Invitation from Donna Winters

If you have not yet seen Traverse City and the Leelanau Peninsula, or even if you have and are considering a return visit, I personally invite you to discover or renew your acquaintance with this fascinating scenic and historic region. The landscape, bay shore, and lake shore offer a refreshing retreat from the hustle and bustle of the workaday world. When you go, be sure to drive to the very tip of the peninsula for a firsthand look at the Grand Traverse Lighthouse!

BOOKS

For more information on the Leelanau Peninsula, see *A History of Leelanau Township*.

ABOUT DONNA WINTERS

Donna adopted Michigan as her home state in 1971 when she moved there from a small town outside of Rochester, New York. She began penning novels in 1982 while working full time for an electronics company in Grand Rapids.

She resigned in 1984 following a contract offer for her first book. Since then, she has written several romance novels for various publishers, including Thomas Nelson Publishers, Zondervan Publishing House, and Guideposts.

Her husband, Fred, an American History teacher, shares her enthusiasm for history. Together, they visit historical sites, restored villages, museums, and lake ports, purchasing books and reference materials for use in Donna's research and Fred's classroom. Recent excursions took her to the sites described in *Bridget of Cat's Head Point*: Traverse City, Omena, and the Grand Traverse Lighthouse.

Donna has lived all of her life in states bordering on the Great Lakes. Her familiarity and fascination with these remarkable inland waters and her residence in the heart of Great Lakes Country make her the perfect candidate for writing *Great Lakes Romances*®. (Photo by Renee Werni.)

More Great Lakes Romances ®
For prices and availability, contact:
Bigwater Publishing
P.O. Box 177
Caledonia, MI 49316

Mackinac
by
Donna Winters
First in the series of *Great Lakes Romances*
(Set at Grand Hotel, Mackinac Island, 1895)
Her name bespeaks the age in which she lives . . .but
Victoria Whitmore is no shy, retiring Victorian miss. She
finds herself aboard the *Algomah*, traveling from staid
Grand Rapids to Michigan's fashionable Mackinac Island
resort. Her journey is not one of pleasure; a restful holiday
does not await her. Mackinac's Grand Hotel owes the
Whitmores money—enough to save the furniture manufac-
tory from certain financial ruin. It becomes Victoria's
mission to venture to the island to collect the payment. At
Mackinac, however, her task is anything but easy, and she
finds more than she bargained for.

Rand Bartlett, the hotel manager, is part of that
bargain. Accustomed to challenges and bent on making the
struggling Grand a success, he has not counted on the
challenge of Victoria—and he certainly has not counted on
losing his heart to her.

The Captain and the Widow
by
Donna Winters
Second in the series of *Great Lakes Romances*
(Set in Chicago, South Haven, and
Mackinac Island, 1897)
*Lily Atwood Haynes is beautiful, intelligent, and ahead of
her time* . . . but even her grit and determination have not

prepared her for the cruel event on Lake Michigan that leaves her widowed at age twenty. It is the lake—with its fathomless depths and unpredictable forces—that has provided her livelihood. Now it is the lake that challenges her newfound happiness.

When **Captain Hoyt Curtiss**, her husband's best friend, steps in to offer assistance in navigating the choppy waters of Lily's widowhood, she can only guess at the dark secret that shrouds his past and chokes his speech. What kind of miracle will it take to forge a new beginning for *The Captain and the Widow? Note:* The Captain and the Widow *is a spin-off from* Mackinac.

Sweethearts of Sleeping Bear Bay
by
Donna Winters
Third in the series of *Great Lakes Romances*
(Set in the Sleeping Bear Dune region of
northern Michigan, 1898)

Mary Ellen Jenkins is a woman of rare courage and experience . . . One of only four females licensed as navigators and steamboat masters on the Western Rivers, she is accustomed to finding her way through dense fog on the Mississippi. But when she travels North for the first time in her twenty-nine years, she discovers herself unprepared for the havoc caused by a vaporous shroud off Sleeping Bear Point. And navigating the misty shoals of her own uncertain future poses an even greater threat to her peace of mind.

Self-confident, skilled, and devoted to his duties as Second Mate aboard the Lake Michigan sidewheeler, *Lily Belle,* **Thad Grant** regrets his promise to play escort to the petticoat navigator the instant he lays eyes on her plain face. Then his career runs aground. Can he trust this woman to guide him to safe harbor, or will the Lady Reb ever be able to overcome the great gulf between them?

Note: Sweethearts of Sleeping Bear Bay *is a spin-off from* The Captain and the Widow.

Charlotte of South Manitou Island
by
Donna Winters
Fourth in the series of *Great Lakes Romances*
(Set on South Manitou Island, Michigan, 1891-1898)
Charlotte Richards' carefree world turns upside down on her eleventh birthday . . . the day her beloved papa dies in a spring storm on Lake Michigan. Without the persistence of fifteen-year-old **Seth Trevelyn**, son of South Manitou Island's lightkeeper, she might never have smiled again. He shows her that life goes on, and so does true friendship.

When Charlotte's teacher invites her to the World's Columbian Exposition of 1893, Seth signs as crewman on the *Martha G.,* carrying them to Chicago. Together, Seth and Charlotte sail the waters of the Great Lake to the very portal of the Fair, and an adventure they will never forget. While there, Seth saves Charlotte from a near fatal accident. Now, seventeen and a man, he realizes his friendship has become something more. Will his feelings be returned when Charlotte grows to womanhood?

Aurora of North Manitou Island
by
Donna Winters
Fifth in the series of *Great Lakes Romances*
(Set on North Manitou Island, Michigan, 1898-1899)
Aurora's wedding Day was far from the glorious event she had anticipated when she put the final stitches in her white satin gown, not with her new husband lying helpless after an accident on stormy Lake Michigan. And when Serilda Anders appeared out of Harrison's past to tend the light and nurse him back to health, Aurora was

certain her marriage was doomed before it had ever been properly launched.

Maybe Cad Blackburn was the answer—Cad of the ready wit and the silver tongue. But it wasn't right to accept the safe harbor *he* was offering.

Where was the light that would guide her through these troubled waters?

Jenny of L'Anse Bay
by
Donna Winters
Special Edition in the series of
Great Lakes Romances
(Set in the Keweenaw Peninsula of Upper Michigan in 1867)
A raging fire destroys more than Jennifer Crawford's new home . . . it also burns a black hole into her future. To soothe Jennifer's resentful spirit, her parents send her on a trip with their pastor and his wife to the Indian mission at L'Anse Bay. In the wilderness of Michigan's Upper Peninsula, Jennifer soon moves from tourist to teacher, taking over the education of the Ojibway children. Without knowing their language, she must teach them English, learn their customs, and live in harmony with them.

Hawk, son of the Ojibway chief, teaches Jennifer the ways of his tribe. Often discouraged by seemingly insurmountable cultural barriers, Jennifer must also battle danger, death, and the fears that threaten to come between her and the man she loves.

Sweet Clover: A Romance of the White City
Centennial Edition in the series of
Great Lakes Romances
The World's Columbian Exposition of 1893 brought unmatched excitement and wonder to Chicago, thus inspiring this innocent tale by Clara Louise Burnham, first published in 1894.

A Chicago resident from age nine, Burnham penned her novels in an apartment overlooking Lake Michigan. Her romance books contain plots imbued with the customs and morals of a bygone era—stories that garnered a sizable, loyal readership in their day.

In *Sweet Clover*, a destitute heroine of twenty enters a marriage of convenience to ensure the security and well-being of her fatherless family. Widowed soon after, Clover Bryant Van Tassel strives to rebuild a lifelong friendship with her late husband's son. Jack Van Tassel had been her childhood playmate, and might well have become her suitor. Believing himself betrayed by both his father and the girl he once admired, Jack moves far away from his native city. Then the World's Columbian Exposition opens, luring him once again to his old family home.

Hearts warmed by friendship blossom with affection—in some most surprising ways. Will true love come to all who seek it in the Fair's fabulous White City? The author will keep you guessing till the very end!

READER SURVEY—*Bridget of Cat's Head Point*

Your opinion counts! Please fill out and mail this form to:

Reader Survey
Bigwater Publishing
P.O. Box 177
Caledonia, MI 49316

Your
Name:_____

Street:_____

City,State,Zip:_____

In return for your completed survey, we will send you a bookmark and the latest issue of our *Great Lakes Romances*®*Newsletter*. If your name is not currently on our mailing list, we will also include four note papers and envelopes of the historic Grand Traverse Lighthouse (while supplies last—see the page opposite the map in the front of this book).

1. Please rate the following elements from A (excellent) to E (poor).

_____Heroine   _____Hero   _____Setting   _____Plot

Comments:_____

_____

2. What setting (time and place) would you like to see in a future book?

_____

(Survey questions continue on next page.)

3. Where did you purchase this book?

_____

4. What influenced your decision to purchase this book?

_____Front Cover _____First Page _____Back Cover Copy

_____Title _____Friends

_____Publicity (Please describe)_____

_____

5. Please indicate your age range:

_____Under 18 _____25-34 _____46-55

_____18-24 _____35-45 _____Over 55

If desired, include additional comments below.